PENGUI

I'm the King of the C...

⊔san Hill was born in Scarborough in 1942, and educated at ⸗ammar schools there and in Coventry. She read English at King's ⸗ollege, London, of which she is now a Fellow. As well as *I'm the ⸗ng of the Castle*, her novels include *The Albatross, Strange Meeting, ⸗he Bird of Night, In the Springtime of the Year, Air and Angels, The ⸗rvice of Clouds, The Various Haunts of Men, The Pure in Heart, The ⸗ise of Darkness, The Beacon* and *The Vows of Silence*. She has written ⸗ree volumes of short stories, including *A Bit of Singing and ⸗ancing*; two ghost novels, *The Woman in Black* and *The Mist in the ⸗irror*; and a number of stories for children. Her autobiographical ⸗ooks are *The Magic Apple Tree* and *Family*. She is married to the ⸗hakespeare scholar Stanley Wells, and they live in a Gloucestershire village from which she runs a small publishing company called Long Barn Books.

Susan Hill has described how in 1968 she went to stay in a remote farm cottage where the farmer's grandson and his friend often came by. Out of that experience grew *I'm the King of the Castle*, which was published in 1970. Written as a novel for adults, it has been set for many years as a GCSE text and is therefore read by young readers too – an early example of a crossover novel. Described by the *Guardian* as 'a brilliant tour de force', *I'm the King of the Castle* won the 1970 Somerset Maugham Award.

Esther Freud was born in London in 1963. She is the author of *Hideous Kinky, Peerless Flats, Gaglow, The Wild, The Sea House* and *Love Falls*.

I'm the King of the Castle

SUSAN HILL

PENGUIN BOOKS

PENGUIN BOOKS

Published by the Penguin Group
Penguin Books Ltd, 80 Strand, London WC2R ORL, England
Penguin Group (USA), Inc., 375 Hudson Street, New York, New York 10014, USA
Penguin Group (Canada), 90 Eglinton Avenue East, Suite 700, Toronto, Ontario, Canada M4P 2Y3
(a division of Pearson Penguin Canada Inc.)
Penguin Ireland, 25 St Stephen's Green, Dublin 2, Ireland (a division of Penguin Books Ltd)
Penguin Group (Australia), 250 Camberwell Road, Camberwell, Victoria 3124, Australia
(a division of Pearson Australia Group Pty Ltd)
Penguin Books India Pvt Ltd, 11 Community Centre, Panchsheel Park,
New Delhi – 110 017, India
Penguin Group (NZ), 67 Apollo Drive, Rosedale, North Shore 0632, New Zealand
(a division of Pearson New Zealand Ltd)
Penguin Books (South Africa) (Pty) Ltd, 24 Sturdee Avenue, Rosebank, Johannesburg 2196,
South Africa

Penguin Books Ltd, Registered Offices: 80 Strand, London WC2R ORL, England

www.penguin.com

First published by Hamish Hamilton Ltd 1970
Published in Penguin Books 1974
Reissued with an afterword 1989
Reissued with a new introduction in Penguin Books 2010

2

Set in 11/13 pt Dante MT
Typeset by Ellipsis Books Limited, Glasgow
Printed in Great Britain by Clays Ltd, St Ives plc

A CIP catalogue record for this book is available from the British Library

ISBN: 978-0-141-04194-0

www.greenpenguin.co.uk

Introduction

In the spring of 1977, not so long after Susan Hill wrote *I'm the King of the Castle*, I set off on a French exchange in the hope that four weeks of exposure to the language would make up for all the years of not having paid attention in class. The family I was going to sounded sympathetic, kind and, more importantly, had a teenage daughter of my age. I don't remember feeling nervous. Back home I had a large circle of friends, and I considered myself rather fabulous with a trip to see The Clash behind me and a packet of ten Marlboro Lights in my pocket. As soon as I saw Catrin I felt less sure. She was another species, a different kind of girl. She wasn't interested in boys, music or smoking, or even pretending that she was. She went on bike rides with her friends, attended percussion classes on Saturday mornings and sat diligently over homework even in the holidays. We were to share a room. At first I tried to impress Catrin, draw her into the glamour of my life. I told her about my trips to London, how I'd once seen two members of the Sex Pistols on the Kings Road, how a friend had pierced her own ear in three places and fainted in the school loos. But I soon learnt there was nothing to be gained from this kind of talk, so I decided to stay quiet. I'd wait and listen and find a way of joining in with her. I didn't have any other choice.

But Catrin didn't want me. If I went cycling with her, she sped off ahead on her long, athletic legs; if I attempted to start up a conversation in my desperate French, she turned her back. The terrible thing was that I cared. I didn't want to care. I loathed myself for it. But four weeks is a long time to spend alone. Soon I actively hated her, and then, when she showed me the smallest glimmer of attention, I found to my dismay I forgot my grievances and leapt at the chance to be her friend. But ten minutes later it was over. She'd turn her back on me again. Wretched and lonely, I retreated to the bathroom, smoked a Marlboro Light and cried.

Those years seem a world away from now. Why didn't I call home, ask for my trip to be cut short, beg to be placed with another family?

Never once did it occur to me, just as in the dark and taunting world which Susan Hill creates, that children had any choice in their fate. 'Some people are coming here today,' Hooper's father tells him at the start of this bleak and gripping novel. 'Now you will have a companion.' But it is clear that Hooper doesn't want a companion, and when eleven-year-old Charles Kingshaw arrives to find a note telling him that he's not welcome, rather than rebel, he begins to withdraw. It would be so easy, and ideal, if these two boys could be friends. But that's not how it is. They are both damaged. They have both lost a parent, and they find themselves, through no wish of their own, living under the same oppressive roof.

I'm the King of the Castle inhabits the world of post-war austerity – sombre, unheated country houses, boarding schools, stiff upper lips. The instruments of torture with which one child persecutes another are simple but nonetheless effective. Dead animals, locked rooms, darkness, crows. With a child's instinct to be cruel, Hooper homes in on the other boy's vulnerability, and he's helped in his campaign by the gloomy isolation of the house, and the wilful blindness of the adults whose only desire is to see the two boys become friends. Susan Hill is a master of suspense, leading us on with flashes of hope, and a sharp insight into the tormented child's state of mind. 'Kingshaw stood for a long time after Hooper had gone. He thought, there is nobody. The whole summer stretched ahead of him. After a while he began to cry, though without making any sound, and swallowing hard to try and stop himself. He couldn't stop. But there was nothing that he would say, nobody to say it to.'

If only Kingshaw could confide in someone. But Susan Hill knows that there is no more terrible risk for a child than to let an adult into their secret world of terror and not be understood. '. . . when you spoke a thing out loud, that was that, and if you didn't, there might be some mistake, some hope.' And maybe he was right not to tell anyone. Maybe even his mother wouldn't have understood.

Sunday, in Catrin's household, was the one day of respite. The family would rise early, pack an enormous picnic and set off into the hills above Marseilles. They met up with other hiking friends and, choosing a new route each weekend, went scrambling over the thyme-scented countryside, stopping eventually for a feast of immense proportions and gastronomic delights. Afterwards, for an hour at least, everyone sat propped against boulders, recovering in the sun. I liked these days. They felt companionable and safe, and with the murmur of small talk, and the exertion, I didn't need to rely on anyone for anything. But on the last Sunday of my visit when Catrin had ignored me for three days, I used the only power I had in my possession, and refused to go. The parents turned towards me. They frowned, they shrugged, while Catrin gave a little moue of irritation. And it was decided. If I wanted to stay at home, then I should.

Wretched, I watched them as they prepared to leave, and I imagined another day, alone, in the shared bedroom, listening to Edith Piaf belting out her heartbreak. I felt as miserable as if I were to be locked up, like Kingshaw, in a dark, spidery shed. Wait, I said. I'll come. And as I stomped across the landscape, all I could think of was exactly how, when it was Catrin's turn to come to England, I'd punish her for being so unkind.

Esther Freud

Chapter One

Three months ago, his grandmother died, and then they had moved to this house.

'I will not live there again, until it belongs to me,' his father had said. Though the old man lay upstairs, after a second stroke, and lingered, giving no trouble.

The boy was taken up to see him.

'You must not be afraid,' his father said, nervously, 'he is a very old man, now, very ill.'

'I am never afraid.' And that was no more than the truth, though his father would not have believed it.

It will be very moving, Joseph Hooper had decided, with the three generations together and one upon his death bed, the eldest son of the eldest son of the eldest son. For, in middle age, he was acquiring a dynastic sense.

But it had not been moving. The old man had breathed noisily, and dribbled a little, and never woken. The sick room smelled sour.

'Ah, well,' Mr Hooper had said, and coughed, 'he is very ill, you know. But I am glad you have seen him.'

'Why?'

'Well – because you are his only grandson. His heir, I suppose. Yes. It is only as it should be.'

The boy looked towards the bed. His skin is already dead, he thought, it is old and dry. But he saw that the bones of the eye-sockets, and the nose and jaw, showed through it, and gleamed. Everything about him, from the stubble of hair down to the folded line of sheet, was bleached and grey-ish white.

'All he looks like,' Edmund Hooper said, 'is one of his dead old moths.'

'That is not the way to speak! You must show respect.'

His father had led him out. Though I am only able to show respect now, he thought, to behave towards my father as I should, because he is dying, he is almost gone away from me.

Edmund Hooper, walking down the great staircase into the wood-panelled hall, thought nothing of his grandfather. But later, he remembered the moth-like whiteness of the very old skin.

Now, they had moved, Joseph Hooper was master in his own house.

He said, 'I shall be away in London a good deal. I cannot live here the whole time, even in your holidays.'

'That won't be anything new, will it?'

He looked away from his son's gaze, irritated. I do my best, he thought, it is not the easiest of tasks, without a woman beside me.

'Ah, but we shall be looking into things,' he said, 'I shall see about getting you a friend, as well as someone to look after us in this house. Something is soon to be done.'

Edmund Hooper thought, I don't want anything to be done about it, *nobody* must come here, as he walked between the yew trees at the bottom of the garden.

'You had better not go into the Red Room without asking me. I shall keep the key in here.'

'I wouldn't do any harm there, why can't I go?'

'Well – there are a good many valuable things. That is all. Really.' Joseph Hooper sighed, sitting at his desk, in the room facing the long lawn. 'And – I cannot think that it will be a room to interest you much.'

For the time being, the house was to be kept as it was, until he could decide which of the furniture to be rid of, which of their own to bring.

He moved his hands uneasily about over the papers on his desk, oppressed by them, uncertain where he should begin. Though he was accustomed to paperwork. But his father's affairs had been left in disarray, he was ashamed of the paraphernalia of death.

'Can I have the key now, then?'

'May . . .'

'O.K.'

'The key for the Red Room?'

'Yes.'

'Well . . .'

Mr Joseph Hooper moved his hand towards the small, left-side drawer in the desk, underneath the drawer where sealing wax had always been kept. But then, said, 'No. No, you had really much better be playing cricket in the sun, Edmund, something of that sort. You have been shown everything there is in the Red Room.'

'There's nobody to play cricket with.'

'Ah, well now, I shall soon be doing something about that, you shall have your friend.'

'Anyway, I don't like cricket.'

'Edmund, you will not be difficult, please, I have a good deal to do, I cannot waste time in foolish arguments.'

Hooper went out, wishing he had said nothing. He wanted nothing to be done, nobody should come here.

But he knew where to find the key.

He is like his mother, thought Mr Joseph Hooper. He has the same way of not bothering to explain, and of making secrets, the same hardness and cool way of looking. It was six years since the death of Ellen Hooper. The marriage had not been happy. When his son, who so resembled her, was away at school, there were long spells when it was hard for him to remember what she had looked like.

Joseph Hooper turned back to answering the letter which had come in reply to his advertisement.

The house, which was called Warings, had been built by the boy's great-grandfather, and so it was not very old. In those days, there had been a large village, and the first Joseph Hooper had owned a good deal of land. Now, the village had shrunk, people had left for the towns and there had been few newcomers, few new buildings. Derne became like an old busy port which has been deserted by the sea. All the Hooper land had been sold off, piece by piece. But there was still Warings, built on a slope leading out of the village, some distance from any other house.

The first Joseph Hooper had been a banker, and rising in the world, when, at the age of thirty, he had built the house. 'I am not ashamed of it,' he had told his friends in the City. And indeed, he had spent more on it than he could well afford. He hoped to grow into it, as a child grows into over-large shoes. He was an ambitious man. He had brought the younger daughter of a minor baronet here, as his bride, and set about founding his family, consolidating a position, so that he could afford the house he had built. He had succeeded with no margin, so

3

that, bit by bit, the surrounding land which belonged to him had been sold.

'That is the history of Warings,' the present Joseph Hooper had told his son, Edmund, taking him solemnly around. 'You should be very proud.'

He did not see why. It was an ordinary house, he thought, an ugly house, nothing to boast of. But the idea that it was *his,* the idea of a family history, pleased him.

His father said, 'You will come to understand what it means to be a Hooper, as you get older.'

Though he thought, what does it mean, it means little, to himself. And he shrank from the expression in the boy's eyes, from his knowingness. He was his mother's son.

Warings was ugly. It was entirely graceless, rather tall and badly angled, built of dark red brick. At the front, and on both sides, there was the lawn, sloping downwards to a gravelled drive, and then into the lane, and without any tree or flower-bed to relieve the bald greenness. Up the drive, and at the back of the house, bunched between the yew trees, were the great bushes of rhododendron.

The yew trees had stood here before the house, Warings, had been built around them, for the first Joseph Hooper had admired their solidity and denseness, the fact that they grew so slowly and were the longest lived of all trees. He had planted the rhododendrons, too, not at all for their brief, dramatic show of colour in May and June, but for their dark green, leathery leaves and toughness of stem, their substantial look. He liked their gathered shapes, seen from the end of the drive.

Inside the house, everything was predictable, the high-ceilinged rooms, with heavy, sashed windows, the oak wall panelling and the oak doors, and the oak staircase, the massive furniture. Little had been changed since the beginning.

Joseph Hooper had spent that part of his childhood before school, and between terms, in this house, and he did not like it, he had unhappy memories of Warings. Yet now, at the age of fifty-one, he admitted that he was a Hooper, his father's son, and so he had come to admire the solidity and the gloom. He thought, it is a prepossessing house.

For he knew himself to be an ineffectual man, without any strength or imposing qualities, a man who was liked and humoured but little regarded, a man who had failed – but not dramatically, as one falling from

4

a great height, who attracts attention. He was a dull man, a man who got by. He thought, I know myself and am depressed by what I know. But now, with his father gone, he could stand before this house, and have it lend him both importance and support, he could speak of 'Warings – my place in the country', it would make up for a good deal.

A narrow path led down between the yew trees into a small copse. That, and a field beyond it, were all that was now left of the Hooper land.

The boy's room, high up at the back of the house, overlooked the copse. He had chosen it.

His father had said, 'But look at all the others, so much larger and brighter. You had much better take the old playroom and have that to yourself.' But he had wanted this, a narrow room with a tall window. Above him, there were only the attics.

When he woke, now, there was an enormous moon, so that at first, he thought it was already dawn, and that he had missed his chance. He got out of bed. There was a slight, persistent movement of wind through the yew tree branches, and the elms and oaks of the copse, and a rustling of the high grasses in the field. The moonlight, penetrating a thin space between two trees, caught the stream that ran through its centre, so that, now and then, as the branches stirred, there was a gleam of water. Edmund Hooper looked down. The night was very warm.

Outside, on his landing, there was no moonlight, and he felt his way in the dark, first on the carpeted upper staircase, and then, for the last two flights, on the bare, polished oak. He went forward quite deliberately, being sure of his way, and unafraid. There was no sound from the room where his father slept. Mrs Boland only came here during the day. Mrs Boland did not like Warings. It is too dark, she said, it smells un-lived in, of old things, like a museum. And she had gone about trying to let in light and fresh air, where she could. But Derne was low-lying, and the air that summer was close and still.

Hooper crossed the wide hall, and here too, because it was the front of the house, no moonlight came. Behind him, the wood of the staircase settled back upon itself, after he had trodden it.

At first, he could not decide which key it might be. There were three together in the left-hand drawer. But one was longer, with a smudge of red paint across the rim. Red paint for the Red Room.

It was at the back of the house, facing the copse, so that when he

5

pushed open the door, he saw it in full moonlight, almost as bright as day, when the lights always had to go on, because of the yew branches, overhanging the windows.

Hooper stepped inside.

It had been designed, by the first Joseph Hooper, as a library, and there were still the glass cases, reaching from floor to ceiling, all around the room, filled with books. But nobody ever read, here. The first Joseph Hooper had not even done so.

Edmund Hooper examined the titles of some of the books the day he was brought here to see his dying grandfather, and they were of no interest. There were bound volumes of the *Banker's Journal* and the *Stockbroker's Gazette,* and complete sets of the Victorian novelists, never opened.

It was his grandfather, recently dead, who had started to make use of the Red Room. He had been a lepidopterist; he had filled it with glass showcases of moths and butterflies. It was like the room of a museum, for here was no carpet on the polished oak boards, and the display cases stood in two long rows, from one end to the other. There were trays of insects, too, which you could pull out from recesses in the walls.

'Your grandfather was one of the most important collectors of his day,' Joseph Hooper had said, showing the boy round. 'He was known and respected the world over. This collection is worth a great deal of money.'

Though what use is it, he thought, what use, why should I not sell it? He hated it violently. He had been brought in here, afternoon upon afternoon, during the summers of his boyhood, led all about the room from cabinet to cabinet, he was lectured and instructed, he had been forced to watch as the insects were removed from their poison-fume bottles with tweezers, spread out and then pinned down through their horny bodies on to the card.

'This will all belong to you,' his father had said, 'you must learn the value of what you are to inherit.'

He had not dared to rebel, he had gone back into the Red Room every holiday, feigning interest, acquiring knowledge, disguising his fear. Until, at last, he had grown older and found excuses for spending all of his holidays away from the house.

'It is easy for you to despise and shrug your shoulders,' his father had said, seeing how it was. 'You pay no attention to what a man has done.

6

I am an international authority, but you think nothing of that. Well, let me see you make a name for yourself, in some way or other.'

Joseph Hooper had known that he would never do so.

He tried to salvage a little conscience by teaching his own boy. 'It is a splendid thing for a man to become world famous in that way,' he said. 'Throughout his life, your grandfather devoted all of his free time – for it was not his profession, you understand, it was only his hobby, he had a job of work to do. Every ounce of his energy apart from that went into building up this collection.'

For ought not a boy to feel some pride in his family's importance?

Edmund Hooper had gone about the Red Room, looking closely, saying nothing.

'I have seen you catching butterflies in jam jars and so on,' Joseph Hooper said, 'I daresay that is a sign of interest, I daresay that you will follow in his footsteps more than I ever did.'

'The butterflies were just a craze last term. We caught larvae and watched them hatch. Nobody's interested now.'

He walked to the window and looked out onto the copse, swept by the first heavy rain of summer. He did not say whether the stiff moths, inside their glass cases, interested him or not.

'Why didn't you bring me here before?'

'You came – you were brought here as a baby.'

'That's years ago.'

'Well – yes.'

'I suppose you quarrelled with grandfather then.'

Jospeh Hooper sighed. 'That is not the sort of thing to say, it is not something we need be concerned with now.'

But he understood, looking at the boy, a little of how it had been with his own father, he felt the need to make some kind of reparation. I am not a hard man, he thought, I have more to regret about my own son than he had about me. For he knew that he had failed, from the very beginning, to ingratiate himself with Edmund.

The small key that fitted all the glass cases was kept inside a Bible on one of the lower shelves.

At first, Hooper walked up and down the room softly, looking at all the moths, laid out on white card, and at the labels beneath them. The names pleased him – Hawk Moths, Footmen Moths, Lutestring Moths.

He read some of them out to himself, in a low voice. Moonlight came through the window, coldly, on to the glass.

Above the wooden panelling of the Red Room were the animals, the stag's head with antlers branching out over the doorway, and the cases of grey fish, against their painted backgrounds of weed and water, the stuffed bodies of weasel, stoat, and fox, glass-eyed and posed in stilted attitudes. Because of the old man's long last illness, and the neglect of the housekeeper, it was some time since they had been cleaned. Mr Joseph Hooper had said that the animals should be sold, they were not a matter of family pride, they had only been bought in a lot by the first Joseph Hooper, who wanted to equip his library in the manner of a sporting person.

Hooper stopped in front of a case at the far end of the room, beside the uncurtained window. He looked down at the flat, fragile shapes. He was fascinated by them, excited. He inserted the small key and lifted up the glass lid. It was very heavy and stiff from disuse. A puff of old, stale-smelling air came into his face.

The largest moth of all was in the centre of the case – *'Acheroptia atropos'* – though he could only just make out the writing on the card, the ink had faded to a dark yellow in the sun. 'Death's Head Hawk Moth.'

He stretched out his hand, put his finger under the head of the pin and slid it up, out of the thick, striped body. At once, the whole moth, already years dead, disintegrated, collapsing into a soft, formless heap of dark dust.

Chapter Two

'Some people are coming here today,' said Joseph Hooper, 'now you will have a companion.'

For he had been much impressed by the graceful letters of Mrs Helena Kingshaw, by their honesty and lightness of tone, and by her voice over the telephone, later. She was widowed, she was thirty-seven, and she was to become what he had termed an informal housekeeper. There would be Mrs Boland for the cleaning and some cooking.

'Perhaps you might agree to come for the summer, just at first,' he had written, 'to see how you and your boy settle, and how we all of us rub along.'

'Warings,' Mrs Helena Kingshaw had replied, 'sounds so much like the home we have been looking for.'

Joseph Hooper had been greatly touched. That night, he examined his own, thin figure in the cheval mirror. 'I am a lonely man,' he had said, and was not ashamed, afterwards, of having admitted it.

'His name is Charles Kingshaw, and he is just your age, he is almost eleven. You must make a good effort to welcome him and be friendly.'

Edmund Hooper went slowly up the four flights of stairs to his own bedroom. It was raining hard again, and great, bruise-coloured clouds hung low over the copse. He had thought of going in there today, but the grass would be too wet.

And another boy was coming, after all, with his mother, so that there would always be someone about the house to notice him. She would start making them play games and go on expeditions, that was how the mothers of some boys at school were. Once, recently, he had wondered if he ought to feel his own mother's absence, to want things that only she might provide. But he had been unable to imagine what these things might be. He remembered nothing at all about her.

His father had said, 'I know that you are not quite happy, that we are only making the best of a bad job. But you must come to me and tell me about things, you must not be afraid to admit when something is wrong.'

'I'm quite all right. There isn't anything wrong at all.' For he hated

9

his father to talk to him in that way, wanted to stop his ears to keep him out. 'There's nothing wrong.' And he only spoke the truth. But Joseph Hooper looked for subtleties beneath the surface of things, anxious, because he had been warned of how much the boy would suffer.

Hooper began to mould plasticine between his hands, for another layer to the geological model, standing on a board beside the window. He thought of the boy called Kingshaw, who was coming.

'It is my house,' he thought, 'it is private, I got here first. Nobody should come here.'

Still, he would not give anything of himself away, the other boy could be ignored, or evaded, or warned off. It depended what he was like. All sorts of things could be done.

He laid down a flat strip of dark red plasticine, following the colouring of strata on a map. The model was humped in the shape of a barrow, like one of those on the downs. When it was finished, he would slice it down like a cake, and all the layers would be revealed. Then he could get on with his Battle of Waterloo map. There were so many things to do, and he wanted to do them by himself, he did not want the boy called Kingshaw here. That afternoon, when they arrived by car, he locked his door. But he watched them, tilting the mirror so that he could look down into the drive without being seen himself. They all stood about nervously. Kingshaw had red hair. 'Edmund!' his father had been calling, up and down the house. 'Edmund! Now your friend is here, I wish you would not lurk about the place, it is so very ill-mannered. Come out here, please. Edmund!'

Joseph Hooper busied himself, for he was suddenly alarmed at the arrival of this woman, alarmed by what he had done. They were to make their home here, they were all to live together in the same house, and he might suffer from it, might know the consequences of a terrible mistake.

He is very uncertain of himself, thought Mrs Helena Kingshaw, who had also, for some years past, been much alone.

'Edmund, you will come down here at once!'

Edmund Hooper took up a small piece of paper from the table, wrote something on it and attached the paper carefully to a lump of grey plasticine. He looked out of the window again. The boy, Charles Kingshaw, was glancing up, seeing the sudden flash of the mirror. Hooper dropped the plasticine, it fell straight as a stone. He moved back from the window. Kingshaw bent down.

'Come along, Charles dear, you must help me with the cases, we cannot leave everything to Mr Hooper.' Mrs Helena Kingshaw wore a jade green suit and worried about it, lest it should be thought too smart.

'Oh – what is it, what have you found?' She was anxious that he should like it here, should very soon feel at home.

Kingshaw thought, I didn't want to come, I didn't want to come, it is one more strange house in which we do not properly belong. But he had dropped the lump of plasticine. 'Nothing, it's nothing. It's only a pebble.'

Walking behind his mother, into the dark hall, he managed to open out the scrap of paper.

'I DIDN'T WANT YOU TO COME HERE' was written.

'Now let me show you to your rooms,' said Mr Joseph Hooper.

Kingshaw stuffed the message fearfully into his trouser pocket.

Hooper said, 'Why have you come here?' facing him across the room. Kingshaw flushed brick red. He stood his ground, not speaking. There was a small round table between them. His trunk and a suitcase stood on the floor. 'Why did you have to find somewhere new to live?'

Silence. Hooper thought, now I see why it is better to have a house like Warings, I see why my father goes about clutching the big bunch of keys. We live here, it is ours, we belong. Kingshaw has nowhere.

He walked round the table, towards the window. Kingshaw stepped back as he came.

'Scaredy!'

'No.'

'When my father dies.' Hooper said, 'this house will belong to me, I shall be master. It'll all be mine.'

'That's nothing. It's only an old house.'

Hooper remembered bitterly the land that his grandfather had been forced to sell off. He said quietly, 'Downstairs is something very valuable. Something you've never seen.'

'What then?'

Hooper smiled, looking away out of the window, choosing not to tell. And he was uncertain how impressive the moth collection might really be.

'My grandfather died in this room. Not very long ago, either. He lay and died in that bed. Now it's your bed.' This was not true.

Kingshaw went to the suitcase and squatted down.

II

'Where did you live before?'

'In a flat.'

'Where?'

'London.'

'Your *own* flat?'

'Yes – no. Well, it was in somebody's house.'

'You were only *tenants*, then.'

'Yes.'

'It wasn't really yours.'

'No.'

'Why didn't your father buy you a proper house?'

Kingshaw stood up. 'My father's dead.' He was angry, not hurt. He wanted to put his fists up to Hooper, and dared not.

Hooper raised his eyebrows. He had learned to do it from a master at school. It seemed an impressive way of looking.

'Well, my mother can't afford to buy us a house, can she? We can't help that.'

'Your father should have left you some money, then, shouldn't he? Didn't *he* have a house.'

'Yes, he did, it had to be sold.'

'Why?'

'I don't know.'

'To pay off all his debts.'

'No, no.'

'Do you remember your father?'

'Oh, yes. Well – a bit. He was a pilot, once. He was in the Battle of Britain. I've got . . .' Kingshaw went down on his knees again, and began to search feverishly through the tartan suitcase. ' . . . I've got a picture of him.'

'Is it a picture of him in the Battle?'

'No. But . . .'

'I don't believe you, anyway, you're a liar, the Battle of Britain was in the war.'

'Well, I know that, everybody knows that.'

'It was years ago, dozens of years. It was history. He couldn't have been in it.'

'He was, he was.'

'When did he die, then?'

'Here's the picture, look – that's my father.'

When did he die, I said.' Hooper moved nearer, menacing.

'A few years ago. I was about five. Or six.'

'He would have been pretty old by then. How old was he?'

'I don't know. Quite old, I suppose. Look, then, there's the photograph.' Kingshaw held out a small, brown wallet. He was desperate for Hooper to see it, to believe him, he felt that he must make some mark on this house, must be believed about something. After a second, Hooper bent down slightly, and took the picture. He had expected someone different, courageous-looking, interesting. But it was only a bald, cadaverous man with a mole on his chin.

'He's old,' he said.

'I told you. When he was in the Battle of Britain, he was twenty. That was the war.'

Hooper said nothing. He threw the photograph down into the suitcase and walked back to the window. Kingshaw knew that he had won, but he did not *feel* the winner; Hooper had conceded him nothing.

'Where do you go to school?'

'In Wales.'

Hooper raised his eyebrows, 'I should think there would be about a hundred schools in Wales. More than a hundred.'

'It's called St Vincent's.'

'Is it a proper school?'

Kingshaw did not answer. He was still on the floor beside his case. He had been going to start unpacking, but now he would not, unpacking would make it seem final, as though he had accepted the fact that he was going to stay here, as though there were a future to be considered. He had been brought up sharp, by Hooper.

He said, 'You needn't think I wanted to come, anyway.' Hooper considered this. He remembered when he had been told of his grandfather's death. He had said, 'I don't want to live in that house.'

He pushed open the window. It had stopped raining. The sky was the colour of dirty sixpences. The rhododendrons still shone with wetness, all down the drive.

'You'd better shut the window,' Kingshaw said, 'it's my window now.'

Hooper turned, hearing the new note in his voice, considering what it meant, and hearing the tremor of anxiety, too. He raise his fists and came at Kingshaw.

The scrap was brief and wordless and violent. It died down quite quickly. Kingshaw wiped his bloody nose and then examined the hand-kerchief. His heart was thumping. He had never fought another boy like that before. He wondered what the future would be like now.

Outside, in the corridor below, he heard the voice of his mother, answering Mr Hooper gaily, and then the banging of a door. He thought, it's her fault that we came here, it's her fault.

Hooper was beside the window again. It was still open. For some time, neither of them spoke. Kingshaw wished that he would go.

Hooper said, 'You needn't think you've got to stick about the place with me, I've got my own things to do.'

'I'm supposed to, that's what your father said.'

'You do what I say.'

'Don't be stupid.'

'I'll bash you again, just watch it.'

Kingshaw backed. He said, 'Look, you needn't think I wanted to come here, you needn't think I like it.'

Though he had expected to get used to things. He had not bargained for Hooper. He began to pick up the things which had fallen out of his tartan suitcase.

'Is your school a proper boarding school?'

'Yes.'

'Well how does your mother afford to pay for you at a boarding school if she can't afford for you to live in a house?'

'I think . . . I don't know. I think it's free.'

'No schools are free.'

'Yes, they are.'

'Only schools for poor people. Boarding schools aren't free.'

'It's . . . I don't know. I daresay my father paid them a lot of money when I first went there. I daresay he paid all of the fees at once, and so now it doesn't cost anything. Yes, yes, he did do that, I know he did.'

Hooper looked at him coldly. He had won, and Kingshaw knew it. He could afford to turn away, letting the subject drop.

Kingshaw wondered whether there might now be some sort of truce between them, whether he might somehow have won his right to stay here. He had come prepared to get on with Hooper, as he got on with most people, because it was safer to do so. He was too vulnerable to let himself indulge in the making of enemies.

But Hooper was something different again, he had never faced this sort of hostility. He was unbalanced by it, and by Hooper's self-possession, not knowing what to do, and ashamed because he did not know. It was like the first time of going away to school, trying to find his way around, watching other people to see what they did.

He wanted to say, I've come here and I don't like it, I don't want to stay, I want to be somewhere by myself, in our own place, not in somebody else's place, we always go to live in somebody else's place. But I can't, I've got to stay here, why can't we make the best of things? He was willing to put himself out, he would even, just at this moment, have said he would do whatever Hooper wanted, would acknowledge him as master of his own territory. But he couldn't put any of it into words, not even to himself, it was only a series of feelings, overlapping one another like small waves. He was confused.

Hooper was looking at him across the table. A bruise was coming up on his left cheekbone, and swelling slightly, where Kingshaw's fist had struck. He looked the older of the two boys, though in height he was shorter. There was something about the way he walked, about the cast of his eyes.

He waited for a moment, and then walked slowly out of the room. But at the door, he turned. 'You still needn't think you're wanted here,' he said, 'this isn't your place.'

Kingshaw stood for a long time after Hooper had gone. He thought, there is nobody. The whole summer stretched ahead of him. After a while, he began to cry, though without making any sound, and swallowing hard to try and stop himself. He couldn't stop. But there was nothing that he would say, nobody to say it to.

In the end, he stopped. He might as well get the rest of his things out, and put them away. His mother had brought him here, she had been very excited about it, she had told him it was the answer to a prayer. He was ashamed of the way she had spoken.

He walked deliberately over to the window. 'It is my window, now,' he said, and pulled it tight shut.

Turning back into the room, he remembered what Hooper had told him about his grandfather, that it was here, in this room, in this bed, that he had died. It did not occur to Kingshaw to question the truth of it. He tried not to think of his own fears to come.

*

'Edmund, why have you locked yourself in here? You will please open the door.'

Hooper stood very still, turning the pencil round and round inside the sharpener, and watching the shaving of wood uncurl itself out of the side, like a moth emerging from the larva.

'I am quite sure that you are in there, you need not pretend.'

Silence.

'Edmund!'

In the end, he had to open the door.

'What are you doing, locked away here? It does not seem to me a very normal way to behave. You should be outside, getting plenty of fresh air, you should be showing Charles Kingshaw about the village.'

A great sheet of white paper was pinned on the wall, covered with curious lines, and little coloured dots, in blocks, together. In one corner, there was written:

Green = Napoleon's infantry
Blue = Napoleon's cavalry
Red =

Joseph Hooper looked at it. But he felt unwelcome here, his son stood, moving the pencil sharpener from hand to hand, waiting.

'But that is not what any battlefield ever was, that . . .' he made a gesture – for he wanted to talk, he did not wish to feel an intruder, a stranger in his son's room. He thought, we should be close together, we have only one another, I *ought* to be able to talk freely with him. But more than anything, it angered him to see his son's careful map, he wanted to say, this is *nothing*, nothing, this tight, neat, careful little plan, he wanted to tell the truth of the matter, to impart a vision of men and blood and horses, the boom and stench of gunfire and the noise of pain, the terrible confusion of it all. But he could not begin. Edmund Hooper stood, watching, sullen.

'Where is Charles Kingshaw?'

'He might be anywhere. *I* don't know where.'

'Then you should know, Edmund, you should be with him. I am not very pleased by this way you are behaving. *Why* are you not with him?'

'Because I don't know where he is.'

'Do not answer me back, please.'

Hooper sighed.

Joseph Hooper thought, if he were older, I could deal with him, if he were older and different, all could be understood and explained away by his adolescence. Or so one reads. But he is still a child, he is not yet eleven.

'Well you had better look for him, and then take him around the place, show him the house and the village and so on, make him feel – well, feel at home. I am very anxious that he should do so. Yes. This *is* his home, now.'

'Oh. Are they going to stay, then?'

'They will stay for the summer, certainly. And I am quite sure . . .' His voice trailed off, as he stood in the doorway. He would not speak to his son about what he felt, how much he wished that everything here would please Mrs Helena Kingshaw.

Edmund Hooper thought, how old my father looks. He has a thin face.

'I want you to get on with Charles, and with Mrs Kingshaw, too. There will be days when I shall not come back until very late, nights when I have to stay up in London altogether. You will . . .'

'What?'

'Well – the Kingshaws are here, everything is for the best. You will have company.'

Hooper turned away.

'Edmund, you are behaving in a very uncivil way towards a visitor.'

'I thought you said this was his home. If it's his home, then he can't be a visitor, can he?'

Perhaps I should strike him, Joseph Hooper thought, for speaking to me in that way, perhaps it is very foolish to let him get the upper hand, to allow such insolence. I do not like his supercilious expression. I should assert myself. But he knew that he would not. He deliberated too long, and then it could not be done. I have tried to avoid my own father's mistakes, he said, but I have only succeeded in replacing them with so many of my own.

It was his wife who had known the way, and she had died without leaving a set of rules for him to follow. He blamed her for it.

He went away.

Hooper added two more circles, meticulously, to a triangular block of them, on the right of his map. He coloured them in very slowly, round and round and round, with his tongue sticking out, and breathing heavily onto the paper, like a much smaller child crayoning. Then he went downstairs.

'You've got to come with me now.'

'Where to?'

'You'll see.'

He had found Kingshaw in the conservatory, poking into the geranium pots with a cane. It was very hot.

'Come on.'

'Suppose I don't want to.'

'You've got to, that's all, my father said so. And if anyone catches you bashing those flowers there'll be trouble, as well.'

'I haven't bashed them.'

'Yes, you have, some petals have fallen on to the floor, look here.'

'They do fall. They fall on their own.'

The sun came beating through the glass on to Kingshaw's face. The skin of his neck was already burned red. But he liked the conservatory. It smelled of old, dry leaves and blistering paint, where the sun struck a broken green bench. There were a lot of spiders' webs, too. Nobody seemed to come here.

Hooper stood, waiting, with the door open. He had not thought that Kingshaw would refuse to obey him.

'So you are both going on a tour of the estate!' Mrs Helena Kingshaw said, appearing in the doorway. She wore the same bright, hopeful expression with which she had arrived at Warings. Things must not go wrong, this is my chance, and I shall not waste it. I mean us all to be very happy.

So they were forced to go, trudging slowly out of the conservatory and down the path, one behind the other, watched by Mrs Kingshaw, not speaking.

'You needn't think I want to take you anywhere. I shall run now, you'd just better keep up with me.'

'What are you going back into the house for? I've seen all the house, haven't I?'

'My father said to show you everywhere, and don't I always do what my father says?' Hooper made a mocking face, and then began to run, through the front door, across the hall, up the oak staircase, in and out of rooms, one after another, banging the doors. He chanted as he went.

'This is my father's room, this is a spare room, this is where trunks are kept, this is your mother's sitting room, now we go up the back staircase, this is a bathroom, this is a cupboard, this is another bathroom . . .' Thump, thump, thump, thump, bang, bang, bang . . .

After a while, Kingshaw stopped following behind him. He sat down on the bottom step of the back staircase. It was very dark and cool.

He thought, I would like to get right away from Hooper, I would like to find a stream or a wood by myself. Anything to get away. But he dared not go anywhere outside the gate of the house, by himself.

He heard Hooper banging in and out along the corridor above. Then, suddenly, he was there again, standing at the top of the stone staircase, above Kingshaw's head.

'You were told to follow me.'

'So what? I don't have to take orders from you.'

'I'm showing you around!' Hooper said loftily.

'You're just a fool, that's a stupid way to behave.'

Hooper began to come very slowly down the stairs, putting one foot out delicately before the other, and stopping, for a moment, each time. Kingshaw heard his breathing. He did not turn round. Hooper's legs, in blue jeans, came up behind his neck. Stopped. Kingshaw had only to move his hand, and he could pull him over, grab him behind the knees and overbalance him, so that he would topple through the well of the staircase. He was terrified of the thought, as it came to him. He did not move.

Hooper walked on, stepping past him with elaborate care, avoiding even the touching of clothes. Somewhere, a mouse scuttled across floor-boards and under a door.

Hooper went away, down the next flight of stairs and then along the corridor leading back into the main part of the house. After a moment, Kingshaw heard the opening and closing of a door. Somewhere else, probably in the kitchen, there was music on a radio.

For a long time, he went on sitting.

Chapter Three

A path led through the rough field, at the back of the house, and beyond this were only more fields, sloping this way and that, overlapping like so many pillows. It was perhaps two miles to Hang Wood, which ran up along the ridge. Below this, a bit of open scrubland dropped sharply down into the forest proper.

That was to the west. To the east of Warings there was only the village of Derne, and then flat farmland, until the first of the main roads.

Kingshaw had studied all of it, but only on the map, half-inch by careful half-inch, before they came here. He had not seen any of it, only gone a little way down the lane at the bottom of the drive, and leaned on a gate.

Today, he began to walk. They had been here over a week, he was tired of hanging about the house, being spied upon by Hooper. He went through the yew trees and hesitated by the copse. Great black shadows lay across the entrance, and he could not see for more than a few yards inside. Keck and stinging nettles grew up as high as his chest, obscuring the path.

He backed away again, and skirted the copse, coming out into one corner of the field. Then, he walked.

The fields sloped upwards at first. It was very hot, a tractor had made giant ruts in the earth, and the ruts had dried hard, so that his feet kept stumbling in. He tried to walk on the turf-mounds in between the ruts though it was uncomfortable. The grass was thick with clots of sorrel and thistles that pricked his feet, through the sandals.

Kingshaw did not look back. He bent his head and plodded on, in a deliberate rhythm, one-one, one-one, one-one. He was not much interested in where he was going, but he must get away from that house, and from Hooper. And he must prove to himself that he could get by, somehow, alone in this place. He climbed a gate. The third field was of thick corn, almost ripe.

He looked for a path, but there was none, not even around the outside edge. Then he made out a narrow track, running diagonally across the field. He followed that. The corn came up to his waist. But half-way through, he realized that it was only a path made by some animal, or by another person who had gone before him. A little of the corn was trodden down. Kingshaw stopped. Someone might see him, probably he ought not to damage any more. He ought to go back.

The cornfield was high up. He stood in the very middle of it, now, and the sun came glaring down. He could feel the sweat running over his back, and in the creases of his thighs. His face was burning. He sat down, although the stubble pricked at him, through his jeans, and looked over at the dark line of trees on the edge of Hang Wood. They seemed very close – all the individual branches were clearly outlined. The fields around him were absolutely still.

When he first saw the crow, he took no notice. There had been several crows. This one glided down into the corn on its enormous, ragged black wings. He began to be aware of it when it rose up suddenly, circled overhead, and then dived, to land not very far away from him. Kingshaw could see the feathers on its head, shining blank in between the butter-coloured cornstalks. Then it rose, and circled, and came down again, this time not quite landing, but flapping about his head, beating its wings and making a sound like flat leather pieces being slapped together. It was the largest crow he had ever seen. As it came down for the third time, he looked up and noticed its beak, opening in a screech. The inside of its mouth was scarlet, it had small glinting eyes.

Kingshaw got up and flapped his arms. For a moment, the bird re-treated a little way off, and higher up in the sky. He began to walk rather quickly back, through the path in the corn, looking ahead of him. Stupid to be scared of a rotten bird. What could a bird do? But he felt his own extreme isolation, high up in the cornfield.

For a moment, he could only hear the soft thudding of his own footsteps, and the silky sound of the corn, brushing against him. Then, there was a rush of air, as the great crow came beating down, and wheeled about his head. The beak opened and the hoarse caaw came out again and again, from inside the scarlet mouth.

Kingshaw began to run, not caring, now, if he trampled the corn, wanting to get away, down into the next field. He thought that the corn might be some kind of crow's food store, in which he was seen as an invader. Perhaps this was only the first of a whole battalion of crows, that would rise up and swoop at him. Get on to the grass then, he thought, get on to the grass, that'll be safe, it'll go away. He wondered if it had mistaken him for some hostile animal, lurking down in the corn.

His progress was very slow, through the cornfield, the thick stalks bunched together and got in his way, and he had to shove them back with his arms. But he reached the gate and climbed it, and dropped on to the grass of the field on the other side. Sweat was running down his forehead and into his eyes. He looked up. The crow kept on coming. He ran.

But it wasn't easy to run down this field, either, because of the tractor ruts. He began to leap wildly from side to side of them, his legs stretched as wide as they could go, and for a short time, it seemed that he did go faster. The crow dived again, and, as it rose, Kingshaw felt the tip of its black wing, beating against his face. He gave a sudden, dry sob. Then, his left foot caught in one of the ruts and he keeled over, going down straight forwards.

He lay with his face in the coarse grass, panting and sobbing by turns, with the sound of his own blood pumping through his ears. He felt the sun on the back of his neck, and his ankle was wrenched. But he would be able to get up. He raised his head, and wiped two fingers across his face. A streak of blood came off, from where a thistle had scratched him. He got unsteadily to his feet, taking in deep, desperate breaths of the close air. He could not see the crow.

But when he began to walk forwards again, it rose up from the grass a little way off, and began to circle and swoop. Kingshaw broke into a run, sobbing and wiping the damp mess of tears and sweat off his face with one hand. There was a blister on his ankle, rubbed raw by the sandal strap. The crow was still quite high, soaring easily, to keep pace with him. Now, he had scrambled over the third gate, and he was in the field next to the one that belonged to Warings. He could see the back of the house. He began to run much faster.

This time, he fell and lay completely winded. Through the runnels of sweat and the sticky tufts of his own hair, he could see a figure, looking down at him from one of the top windows of the house.

Then, there was a single screech, and the terrible beating of wings, and the crow swooped down and landed in the middle of his back.

Kingshaw thought that, in the end, it must have been his screaming that frightened it off, for he dared not move. He lay and closed his eyes and felt the claws of the bird, digging into his skin, through the thin shirt, and began to scream in a queer, gasping sort of way. After a moment or two, the bird rose. He had expected it to begin pecking at him with his beak, remembering terrible stories about vultures that went for living people's eyes. He could not believe in his own escape.

He scrambled up, and ran on, and this time, the crow only hovered above, though not very high up, and still following him, but silently, and no longer attempting to swoop down. Kingshaw felt his legs go weak beneath him, as he climbed the last fence, and stood in the place from which he had started out on his walk, by the edge of the copse. He looked back fearfully. The crow circled a few times, and then dived into the thick foliage of the beech trees.

Kingshaw wiped his face with the back of his hand again. He wanted to go to his mother. He was trembling all over. But he never did go to her, he made himself cope alone, he would not go because of a stupid bird. Then his eye caught a quick movement. He looked up. Hooper stood in the window of his bedroom. He watched and watched.

After a moment, Kingshaw glanced away, turned slowly, and went up between the yew trees and into the house, by the back door.

'You were scared. You were running away.'

'This is my room, you can't come in here just when you want, Hooper.'

'You should lock the door, then, shouldn't you?'

'There isn't any key.'

'Scared of a bird!'

'I was not, then.'

'*You* were crying, I know, I can tell.'

'Shut up, shut up.'

'It was only a *crow,* a crow isn't anything, haven't you ever seen a crow before? What did you think it would do?'

'It . . .'

'What? What did it do?' Hooper puckered up his face. 'Was it a naughty crow, then, did it frighten Mummy's baby-boy?'

Kingshaw whipped round. Hooper paused. The recollection of Kingshaw's fist on his cheekbone was vivid. He shrugged.

'Why did you go off, anyway? Where did you think you'd get to?'

'Mind your own business. I don't have to tell you anything.'

'Shall I tell you something, Kingshaw?' Hooper came up close to him suddenly, pressing him back against the wall and breathing into his face,

'You're getting a very rude little boy, aren't you, you're very cocky all of a sudden. Just watch it, that's all.'

Kingshaw bit him hard on the wrist. Hooper let go, backed a step or two, but went on staring at him.

'I'll tell you something, baby-baby, you daren't go into the copse.'

Kingshaw did not reply.

'You went and looked and stopped, because you were a scaredy, it's dark in there.'

'I changed my mind, that's all.'

Hooper straddled a chair beside the bed. 'All right,' he said, in a menacing, amiable voice, 'O.K., go in there, I dare you. And I'll watch. Or into the big wood, even. Yes, you daren't go up into the big wood. If you do, it'll be O.K.'

'What will?'

'Things.'

'I'm not afraid of you, Hooper.'

'Liar.'

'I can go into the wood any time I want.'

'Liar.'

'I don't care if you believe me or not.'

'Oh, yes you do. Liar, liar, liar.'

Silence. Kingshaw bent down and began to fiddle with his sandal strap. He had never been faced with such relentless persecution as this.

'I dare you to go into the copse.'

'Oh, stuff it.'

Hooper stuck his hands up on either side of his head, and waggled his fingers about. He found Kingshaw frustrating. He was at a loss to know how to get past this stone-walling, the dull, steady stare. All he could do was bait and bait, seeing how far he could go, trying to think of new things. He despised Kingshaw, but he was curious about him. He had watched him change, even in the week since they came here. He was closer, more suspicious. Hooper wanted to know what was going on inside his head. He sat on the chair again, and watched.

'Stare you out,' he said coolly.

Kingshaw wanted him to go. But, after that, he had no idea what he might do. He was not very resourceful. He could make a model, or read. If he could make a galleon model it would last a long time, they were difficult. He could think no further ahead than that.

He was anxious about the copse and the woods. He would have to go there, now. He always had to do things when people dared him. Terrible things.

When he was about five, he had gone with his father to an open-air swimming pool. There had been a boy called Turville. Turville had seen that he was afraid of the water, not just because he could not swim, but for other reasons, quite inexplicable. The glassy, artificial blueness of it, and the way people's limbs looked huge and pale and swollen underneath. But the more afraid he had become, the more he had known he would have to jump in. There had been a hard ball in the centre of his belly. He felt sick. As he jumped, and after he had jumped, he felt no better, he felt worse, the reality of it was far more appalling than he could have imagined.

Turville had made him do it again and again, until he was satisfied, and Kingshaw's father and Turville's father had watched and laughed, and looked away again, blind, unaware. Kingshaw had gone on diving and gone on being afraid, it was the fear that had driven him on, and his shame because of it.

Now, he would have to go into the copse, or up to the wood. He sighed, looking down from his bedroom window, on to the dull front lawn. He thought, make him go away, make him go.

Hooper went, suddenly, banging the door without speaking to him again. Kingshaw went on staring out of the window. He thought, we keep on going to new places, awful places, we keep on not belonging. I want to go back to school.

There was nothing at all to do.

Hooper went up to the attic. As soon as the idea had come into his head, it had filled him with excitement, though he was startled by it, he had never done such a thing before. He could not have imagined the charm it afforded him, having Kingshaw here, thinking of things to do to him.

There were several attics, leading out of one another, through little, narrow arches, like catacombs. Everything was standing about in piles and the piles were thick with dust. He had spent an afternoon here, before Kingshaw had come, and found a trunk full of odd lumps of rock, of different textures and colours. He wanted them. There were things of his grandfather's, too, lights and jars and nets, all to do with the moth collecting. The nets were rotting. They had a queer smell.

The thing he wanted to find now was in the last attic, on the floor. He remembered having seen it the day before, when he came looking for a stamp album. The sun shone in straight through the tall windows, making the dust dance, and falling into odd shapes, on the floor boards. Everything smelled old and dry and hot. He moved aside a cardboard box, and a huge spider, with a lumpy, greenish-grey back, scuttled out, and over some piles of newspapers. Hooper half thought of trying to catch it. But it would be a lot of trouble and they always died. He would have used it to frighten Kingshaw, if the new idea hadn't come to him.

He shoved the box farther away, so that the unsettled dust rose up, making him sneeze. Then, he bent down and lifted the thing up carefully. He thought that it might disintegrate, like the moth in the Red Room. But there was only dust. He stroked it. It was very large. And old, he supposed. For a moment, Hooper thought he might change his mind, for he was a little afraid of it himself, now. He held it gingerly, and rather away from his body. Then, he found a box of old, torn-up shirts, took one out and wrapped it up carefully inside. The cloth smelled peculiar, too. He left the attic.

Kingshaw woke. The room was quite silent. He had dreamed it, then.

He lay on his back, keeping his eyes tightly closed, and thinking about why Hooper might have disappeared for the rest of that day. He had been waiting for him to come and say, 'You've got to go into the copse, now, I shall come to the window and watch you, you've got to go right in, and if you don't . . .' But Hooper had not come near.

What Kingshaw thought was, Hooper is not very used to being a bully. He is trying it out, he is just learning. Because he was not like the usual bullies he had known at school. He could cope with them, they had simple, and transparent minds. In any case, they rarely bothered him, now. He had ways of dealing with them. But Hooper was unpredictable. Clever. Inventive.

There was a sound outside on the landing, a sort of shuffle. But Warings was that sort of house, it moved and creaked all the time, it was old and the doors and windows did not shut properly.

Kingshaw turned his head and then opened his eyes, to look at the clock. He never liked to open his eyes in this room, at night, he could not stop himself thinking about Hooper's grandfather, lying dead.

What he saw first was not the clock. There was a thin beam of moonlight coming into the room, and a shape upon his bed, about half way down. He could not at all make out what it was. He listened. Somebody had been in his room, but there was no sound, now, from outside the door.

He thought, make me put the light on, I mustn't be too scared to put the light on, I've got to see. But he dared not reach out his hand, he lay stiff, his eyes wide open. Nothing moved. He did not move.

But he had to see, had to know. Make me, make me put on the light . . .

He reached out his left hand swiftly, and found the switch and pressed it before he could stop himself. He looked.

He knew at once that the crow was not real, that it was stuffed and dead. Somehow, that only made it so much worse. Its claws were gripping the sheet. It was very big.

Kingshaw lay stiff, and did not scream, did not make any sound at all. He was dry and faint with fear of the thing, though his brain still worked, he knew who had brought it, he knew that Hooper was still waiting out in the corridor, must have seen the light go on. Hooper wanted him to be frightened, to scream and cry and shout for his mother. He would not do that. There was nothing, nothing at all, that he could do to help himself. He wanted to lift up his leg quickly, and topple the terrible bird on to the floor, out of sight, not to have it there, pressing down on his thigh. But if he moved at all, it might fall the wrong way – forwards, nearer to him. He would not be able to touch it with his hand.

He must put out the light. Hooper was still waiting, listening. He managed it, eventually, but he dared not draw his hand back into the bed. He lay with his eyes squeezed shut, and a burning pain in his bladder. He was afraid of wetting the bed. He wished to be dead, he wished Hooper dead. But there was nothing, nothing he could do. In the end, towards morning, he half-slept.

When he woke again, it was just after six o'clock. The crow looked even less real, now, but much larger. He lay and waited for the beak to open so that he would see the scarlet inside of its mouth, for it to rise up and swoop down at him, making for his eyes. He thought, it's stupid, it's stupid, it's only a stupid, rotten bird. He took one deep breath, and then closed his eyes and rolled over, out of bed on to the floor. Then, ran. He sat for a long time on the lavatory. The house was quite silent.

He wondered what he could do with the thing, how he could possibly get rid of it. Now it was daylight, he would be even more afraid of touching it with his bare hands, but he wouldn't tell anyone about its presence in his room. It would have to stay there, then, lie on the floor beside his bed, night after night, until Mrs Boland came to clean and took it away.

But when he got back, the crow had gone.

Hooper returned the bird to the attic. He knew that Kingshaw had woken in the night, had switched on the lamp and then had done nothing else, for there had been no sound at all. The light had gone back off again. There had been silence. In the end Hooper had got up and walked back quietly to his own bedroom, stiff with cold.

At breakfast, he stared and stared, trying to catch Kingshaw's eye, to find out. Kingshaw did not look at him, and did not speak.

At the bottom of the cornflakes packet there was a plastic model of a submarine. You submerged it in a bath of water, and then it rose gradually up to the surface, on a stream of bubbles. It was Kingshaw who reached the bottom of the packet. He pulled out the greaseproof bag, and then fished down for the submarine. Hooper waited.

Kingshaw examined the model carefully. He read the instructions that were attached to it by a rubber band. After that, he put it down on the table, some distance away from him, and went on eating his cornflakes, not looking up.

'It's O.K.,' Hooper said, 'you can keep it if you like.' He smiled a sweet smile.

Kingshaw raised his head slowly, and gave Hooper a long look of hatred. Then, he went on eating. The plastic submarine remained, untouched between them, on the table.

'Well, it is so nice to see them shaking down together, after all,' said Mr Joseph Hooper to Mrs Kingshaw, a little later, after the boys had left the room. 'I think they may be friends.'

Hooper saw him as he was coming up the drive. At once, he stepped off the gravel on to the lawn, and walked carefully around the edge, until he was within a few yards of him.

Kingshaw was standing with his hands cupped on either side of his face, trying to see through the window of the Red Room. Hooper waited, trying not to be reflected in the glass. Kingshaw shifted a little, standing on tiptoe.

'What are you prying at?'

He spun round. Hooper came towards him.

'You can't get in there, it's locked. It's the Red Room and it's private. My father keeps the key.'

'What for? It's only a lot of old books and dead fish.'

'That's all you know.'

'What then?'

'Valuable things, I told you that before. Things you'll never even have seen.'

Kingshaw was curious, he had been trying to imagine what the glass cases might contain. But he did not like the look of the Red Room, in spite of that, he did not think he would want to go inside. He moved away from the window.

'Want me to show you?'

Kingshaw shrugged. He thought, I mustn't let Hooper know what I truly think, never, not about anything. He did not want to go into the room.

'You can come with me after supper,' Hooper said.

Kingshaw stood about in the hall. Hooper did not come. Perhaps it was all right, and he had forgotten or changed his mind, perhaps he would not come. Kingshaw turned away.

'I've got the key now,' Hooper said, coming up behind him.

It was very dark inside the Red Room. Beyond the windows, the sky was steely grey, the rain teemed down. The branches of the yew trees were bent against them.

Kingshaw went only a little way into the room, and then stopped. He had known that it would be like this, that he would not like it. There was a dead smell and his shoes screeched faintly on the polished wood floor. Hooper stayed beside the doors, the keys in his hand.

'Go on then,' he said in a soft voice, 'you've got to look now. You should just think yourself lucky I've brought you. Go on.'

Kingshaw stiffened and moved slowly towards the first of the glass cases. He drew in his breath sharply.

'Moths.'

'Yes, every sort of moth in the world.'

'Who . . . where did they come from?'

'My grandfather. Haven't you ever heard of him? You're thick, aren't you? My grandfather was the most famous collector in the whole world. He wrote all sorts of books about moths.'

Kingshaw did not know which were worse, moths alive, with their whirring, pattering wings, or these moths, flattened and pinned and dead. You could see the way their eyes stuck out, and the thin veins along their wings. The skin prickled across the back of his neck. Since he was very young, he had been terrified of moths. They used to come into his bedroom at night, when they lived in their own house and his father had always made him have a window open, and he had lain in bed, in the darkness, hearing the soft flap of wings against the walls and the furniture, and then silence, waiting, dreading that they were coming near him and would land on his face. Moths.

Hooper came up behind him. 'Open one of the cases, then,' he said. 'I'll let you.' He held out a small key.

'No.'

'Why not?'

'I – I can see them all right, can't I?'

'Yes, but you can't touch them, can you. You've got to touch them.'

'No.'

'Why not? Scaredy-baby, scared of a moth!'

Kingshaw was silent. Hooper moved forward, inserted the key and pushed the heavy lid up.

'Pick one up.'

Kingshaw backed away. He could not have touched one for anything, and he did not want to watch Hooper do it. 'What's the matter, baby?'

'Nothing. I don't want to touch one, that's all.'

They won't *hurt* you.'

'No.'

'They're dead, aren't they? They've been dead for years and years.'

'Yes.'

'What are you scared of? Are you scared of dead things?'

'No.'

Kingshaw went on moving backwards. He only wanted to get out of the room. If Hooper tried to grab him and force his hand down on to one of the moths, he would fight, he didn't care how much he fought.

'Come here and look, Kingshaw.'

'I don't want to.'

'Well *I* dare touch it, I'll pick one up and hold it. I dare do anything.'

'You'd better not.'

'Why?' Hooper was peering curiously into his face. 'Why?'

'You might damage it. If they're valuable you'll get into trouble, won't you?'

He imagined the furry body of the moth against the pads of Hooper's fingers. He was ashamed of being so afraid, and could not help it, he only wanted to get out, to stop having to see the terrible moths. Hooper watched him.

There was a moment when they both stood, quite still, waiting. Then, Hooper whipped around and pushed past Kingshaw without warning, he was out of the door, turning the key sharply in the lock. After a moment, his footsteps went away down the hall. A door closed somewhere.

At once, Kingshaw went to the window, averting his eyes from the moths. The rain was driving across the lawn now, into the yew trees, battering against the window. It was gone nine o'clock, and already dusk, because of the heavy clouds.

The windows were bolted. It took him a long time to ram back the stiff metal, and he split his thumbnail down one side. The window-ledges were filthy. He dared not turn round and look back into the room, at the stiff, animal bodies and the dead fish, and the rows of outstretched moths underneath their glass lids. He tugged and heaved at both the tall windows, until his arms felt wrenched from their sockets, and his chest ached. He could not move them, nobody had opened them for years. He went on trying, though, long after he knew that it was useless, because, as long as he pulled desperately at the windows, he was not having to turn and face the silent room. But in the end, he let go, and began to cry with frustration.

After a time he thought, it's only about eight o'clock, everybody's up, if I shout and shout they'll come for me. But he knew that he would not shout, he would not do anything to make Hooper feel that he had won. Eventually, his mother would go up to bed, and then he could bang on the door, someone would come to him. He just had to wait, that was all.

He sat on the window-ledge. If Hooper had come back now, he would have . . . but he could not imagine what he might do. The fight with

31

Hooper on the first day had shocked him, though he had not been hurt himself.

A burst of rain spattered against the window.

Looking out onto the lawn, he could see the shadows of the yew trees, tossing in the wind. He thought suddenly of the figures of men, hiding out there, watching him, lying in wait. The rhododendrons were bunched together in peculiar shapes, on either side of the long drive. He dared not go on looking, he turned his back on the garden and walked forward a little way, into the room.

He thought, I ought to switch on the standard lamp and look in the cupboards for a book to read, I ought not to be a baby. When they come past, I shall call out, that's all. He would not tell them about Hooper.

He knew that the lamp would cast shadows, but only in this one small corner, by the bookcases, the rest of the room would be in darkness. He did not think he would mind, if he sat up close to the books, in the circle of the lamp . . .

It was very important to stand up to Hooper, even if only he himself knew that he had done so. It was the most important thing of all.

Kingshaw lifted his arm up to the standard lamp. As the light came on, a moth emerged from inside the shade, brushing against his hand as it flew, and began to beat about the glow.

In the end, they did come, through the hall on their way upstairs, laughing together. He called out. They opened the door.

He said stiffly, 'I got locked in.'

His mother stood, frowning, looking to Mr Hooper for guidance. Mr Hooper took a few steps nearer to Kingshaw.

'I'm all right,' he said. 'It's O.K. I just got locked in. Good-night,' and raced for the stairs, before the questions could begin. In the lavatory he was violently sick.

Hooper said the next morning, 'He's stupid. Why didn't he shout, then? I didn't know he was in there, I never know what Kingshaw does.'

All that Kingshaw thought was, it can't go on for ever. Because, in the end, the time would pass and then there would be no more of this terrible house, no more of Hooper. It was just a question of waiting, of finding things to do. He would not think about next holiday. By then, everything might be changed, they might be living somewhere else. Since his father died, things did change, often. Once, they had lived in a hotel. He had hated that.

At night, he said, dear God, make Mr Hooper not like us, make him not be happy to have us here, make him ask us to go away. Though he wondered about what would happen then, whether the next place they went to might not be worse.

He thought about school. There, he belonged, they knew him, he had become the person they had all decided that he would be. It was safe. The first day he had arrived, when the car had stopped in front of Main Block, he had known it would be all right, it was what he wanted. Lots of the others had been crying, and white in the face, their mothers held their hands. He had not cried. He had wanted to go inside and see everything, to look at the faces of those who were already there, touch the walls and the doors and the cover of his bed, smell the particular smells. He had been tense with excitement, feeling his feet crunch on the gravel, he had wanted to say to his mother, go away, go away, so that it could all begin.

'How brave!' somebody else's mother had said.

'Oh, but they do not always show everything, he is bottling it up. He is only seven, and that is no age, no age at all.'

Mrs Helena Kingshaw said, 'Charles is a very sensible little boy. Though – oh, yes, I wonder so often if we are doing the right thing, if he is not still too young . . .'

But they had, they had, Kingshaw thought, fingering the embossed badge on his new blazer. This was all right, it was what he wanted. Though it was different, he could not have imagined what it would be like.

The third week of term, he had been ill. He was in a special room and everybody had come to see him whenever they liked, and he had books and biscuits and any drink that he asked for. The sun had shone through the window on to his bed. He thought this is all right, this is the place to be. When he got up, he could go into the Headmaster's house and watch television and eat fruit.

He wrote home, 'I like it here very much, it is smashing here.'

'He is a brave little boy,' Mrs Helena Kingshaw had said, reading the letter, and weeping a little.

At St Vincent's School, Kingshaw said, let me stay here for ever and ever.

Chapter Four

A week later, Kingshaw found the room. Hooper had gone to London for a day with his father.

It was on the top corridor, at the east end of the house. Nobody slept there. What he liked about it was the smallness, and the fact that it seemed never to have had any particular function of its own. There was a window, looking onto the fields that led towards the village. There was a low chair, heavily stuffed, but without arms, and covered in faded, flowery material, and a rectangular table, up against the window. The table had a drawer, and a blue wicker chair in front of it. Against the opposite wall was a glass-fronted cabinet, and inside this were the dolls, dozens of very small dolls, all female, and made of wool-covered wire, like pipe cleaners, with embroidered-on faces. The gowns and crinolines and veils worn by the dolls were all faded to beige and grey and fawn, and the faces were almost worn away.

Kingshaw had opened the cabinet and examined the dolls, picking each one up in turn. He lifted their skirts and found petticoats underneath, and knickers, embroidered on to the bodies in black wool, the same as the faces. He liked them, liked the feel of them in his hands. He laid them all out on the table and looked at them.

Perhaps, once, this had been some child's nursery, but he did not think so. The furniture seemed to have been dumped here arbitrarily, having served its purpose in another part of the house. The room had no character of its own, and so he thought that he might be able to take it over. He did not like the bedroom he had been given, he only went in there to sleep. He brought the construction kit of the Spanish galleon model, and worked at it in here. There was a lock on the door. If Hooper locked himself away, why shouldn't he do the same? He felt it was a way of defending himself.

He liked being alone, because he was used to it, he was safe with himself. Other people were unpredictable. He had never missed his father. But there was such a lot of time, here, and when the model was finished, he must think again of something to do. That morning, a postcard had come from Devereux, in Norfolk:

'We're sailing every day. It's sunny. There are rather a lot of people here, and high-powered boats. I'm learning everything about them. See you.'

He wished he could have gone with Devereux. They had asked him, Mrs Devereux had written a letter, and other people had asked him, too, he could have gone with the Broughton-Smiths to Italy. But they had been coming to Warings. Besides, his mother had said she did not like the idea of sailing, did not like the thought of his travelling abroad, did not like his going away when she saw so little of him. She said, 'You are all I have left now.' He turned away, embarrassed, hating to listen to those things.

He knew that Hooper was trying to find out where he went now. But he was learning cunning, he would not be followed. He could wait until Hooper was in the lavatory, or else he would tell him that he was wanted somewhere, by Mrs Boland or by his father. Or else he would simply run in the opposite direction, dodging down corridors, go into other rooms and hide, putting Hooper off the scent, waiting. It was surprising how often he had succeeded. It would not last.

He knew that, quite simply, he hated Hooper now. He had never hated anyone before, and the taste was very strong in his mouth, he was astounded by the strength of it. They had been told about how wrong it was to hate, but he had scarcely listened, for it had not seemed an emotion with which he would ever have to do. He liked most people. Though he disliked Crup, for instance – but not liking someone was different, it wasn't hating, and he had a way of dealing with Crup, now. But he had seen after the first few days, that what he felt for Hooper was hatred. He was terrified of the feeling, wished it were gone, and knew that it would never go, not so long as he had to be in this house, with Hooper.

He thought then – perhaps I do not have to be here with him. He laid down the triangle of plastic thoughtfully.

On the train from London, Joseph Hooper said, 'I hope you are friendly with young Charles Kingshaw, now. I have not seen you about the place together very much.'

Hooper looked up from *The Scourge of the Marsh Monster*.

'I can't help it if he locks himself up, can I?'

'In his room?'

'Somewhere. In some room or other. *I* don't know.'

'That sounds to me a very strange way of going on. What is this all in aid of, what does he do?'

Hooper shrugged.

'Slowly, remorselessly, the huge feet carried the hulking beast forward. The stench of the marshes hung about it and the mud on its scaly hide was mud formed at the dawn of history. The blood and death it now sought were . . .'

'I suppose that I must speak to his mother.'

The train crossed over some points.

'But then, I daresay he is a little shy. You will have to be understanding about that, Edmund, there must always be a little give and take in this sort of friendship. That is a lesson I hope that you will learn in life very quickly. He has no father, when all is said and done.'

Hooper looked up briefly, raising his eyebrows.

Mr Hooper coughed, turned his face away, and shifted a little in his seat. There is no telling, he thought, perhaps he does remember something of his mother, after all. We cannot fathom the minds of young children. He was discomforted by his own lack of insight. He tried to find some clue, in his son's facial expression, as to what might be going on in his mind, but there was only a blank. He could recall nothing of himself at the same age except that he had loathed his own father.

But I came through, he said to himself now, I daresay that I am normal enough, that there is nothing so much wrong with me, in spite of it all. I shall not allow myself to feel guilty about it. Edmund will be like any other healthy boy. I am not to blame.

He watched the darkening countryside and then, after a time, returned to his magazine, more settled in his mind. He felt exonerated.

Edmund Hooper stared down at his own finger, as it lay across the comic, at the crinkled skin and the dry, ragged line of nail. He imagined what his hands would be like in a flat solid block of flesh, without the divisions of fingers. Fingers were queer. But it was amazing to realize what things he would not be able to do. Underneath his hand were the gruesome drawings of the Marsh Monster.

He thought, tomorrow I shall find out about Kingshaw, just by waiting and going into every room in the house, one after the next, very quietly. For he was irritated by the feeling that the other boy had somehow slipped through his fingers, had taken a little of the initiative. He had been here almost three weeks.

It was unexpected, Kingshaw was not that sort of a boy. Hooper could see quite clearly that the experience of being tormented and disliked and repelled was new to him. For a while, at the beginning, he had flinched in surprise, retreated, wondering how to cope. But he was quick, his defences had gone up now.

Over the business of the stuffed crow, Hooper had felt a grudging respect, though he had withdrawn it later, in fury, when Kingshaw had derided him the next morning. And now, he had started taking himself off to some other part of the house, a room that Hooper did not know had become Kingshaw's fortress.

Joseph Hooper was saying, 'You had better both go off on some expedition or other, this weather is too good to last. I cannot remember being at a loose end here, in the summer holidays when I was your age.'

Though he remembered that he had rarely been allowed beyond the garden. They had said, the girls will follow, there will be an accident. But it was not because of that. He had been summoned by his father to go and sit in the Red Room, to watch the moths in the poison bottle, to smell the smell of old books and stuffed weasels and watch the sunshine lying across the garden, beyond the high windows.

Looking up now, suddenly, he saw what it was about his own son that reminded him so vividly of himself. He was very pale. The village boys of Derne had always gone about half-naked, their bodies brown as Indians, through the summers, but Joseph Hooper had rarely gone out, and never been allowed to strip off his shirt, and so he had been very pale. Now, his own son was pale.

'You should get out into the fresh air and the sunshine, not mew yourselves up inside the house. It seems to me a very unhealthy way of going on. I shall insist upon your going off into the garden tomorrow, the moment you have eaten breakfast.'

Hooper lifted the comic higher up in front of his face. He would have said out loud, I don't want to go on any expedition, I don't want to do anything or go anywhere with Kingshaw. But he said nothing, wondering whether it might not be Kingshaw who would refuse to go with him. He thought he had made Kingshaw afraid, now.

The train gathered speed through a tunnel. At Warings, Kingshaw went to bed early and lay in the darkness, making plans. He said, it will be all right, I know what to do, it won't go on for ever.

He made plans for a long time, almost a week. Everything was worked out, except the time. He had to find the right day. But, to begin with, it was harder than he had anticipated to get the things together. He was a methodical planner, but he was feeling his way.

Just because it was not the sort of thing he had ever done before, or would be expected to do, Kingshaw knew that he would be taken seriously. Though he was doing it for himself, only, he did not care what any of the others thought about it. It did not occur to him that he might fail, though he failed regularly at other things. For, at the very least, it would be a gesture, and they would understand it as such. It did not seem to him a strange, or ridiculous thing to be planning, and certainly not a lark. It was necessary, that was all. He was neither courageous nor frivolous.

When he got hold of the things, he took them along to the room with the dolls, locking it behind him and removing the key, whenever he left. Though he was certain, now, that Hooper had discovered it. It had only been a question of time.

One day, it rained without stopping, and Mr Hooper caught him, on a bend in the main staircase.

'Ah now, I have been looking for you!'

Kingshaw stopped. His mother had said, 'You should be very, very polite to Mr Hooper. He has been so very kind to us already. He is anxious to take an interest in you, Charles, already he has been talking to me about your schooling and your future.' Her eyes had been very bright, and the bracelets went sliding up and down her arm. Do not spoil everything for me, she wanted to say, do not take away my chance. Kingshaw did not like this new eagerness and hopefulness about her, now that she was at Warings.

She had changed a good deal.

'You are to be polite to Mr Hooper.' But there was never anything he could think of to say.

'Where is Edmund?'

'He might . . . I don't know, I haven't seen him.'

Mr Hooper stooped a little, and wore a very dark blue suit, and kept smoothing his hand back over the receding hair. He had a small, pursed mouth.

'Now I have found two things for you, this morning. I have found the draughts and a bagatelle board. The draughts are very unusual ones, very valuable, they were . . . but I daresay you will not be interested in that kind of thing, you had better find Edmund and then I will bring the things to you. There is a table in the front sitting room, you can go there.'

Kingshaw went slowly on, up the stairs. He thought, Mr Hooper can tell us to do what he pleases, because my mother is paid to work for him, and this is not our house. I shall have to go into the sitting room with Hooper and play draughts.

'Oh, how kind of you! What a good idea!' said Mrs Helena Kingshaw, smiling eagerly, in the breakfast room. That is just right for a rainy morning. They have been so very unresourceful, these last few days, I cannot think . . . but now they can get together over these games, and then we shall really see the friendship cemented. That is a clever suggestion of yours!'

Joseph Hooper smoothed back the receding hair and felt more than ever satisfied with Mrs Helena Kingshaw.

'You needn't think I'm going to stick in here with you. Just wait till my father goes out. He won't know what I do then.'

'My mother's going to be here, though. She'll know. You'll have to stay.'

Hooper made a derisive noise in the back of his throat.

'And what if he doesn't go out, what if he stays here all day and doesn't go to London?'

Hooper did not reply.

Kingshaw thought, suddenly, *it might be all right*. We might go on and on playing draughts and things, he might change, we might be friends. Then I shall go back to school, everything might be all right.

But he knew at once, looking at Hooper's back, that it would never be ail right. He could not go back to the beginning, when he had not wanted to come here but nevertheless had thought he might get Hooper to be friendly. Nothing could change, he had made his plan.

Having decided, it was like a great cloud lifting. He had been tempted and now he couldn't be tempted again. Though he woke up night after night and remembered what he was planning to do, and his mind was blank with fear. But he would still do it. No matter what else happened between him and Hooper.

'That's a bagatelle board,' Hooper said now, 'it's very old. It's worth having, I can tell you.'

Kingshaw glanced across at it.

'We could play, then.'

There was a pause. The bones on the back of Hooper's thin neck stuck out, above the round line of his tee-shirt. Kingshaw stiffened, remembering the stuffed crow on his bed, trying to guess what else Hooper might to do him.

'O.K.,' Hooper said casually, 'We might as well.'

He went over and lifted up the board. 'Move those draughts,' he said. Kingshaw hesitated. Then, did so, because it made no difference, there was no point in having a row. Knowing that he had made up his mind, that everything about the future was settled, he could afford to stay in here, with Hooper, and play the bagatelle game, he might relax for a short time.

They scarcely spoke. Hooper kept the score and they took their turns, concentrating fiercely. The little, silver balls clattered against the nails. Outside, the sky darkened, and it rained harder. Joseph Hooper did not go to London, after all.

At eleven o'clock, Mrs Helena Kingshaw, coming in with glasses of milk, said, 'Well, what a splendid game, what could be better than this, on a rainy morning!' She spoke in a gay voice.

They took their drinks, and said, 'Thank you', and nothing more.

He had two other things to take along to the room with the dolls. He waited until after lunch. And he had to think of something to put them all in, too.

He looked about him carefully, on the landing and up the first flight of stairs. There was nobody. Anyway, if Hooper already knew about the room, it scarcely mattered now.

All the doors up here were painted brown, and after the first landing, there was no carpet. Kingshaw thought, I hate this house, I hate it, it is the very worst of all the places we have lived in. From the first moment he had looked at it, out of the car window, he had hated it. It didn't seem much for Hooper to be so proud of.

He walked along a little, dark passage-way, and turned into the corridor. Then he saw Hooper. He was sitting on the floor, with his back against the door of the room and his legs stretched out. Kingshaw stopped dead.

'Going somewhere?'

'Get lost, Hooper.'

'Where's the key? Look, this isn't *your* house, you know, who do you think you are, going around locking doors?'

'Stuff it.'

'You can't come in here any more unless I say so.'

Kingshaw put down the small box he was carrying, wearily. Hooper was very childish.

'You needn't think I'm going away, either. I can stay here all day. All night as well, if I like. I can stay here for ever. This is my house.'

'Why don't you grow up?'

'I want to know what's in here.'

'Nothing.'

'That means something. You'd better tell me.'

'Shut up.'

'I want to know what you keep coming up here for. You needn't think I don't know where you go to, I've known for weeks, all the time, I've known.'

Kingshaw was silent. He stood some way back from Hooper, his face in the shadows. There was the sound of rain on the roof. He might as well let Hooper in. He'd get in, anyway, fight, or else just stick it out for hours on end. He had no good opinion of his own chances, against Hooper. Or against anyone. He was not cowardly. Just realistic, hopeless. He did not give in to people, he only went, from the beginning, with the assurance that he would be beaten. It meant that there was no surprise, and no disappointment, about anything.

So he might as well let Hooper into the room now, and get it over with. If he was going to find out, he might as well find out because Kingshaw chose to let him. It kept the initiative in his hands, somehow, and he cared about that. Hooper always won.

Kingshaw reached slowly into the back pocket of his jeans, and fetched out the key.

*

'There isn't even anything *in* here – what a footling room. What do you come in here for?'

Silence.

'Was that galleon already here?'

'No.'

'Did you do it?'

'Yes.'

Hooper went over, and examined it closely. 'You haven't done the gluing properly. The joints show.'

'So what?'

'It'll just break, that's all.'

'Leave it alone, leave it alone.'

'What are *those* things, Kingshaw?'

'Things.'

'You're close, aren't you?'

'I don't have to tell you everything.'

'Let's see inside that bag.'

'No. Get off, Hooper.' He struggled, but Hooper reached his arms up high, out of reach.

'I shall open it, I'm going to open it, I'm opening it *now* . . . I'm . . . Oh!'

'Give me that, it's got nothing to do with you, it's my own private things.'

'What do you want matches for?'

Kingshaw turned away, putting his hands in his pockets, and looked out of the window. He thought, let him get on with it, then. Behind him, Hooper's hands scrabbled about in the parcel, splitting open a paper bag. He was laying the things on the table.

'You stole these, all of them. Thief, thief, thief.'

'I did not, so.'

'You couldn't have bought them.'

'Yes, I did, I did.'

'Liar.'

'Well – I didn't buy the matches.'

'Where did you get them, then?'

'They were . . .'

'What?' Hooper came up and pushed his face into Kingshaw's, menacing.

'What?'

'They were lying around. I expect my mother bought them.'

'I expect she did not, pick-thief. Things in this house aren't yours, they belong to us, and if you take them it's stealing. You're a thief.'

Hooper backed away suddenly, as Kingshaw swung round, so that the blow landed nowhere. Hooper went on staring at the things lying on the table, his mind ticking over. Suddenly, his face cleared, eyes widening, and he flushed slightly, with excitement, as the answer came to him.

'You're going to . . .' He stopped, staring at Kingshaw.

Then he let out a long whistle.

'Cunning!'

'You don't know. You don't know anything about it. Think I'd tell you!'

Hooper's face was queerly triumphant.

'I know why you're doing it as well. It's because of me. You're scared of me, Kingshaw, you're Mummy's little scaredy-pet. You don't know what I might do to you, I could do anything at all. That's why.'

'Don't be stupid.'

But Hooper was laughing, knowing that he had the truth. Or part of it, for there was more to it, now, than just fear of Hooper, there were a lot more things, worse things.

'I could tell them.'

'What could you tell them? I haven't said anything, you don't know what it's all about.'

There was silence. Kingshaw saw that Hooper was turning this way and that, uncertain how to take the advantage. He knew that what Kingshaw said was partly true. Nothing had been said, if he told Mrs Kingshaw and his father, they would laugh at him.

He had set all the things out in two very even rows, like museum exhibits, and he was picking each one up and looking at it, wondering. Kingshaw thought, there's nothing he can do, it won't make any difference, just because of what Hooper knows. It will be all right, I shan't have to stay here, even now.

Hooper said, looking sideways at Kingshaw, beneath his lashes, 'I shall come with you.'

Kingshaw knew that he meant what he said. He thought about it for the whole of that week, kept on remembering Hooper's voice, and the queer smile. He was running away because he wanted to get away from Hooper – it was the only way. As long as he stayed here, things would get worse, Hooper might do anything at all, and then he would have to do things back, to defend himself. There was no knowing where it might end. Hooper did not want him here. Well then, he would not stay.

He had seen very early on that there was no possibility of a truce between them. They had each avoided one another, locked themselves away. But that was only the beginning, biding time, it couldn't last. If it had been at school, even, things might have been better, they might have been protected by the crowd. Not here.

He knew that he had gone as far as he could, in defending himself successfully against Hooper. He was no good at it, he would go on losing and losing, he would never be able to cope. Hooper was sly. He hated Hooper.

But there were other things. The way his mother was, now, bright and ingratiating and altogether without pride. He didn't like to watch her. He himself was proud. And there was the house, Warings, the darkness and oldness of it, and the queer smell, he was frightened all the time he was here.

It would not do any longer. So he would go away. It seemed quite simple. He had a map, he had thought about it. Everything was planned. Only now, Hooper had guessed, and said that he would follow him. He would wait and watch and listen, there would be no way of escaping from the house without his knowing. And having Hooper come with him, taunting and bullying, wearing him down, was the worst thing he could imagine. Even worse than going away alone.

Joseph Hooper felt a new man. He planned to call in the decorators, and to turn out the attics, even to give a Sunday morning cocktail party, marking the beginning of his era as master of Warings. His friends would come down from London, and he would make contact with country neighbours, he would consolidate his position in the area.

'You have taken a load off my shoulders,' he said to Mrs Helena Kingshaw. 'You have given me new strength. I no longer feel so much alone.'

He surprised himself, as he spoke in that way, for he was a reticent, even a severe man.

They were gratified with one another, and with this new arrangement of their lives, and so it was easy to say, 'How well the boys have settled

44

down together! How nice to see them enjoying themselves! How good it is for them not to be alone!' For they talked at length about their children, knowing nothing of the truth.

Mrs Helena Kingshaw threw herself eagerly into the planning of the Sunday morning cocktail party, to which so many important people were invited. She thought, my life is changing, everything is turning out for the best. Oh, how right I was to come here!

Chapter Five

His mother said, 'I am going up to London for a day, with Mr Hooper.'

Kingshaw's heart thumped. He knew he would not have another chance like it.

'We shall be leaving here very early in the morning, and catching the first train,' said Mrs Helena Kingshaw, excited as a girl. There was a large number of things to be bought for the cocktail party, and she also hoped to find a smart, new dress. The outing would be a wholly delightful treat. Joseph Hooper had spoken a little stiffly, looking embarrassed, as he suggested it, but she thought that he had been pleased at her enthusiasm, he had given a small, shy smile.

'Oh, but what about the boys? How ever can we both leave the boys for a whole day?'

For she was anxious, now, to care for them both equally, not to make a favourite of her own son.

'But there is Mrs Boland to look after the boys, and they are quite sensible, I think, they are not babies. It will be a bit of an adventure for them, they will enjoy a sense of freedom!'

Mrs Kingshaw looked out of her sitting-room window, and thought, he likes me, he is taking me up to London. Though, in truth, she was only to travel with him, there and back, for he would be spending the day at his City office.

She felt a little ashamed of not wanting to take Charles with her. He said, 'I wouldn't want to go, anyway. I'd rather stay here.' She would not let herself believe it, for she worried a good deal about her own capacity for motherhood, about whether she said the right things and looked sufficiently at ease, in his presence.

Now, she said, I must think of myself a little more, and opened the door of her wardrobe, to begin the choosing of clothes to wear.

He would go very early, even before they did, he would go at dawn. They would never think of looking into his room. Then, there would be the whole day, until very late in the evening, before anyone could possibly find out. Mrs Boland would think he had taken a picnic somewhere, Mrs Boland never noticed.

But when his mother got back from London, she might come up and look into his room. He would have to risk it, that was all, or else do something to the bedclothes. No, that wouldn't work, she always wanted to lean over him and put her face on to his, she would find out if she came into the room at all. If she did not, then he had until breakfast the next morning. More than a whole day and night.

He had plenty of money. He always kept money which he was supposed to put into a Post Office book, in a navy-blue cotton bag, inside a Lego box. People gave him pound and ten shilling notes for Christmas and birthdays, they gave him more because he hadn't got a father, and then there was pocket money. He never spent much. He had almost seven pounds.

If he walked to Crelford station by the road, someone would be bound to see him. He was going across the country, beginning with Hang Wood. He had to make himself go into Hang Wood, whether he needed to or not. And he could hide, they would never think of looking there, first.

'I shall bring you back a present,' said Mrs Helena Kingshaw, that evening, 'I shall bring something very special, you mustn't think I shall forget you.' The bracelet slipped up and down her arm. Kingshaw hated the bracelet, hated the way she waved her arm about, showing it off. They should never have come here.

He took the blue mug of Ovaltine she was holding out for him. 'Good night.'

As he went up the second flight of stairs, he saw Hooper, standing in his own doorway, watching. He wore bottle-green pyjamas that made his skin look more pale. Kingshaw ignored him, but he knew that Hooper was wondering, might even be able to see into his head and find out things. There was no end to what Hooper might do.

He thought, tomorrow, I shall be gone, tomorrow, nothing will matter.

'I have built a good fire in the sitting room,' said Mr Joseph Hooper, smoothing back his hair, hovering in the doorway of the kitchen. 'Perhaps you would care to come and sit in there, keep me company and so forth. Just as a change.'

Mrs Helena Kingshaw blushed, and made a little gesture of surprise and pleasure.

He had set the alarm for half past five, and then, after some more thought, moved it forward to five o'clock. It would be light by then, and he wanted to go as early as he could. He had brought all the things he was taking, along from the other room, very late the previous evening, while Hooper had been watching 'Gunlaw' on the television. Now, they were under his bed.

After searching all over the house for days, he had found an old school satchel, in a drawer in one of the spare bedrooms. It had no straps, but he managed to tie it up with lengths of string, so that it would go over his shoulders.

The food had been the most difficult to get. He had taken it from the kitchen, when his mother was out, and then wondered whether that was stealing. At school, they said that stealing was one of the worst, worst things you could ever do, he had been impressed from the very first week about it. But in the end, he had decided it was not stealing, the food he was taking would be the food he would have eaten, if he had not been going away, it was part of what his mother got for working here. He wasn't taking very much, in any case. Biscuits and two packets of jelly which he could eat, cube by cube, some potato crisps and half a box of processed cheeses. He bought chocolate in the village, and some peppermints in a tube. It looked enough. He had money to buy more, when he got farther away from Derne.

Water was more difficult. He had nothing to put it in. A glass bottle would be heavy and might break, and in any case, he couldn't find one that was empty. In the end, he decided to drink a lot before he set out, and then find a stream, or a shop selling lemonade. He had never been far into the country before, but he thought there would be streams.

Besides the food, he packed a torch, and his penknife, some sticking plaster, a pair of socks and a ball of string. He had not been able to find a map, only the one Mr Hooper had in his desk, which he could look at, but dared not take. There was nothing else he could think of. Besides, the satchel was completely full, though it felt quite light, when he tried it on. He stood in the room, holding the string straps, thinking, I am going away, I am going away. There was a queer feeling in his stomach.

He woke soon after four o'clock. It was still dark. There was no point in going yet. He lay stiffly on his back, eyes open.

He was afraid. He had known how it would be. There was no question of it all being an adventure. That's what Mr Hooper would have said. Perhaps other people might do it because of that, for a lark, like Peverell and Blakey when they went out and up the mountain, last winter term, wanting to cause a stir. 'Adventures are all very well,' the Head had said, afterwards.

But he was the last person to do anything like this unless he had to. All the time he had been planning the journey, there had been a peculiar feeling about it, he couldn't believe it would really happen. He thought, perhaps Hooper will die, or he will have an aunt abroad who will want to see him, perhaps Mr Hooper will quarrel with us and we shall be asked to leave Warings, suddenly. They had lived in a house in London for four weeks, once, and then left very quickly, because of something his mother did not like, some unpleasantness. It had been Christmas, and they had gone to live in the hotel.

He knew that there was no hope, really, that Hooper would stay here and he would go, and that was all. He did not attract luck to himself, he attracted un-luck. Bad things happened, not good things, and it didn't make any difference what he thought or felt or did.

He felt more than afraid. He was dull and numb, with the reality of it, now that the morning had come. His mind kept turning to all the terrible possibilities, and he had to think of other things, quickly.

He knew that what he ought to care about was his mother. He ought to care what she would feel, he had a sense of there being something wrong with him, because he did not care. She had brought him here, and now, she was going to London with Mr Hooper, she looked at him, and did not understand. 'Charles is settling down so happily,' she had said, and Kingshaw had been appalled, hearing it, though not really surprised. She had never known anything about him, he had never wanted it. He liked to keep things inside himself. People never seemed to see as clearly as he did, and he had grown used to being left to cope alone.

He lay until the darkness in the room thinned just perceptibly to grey. It was twenty minutes to five. He would not go yet, he dared not go in the dark. But he could not lie still. He got up and dressed and stood beside the window, forcing himself to count his breaths up to ten, in and out, waiting for the alarm to ring.

Outside, it was very queer. He had never been up so early before. He went out of the back door, and skirted the path, through the yew trees. When he got to the fence, leading into the first field, just beside the copse, he looked back. The house seemed very large, seen from here, with all its windows shuttered and blank, like closed eyes. Kingshaw thought, I hate, hate, hate it.

He turned away.

It was much colder than he had expected. He wore his jeans, a sweater over a tee-shirt, and his anorak. It didn't seem enough. There was a thin, grey mist everywhere, it seeped damply through his clothes.

He climbed over the fence and was immediately startled, because he could not see very far ahead, up the field, the mist was quite thick. But he knew this first mile or so, from before, from the day the crow had followed him. He adjusted the string straps of the satchel, and set off over the tussocky grass. It was very wet. The sorrel and docks brushed against his legs, and damped through his jeans, very quickly. It was slithery, too, he had to watch his footing. Down in the grass, the dandelions shone like doubloons.

He came to a deeper rut, and recognized it as the place where he had fallen, and where the crow had perched on his shoulders. He could remember the feeling of the hard claws as they dug into his flesh, the weight of the bird and the sound of its caawing. He shivered. After a moment, he turned again, and looked back. He could no longer see the house at all, the mist had closed about it completely.

He had never experienced such silence. It had a sort of thickness, partly because of the fog, and because there was no wind, no movement of air at all, only a coldness on his face. He could not even hear any birds, in the middle of the field. There was only the faint, rushing sound, deep inside his own ears. And his feet rustled and squeaked, over the wet grass.

He reached the fence. Still, everything ahead of him was shrouded in mist, but the greyness of the sky was a bit paler. There was a hawthorn hedge, draped with beaded cobwebs. Kingshaw poked his finger into the centre of one, and the fine strands clung to it and came away, cold and slightly sticky. A black insect scuttered over his finger-nail, and down into the torn remains of the web.

He went on. He felt absolutely alone, there might be no other person in the whole world. Walking through the mist, he thought he might be going to fall over the edge of something, down into a sea, or a deep pit. But he was no longer afraid, he was too intent upon plodding ahead. He felt the wet jeans flapping about his ankles.

When he came towards the cornfield, the mist seemed to be much thinner, and he could just make out the dark shapes of the edge of Hang Wood, on the far side. The corn was a curious, dirty beige colour in the early light, and very still. At the edge of the field, there was a tractor. It loomed at him suddenly, out of the mist. It might have taken root, and grown up out of the ground here, it did not seem likely that any person had ever brought it, unless they had dropped it and abandoned it, like something left on the moon landscape.

He went over to it. This had cobwebs on it, too, strung in and out of the steering-wheel spokes, and over the metal hubs. After a moment, he put his foot on the step and hauled himself up. The seat was very hard and cold. He leaned forwards and held on to the steering-wheel. It slipped damply between his fingers. The treads of the huge tyres in front were caked in and out with mud and manure and crushed straw. There was an odd smell about the tractor, of cold oil and rust. Kingshaw felt very high up, and somehow powerful, it was like sitting on the back of a great beast. He could imagine the feel of it, beneath his body, moving off and surging forward, vibrating and heaving over the rough ground, and on, through some dark jungle. Everything would flee before it, he would be master, conqueror.

A thin breeze cut suddenly across the cornfield. Kingshaw struggled to get down, and for a moment, caught the leather satchel against the gear handle of the tractor and was trapped. He was terrified of pulling some lever and dislodging the machine, of its bowling down-hill, backwards, and his being thrown off, pinned under the great wheels. He sweated a little, twisting this way and that, and reaching his left arm round behind him, to try and unhitch the string. It gave, and he half-fell forwards, on to the wet ground. He wasn't hurt, but the string of the satchel broke. It had already started to dig into his shoulders, in a thin, hard line. It was not going to be much use, after all. But he had to make do. He tied the string again, and flattened the knot, as well as he could, then swung the satchel on to his back.

When he had wriggled under the barbed-wire fence, and into the cornfield, he looked back over his shoulder again, and now, he could see much farther, the mist was clearing slowly. The tractor looked far larger, as he moved away from it, but also more ordinary. Just metal.

Ahead, he could see the dark, blue-green line of oak trees, with the black spaces in between their trunks. He set off through the cornfield.

Hang Wood wasn't too big, he thought. It dipped down on the far side. He would go through it and come out into the field of scrub, below. At the bottom of the scrub lay Barnard's Forest, which stretched for about seven miles, lying like a dark animal pelt across the back of the land, and reaching out into the next county. He wouldn't go anywhere near that. When he came out of Hang Wood, he would go across the scrub, and then west, into open farmland, and over the first of the downs. After about ten miles, he could probably join the road. He had no real idea of how far ten miles was, but he ought to be able to manage it easily. After Hang Wood, he would manage anything at all.

There was no question of letting himself off. He had known from the beginning, he always knew, though he twisted and turned in his mind, trying to get away from whatever drove him. It was what he was afraid of, something inside himself which always made him do things. Hang Wood. Hooper had talked about it. He had come up here and seen it for himself, the day he was chased by the crow. It filled his imagination. Hang Wood.

Hooper had dared him to come here, or to go into the copse at the back of the house, that had been the start of it all.

But at least it was the last place they would ever come looking for him. If they had not gone to London, after all, or if Mrs Boland and Hooper came out in search of him, they would first go down into the village. Hooper would, especially, he knew how frightened Kingshaw was of the wood. Because Hooper would know what had happened, of course, he would realize it the moment Kingshaw didn't go in for breakfast. But by then, the others would have set off for the station.

Kingshaw quickened his pace through the cornfield. He felt suddenly exposed. It was very high up here, and once the mist had cleared, he might be seen by anyone, from miles away. You could see the cornfield from the house, and the thing he feared most of all, now, was being found by Hooper.

*

By the time he reached the fringe of the wood, the sun had risen, and was coming faintly through the mist. It was still very cold. Kingshaw saw that the corn on this side, near to the trees, had been eaten away, and flattened, in semi-circles. He didn't know what by. He remembered the crows.

It had been all very well to talk of going into Hang Wood. Now, he saw that it wouldn't be so easy. There was a ditch, overgrown with thick grass and weeds. Above it grew a dense, thorny hedge. There was barbed-wire, too. Kingshaw lowered his foot experimentally into the ditch. The undergrowth came up almost as far as his knees. It was very wet. Then the bank sloped up towards the hedge, there seemed to be no way of getting through. He could see a few yards into the wood, and between the trunks of the first trees. It was dark, and he could smell it, too, even from here, a cold, soily smell.

He got out of the ditch again, and began to walk slowly around the perimeter of the cornfield. All the time, the mist was thinning, and thinning, he could see the tractor quite clearly, and the barbed-wire right on the other side of the field. The sun was stronger. He looked at his watch. It was nearly six o'clock. It always took longer than you expected, walking.

They would be up, now, in the house, they would be getting dressed. If they were going to miss him, before they left, they would do so at any time from now, and for the next half hour. He looked out over the field, expecting to see their figures rising up and marching towards him, his mother in the smart green suit, and Mr Hooper, very tall and thin and dark, like a crow.

He felt happier, now, because there were some noises, birds mostly. Once or twice he caught sight of a flitting shape, in among the trees. The leaves rustled.

The wood curved round and he followed it, until he was out of sight of the fence, and the tractor. There was much more corn, stretching downhill, away and away, and for as far as he could see it was all eaten at the edges, in the curious half-moons. Something, something, had been there. He did not want to think about it, it could be anything.

The sky was a very pale, pearly grey, and the mist lay in great rolls, about the edges of the field, and thick on the horizon. But the sun was very bright, here. He stopped, unhitched the satchel, and peeled off his anorak. It wouldn't go inside, he had to get out the ball of string and his penknife, to cut it with, and then tie the anorak on. It took time.

He was rather proud of himself. There had been all the planning, and now, there was doing it. He warmed to the spirit of the thing, saw no end to the possibilities of his going ahead, solving the problems as he came to them, no limit to what he might do.

He had never been much good at anything. Not *bad*. Not so unfailingly, hopelessly bad that everybody held him up as an example, like they did with Leek. Leek got by, simply because of his monstrous incompetence. People ragged Leek, but they were oddly proud of him, too, he was a freak, he was so bad at everything. Their faces smirked indulgently, when they talked about him. Leek was carried along by everybody.

Kingshaw was not like that. He neither did things very well, nor very badly. He was the sort of boy whose name people forgot. They met him in corridors, and flicked their fingers at him, sending him on messages. He was always being sent on messages. In form, they said, 'You, er . . .'

So he was proud of himself, now, that he had reached the edge of Hang Wood, and everything had gone right, proud of the way he had thought things out, proud of the neatly packed satchel, and of what was inside it.

Everything was all right, then.

But, when he was tying the satchel up again, he noticed a wart on the back of his middle finger. It hadn't been there before. His stomach turned over in fear. It had happened, it was true. They had told him it would.

Broughton-Smith had had the warts, dozens of them, on his knees. They were so bad, he was being sent to the doctor.

Casey said, 'They inject you.'

'They stick a hot needle into the middle of every one. That's what they do.'

'It hurts like hell.'

Broughton-Smith had stared down miserably at his warty knees. He had been the one who cried all night, after he'd had a tooth out. Fenwick had laughed at him. In the end, Gough had gone to fetch his brother. 'You won't have to have the doctor,' he said, 'because my brother knows about black magic, there's something he can do with warts, and then they go away.'

Gough's brother had taken Broughton-Smith into the Fifth form labs, on corridor two, one evening before supper. The rest of them had waited outside on the landing, in the dark. Nobody said anything, nor even dared to look through the glass door of the lab. Kingshaw remembered the smell of them all as they stood close together. He had been afraid. Anything might happen.

In the end, Broughton-Smith had come out, smiling a secret smile.

'What did he do?'

'What happened?'

'Is it a spell?'

'You're not allowed to do black magic, it's a terrible sin.'

'You'll probably die, now.'

'Yes, he's poisoned you, I bet, you'll die in the night.'

'Let's have a *look*.'

But Broughton-Smith had slipped out of their circle, in the darkness, and run away down the stone stairs. The Prep bell had rung.

The next morning, all his warts had turned a brownish-black colour. Broughton-Smith had kept moving his knee out from under the desk, to stare at them. He looked afraid. Two days afterwards, they were all gone. He'd showed them his leg, stretching it out on the bed in dorm, and letting everyone peer at the puckered, wartless skin of his knees. When the lights were out, they'd talked about it.

It was Clarke who had said, 'They go on to someone else. It's part of the spell. To get them away, you have to wish them on to somebody else.'

'Who?'

'Anybody?'

'No, you do it to somebody you don't like.'

Kingshaw lay and thought, they will come on to me. It was inevitable. Broughton-Smith had never liked him. He told himself he didn't believe in any of it, but he had to, because Broughton-Smith's warts were gone, and because the next morning, Kingshaw saw him, looking and looking at him. That was the way things happened.

Now, he stared down at his wart for a long time. He wondered if he could make it turn black and go off to somebody else. On to Hooper. Or whether he ought to try. But he was afraid, he didn't like having it on his own hand.

By the time he had found the gap, right down at the far end of the wood, the sun had come right out, the sky was clear. There was a space in the hedge, and here, the trees were different, a separate group of them, inside the main wood. Kingshaw thought they were larches. The sun was shining directly into them, so that he could see for a long way inside. There was bracken, and curled foliage on the ground, and the light coming out between the branches was a queer coppery green, like the light under the sea. It looked all right, he thought. Safe.

He straddled the ditch for a moment, feeling the sun on his back, though the air ahead of him was very cold. There was a lot of dew, his jeans were very wet, now.

Then, he jumped forward across the ditch, and took a dozen paces quickly forward, eyes closed. When he opened them, he was inside Hang Wood.

Chapter Six

Kingshaw held his breath. There was a continual soughing movement inside the wood, and the leaves rustled together like silk, directly over-head. They were very pale green, and almost transparent where the sun shone through, he could see all the veins. At his feet, in between the creeping foliage, were dead leaves, rusty-coloured and dry on top, but packed to a damp mould just below the surface.

Immediately ahead of him there was the trunk of a fallen tree. He sat down on it. The bark was covered with greenish-grey moss. It felt like moleskin under his fingers. There was fungus, too, issuing out of the cracks, and in the groin of a branch, in weird, spongy shapes.

He liked it here. He had never been anywhere like it, and it was not remotely what he had expected. He liked the smell, and the sense of being completely hidden. Everything around him seemed innocent, and he could see for some way ahead, it was all quite all right. The sun made even the dense holly and hawthorn bushes on the edge of the clearing look harmless.

Different birds kept on singing, though not very near to him, and he did not see any of them, except, now and again, a darting brown shape in the branches. There was a cooing from pigeons, right inside the wood. He saw a rabbit. It came out of the undergrowth, not far away from him, with an odd, bumping movement, and then sat down in a shaft of sunlight, and began to wash itself like a cat. Kingshaw held his breath.

They had rabbits at school, in cages, fat, and white, with pink, vacant eyes. But this was different, it quivered and twitched with life. He watched it for ages. But when he moved, to unhitch the satchel and get out some food, the rabbit bumped away.

Before leaving the house, he had gone down into the kitchen, and cut one thick slice of bread and butter, and he ate that, now, with one of the cheese triangles. As soon as he had finished, he wanted a drink. He had been stupid not to find some sort of bottle. Well, there was no drink, it would be better to try and not think about it. Instead, he got up and crossed to the other side of the clearing. There was a narrow path, but it was very overgrown. Low branches and bushes were spread out on either side, and he had to climb over and under them, lifting briars and brambles out of his way. There was a holly bush, too. He stuck the pad of his thumb accidentally on to a thorn. When he sucked up the great bead of blood, it tasted sweet, and metallic. Then a briar scratched his face. He found he was having to bend lower and lower. But eventually, there was another clearing. He stood upright again.

It was darker here, he could tell that he had come a good way into the wood. The leaves locked together more tightly overhead, and the sun could not get through. He could see birds flitting away in alarm, through the trees ahead of him. He wiped his arm across his nose and upper lip.

Then he heard the sound. At once, he knew that it had come before, seconds ago, but he had taken no notice, mistaking it for a part of the noise he was making himself. Now it came again. It was some distance back, on the edge of the wood. He heard himself breathing. That was all. But the birds had gone quiet. He waited. Nothing. Still nothing. Then, a soft, slithering noise in the bracken.

There was a thick holly bush just beside the path. Kingshaw bent down low and began to creep towards it. He tried to move only on the balls of his feet, but the leaves made sounds. He had no idea what he was hiding from. It might be an animal. He didn't know what there was in here, except for the rabbit he had seen. And whatever it was had eaten away the corn. He thought it could not be one of them from the house. They would have come shouting and shouting across the fields, plunging heavily into the wood. These sounds were stealthy. Perhaps people came shooting here, or else there was a gamekeeper. He supposed he might be trespassing.

He crouched low down behind the holly bush. A small, rust-coloured insect ran over his feet. The dark inside of the holly bush smelled bitter. From deep in the wood, some bird made a screeching sound, and then again, after a pause. It was like a mad person laughing. Then, nothing, not even the crack of a twig.

Just as he was going to get up and come out from behind the bush, the tree branches parted, and there was Hooper.

He had made very little sound, and *said* nothing at all, had not shouted Kingshaw's name. It was as though he knew exactly where he was coming to, had known all along.

Kingshaw only felt a dull sense of inevitability. He was not much afraid, not angry, even. His luck had not held, had probably never been in. Getting out of the house, and as far as this, so easily, had all been an illusion, From somewhere, Hooper had been watching.

He had no idea at all what he could do now.

Hooper had stopped. His arms and legs looked oddly white, in the aqueous light of the wood. He was listening and looking about him, though without moving his head. For a moment, Kingshaw's hopes rose. He thought, perhaps he hasn't come after me, perhaps he is only coming for a walk by himself, perhaps I can stay here and not be noticed, and then, in the end, he will just go back home again.

Hooper said quietly, 'You can come out, Kingshaw.' Kingshaw froze. There was silence. The throaty cooing of the pigeons came again, from inside the wood.

'You're behind that holly, I know, I can see your feet, so you needn't pretend.'

Very slowly, Kingshaw raised himself up, hesitated and then came forward a little way. The two boys faced one another, across the path.

'I told you I'd come after you. I said you wouldn't be able to get away.'

'*How* did you see?'

'How do you think? I've got a window, haven't I?'

'Yes, but I didn't . . .'

Hooper sighed. 'You're stupid, aren't you? It was pretty obvious it would have to be today, wasn't it?'

Kingshaw didn't reply. He thought, I'm stupid, I'm stupid. Because if he had chosen today, Hooper would have known it, it was the only chance there had been for weeks. Besides, Hooper always knew things, that was the way things were.

'You can't come with me, anyway.'

'I can do what I like.'

'They'll come looking out for you.'

'And for you, then, as well.'

Then, Kingshaw noticed a small, canvas bag slung over Hooper's shoulders. So he did mean it, then, he was coming.

'Just because you can't think of anything for yourself,' he said in a babyish voice. 'You've got to do the things I do.'

Hooper sneered.

'You wouldn't be interested in where I'm going, Hooper, the people wouldn't want *you*.'

'Where are you going?'

'Not telling.'

'How do you know they want you?'

'I do.'

'*How?*'

'Never mind.'

'Look, Kingshaw, you can just save your breath, you needn't think you can do anything about me. You only *came* here, it isn't your place, you've got to do what I say because your mother works for us.'

'No, it isn't like that, you shut your face, Hooper.'

'She's a servant, that's all, she gets paid, and she has to do what my father says, and that means you have to do what I say.'

'Who said?'

'My father said.'

Kingshaw thought, it might be true. For, wherever they had lived, he had had to take notice of what the people told him, his mother had said, 'You must be polite, you must not be a nuisance, it is their house, not our house.'

'So if I want to come with you, I will.'

Kingshaw said desperately, 'But what *for*. I don't see why you're coming. You don't want to run away, and it isn't because you want to come somewhere with me, is it, you don't *like* me.'

'No.'

'Why, then?'

Hooper was silent, only smiling a smile. Kingshaw wanted to hit him and hit him, and then he was frightened, at the way Hooper made him feel like this, destroyed every sensible, reasonable idea he might have. There seemed to be a churning and boiling inside his head, when Hooper stood in front of him like this, so that he could only flail out savagely in all directions, missing his target, unable to stop himself, and talking like a baby. Now, he had to brag, he said, 'But I came in here, didn't I? You said I daren't go into the copse, but this is much bigger, I bet you never thought I'd dare come in here by myself.'

Hooper shrugged. 'You needn't think *this* is anything.' He bent down and poked about in the undergrowth, until he found a thick, shortish stick. He beat it about, experimentally, in the air, and it made a whistling noise.

'What are you going to do with that?'

'Anything. You always have a stick when you go in woods.'

He sounded cool, knowledgeable. They stood there, for several minutes. Then, although he didn't want to ask, Kingshaw could not stop himself, he said, 'Did you bring anything to drink, Hooper?'

'Didn't *you?*'

'No.'

'Are you thirsty?'

'A bit.'

'You're *stupid.*'

'It doesn't matter, anyway. I only wondered.'

'You needn't think I'd give anything to you, you should have thought of it yourself, if you're so clever.'

Kingshaw turned away, and began to walk as fast as he could, through the clearing, and towards the next stretch of undergrowth. He knew he would hear Hooper, coming up behind him. After a moment, he did. But for some time he did not speak.

He no longer felt relaxed and happy with being in the wood, he had lost interest in what he saw and heard. He only thought, now, about the fact that he was alone with Hooper, and of what Hooper might do to him. Though perhaps he could do much less than in his own house. That was his territory, he was master. Here, they were somehow more equal.

After a while, Kingshaw realized that the path had disappeared altogether. Now, there was only the thick, greenish-brown carpet of foliage, the sticks and twigs and sinewy roots of the trees, like ropes coming up out of the ground. Everywhere looked the same, they might have taken any direction. He went straight ahead. This was the way out to the other side. But he had no real idea of how far it was, he kept expecting to see the end, and did not.

The sun was spearing, now and again, through the network of leaves, and rippling over the tree trunks like water. But mostly, the leaves were too thick to let much light in. It was very close, too, now that they were well into the wood, the air he took in at his mouth felt warm, and somehow thicker than normal air. Kingshaw felt his skin sticky, under his tee-shirt. Soon, he would have to stop and take off the sweater.

It was hard going. He would push through a lot of undergrowth, and closely packed bushes, scarcely able to see more than a yard ahead, and then come out suddenly into another wide clearing. It went on and on like this for some way. He heard Hooper behind him all the time. But they had both got the feeling of the place, now, and they were moving about less noisily.

It was as they ducked, and then struggled under a great tangle of briars, getting their clothing caught, and having to stop and free it, that Kingshaw first heard the noise. It was an odd, honking sort of sound, like a pig or a horse, but yet not like either. He stopped dead. Behind him, Hooper moved on a few paces, and then stopped too, when he was very close. Kingshaw felt his breath. The honking sound came again, and then there was a movement, the crack of a twig.

'What is it?'

Kingshaw turned his head slightly, and saw Hooper's face. He had square teeth, with ridges down them, and a gap in between the two at the front. There was a fine line of sweat drops on his upper lip. Kingshaw thought, he is real, there is blood and water inside him. He was somehow reassured by Hooper's close presence, by the ordinary smell of him. After all, was there anything he could do to hurt him?

'It's a noise. There's something through there.'

'What?'

'I don't know, do I?'

'It can't be any person, that isn't a person's noise.'

'No.'

'It's stopped now.'

'Perhaps it's gone away, then.'

The twigs cracked again, and then they heard soft, thudding steps, in the leaf-mould out beyond the bushes.

'*Go* and look.'

'It might be . . .'

'What?'

'I don't know.'

'Go and look.'

Silence.

'You're scared.'

'So are you, then.'

'Don't be stupid.'

'Why daren't you go out?'

'I said it first, you've got to go. Go *on* . . .'

They were whispering. After a moment, Kingshaw moved forward a bit farther, pushing the branches aside carefully with his hands, not knowing what he was going to see. He had a sudden vision of things watching him, from in among the trees, of eyes glinting, and spears poised. There was a tension in the wood, a sense of aliveness and secrecy. He remembered reading about wild boars that came plunging through forests, and how the hunters waited, and then leaped out and stuck knives into the throat and heart and eyes of the animal. There were hogs, too, with filthy, poisonous spines. The honking came again. He moved very cautiously forward another step.

There was a small clearing, and a shaft of sunlight, and opposite him, between two trees, a deer. It was the colour of sand, and its body quivered all over, its eyes were huge and glittery. Kingshaw realized that it was frightened, even more than he had been. He slid back into the bushes.

'It's a deer.'

'What sort of a deer?'

'I don't know – like any sort. It's got sort of branchy horns.'

'Antlers, stupid.'

'Yes.'

'I've never seen one.'

'You must have, in the zoo.'

'I've never been to a zoo.'

Kingshaw gave a whistle of amazement. He had never expected that he might outdo Hooper, in any experience.

'What are we going to do, then?'

'Well, it won't *hurt* us.'

'O.K., we'd just better go on, then,' Hooper said.

Kingshaw stood aside. He remembered that he did not want to be with Hooper at all. Hooper pushed past him. The branches fell back straight away, almost concealing him. For a second, Kingshaw felt alone again. Then, the deer began to call again.

'What does it do that for?' Hooper whispered through the bushes at him.

'I suppose it's frightened. Perhaps it's warning some others.'

'Oh. Do you think there are lots of them?'

'I don't know. I thought you were supposed to know everything about everything.'

'Shut up.'

'There wouldn't be one by itself, would there, anybody would know that.'

'No. Look, come on, Kingshaw, we can follow it, we might see hundreds and hundreds of them. We might see *anything*.'

Kingshaw heard Hooper move forward abruptly, and then the sudden noise of the deer, as it crashed away through the bracken. He went forward into the clearing. As he did so, a fox shot away ahead of them, between some trees.

'Come on,' Hooper said.

Kingshaw followed him. They went between the oak trees, where the deer had been standing, and plunged deeper into the wood.

After a bit, Hooper said, 'Shut up making so much noise. You've got to stalk them and be quiet, that's what hunters do.'

'We're not hunters.'

'Yes, we are. You want to follow it, don't you? You won't see anything if you make all that din.'

Kingshaw did not answer. He felt furious with Hooper, because he had so suddenly taken over, walking in front of him and saying what to do. It was his thing, now. But at least, for the time being, he was more interested in tracking down the deer than he was in doing anything to Kingshaw. To him, it was just an expedition, an adventure, it was not serious. After a while, Kingshaw caught some of the idea from him. When Hooper began to run through one of the clearings, he ran, too, though they made so much noise that the deer must by now have gone far off. Hooper made some strange, darting and leaping movements, lunging forwards now and then. Then he dropped down on all fours, and began to edge his way round a tree.

'We're hunters,' he said. 'You've got to be dead quiet now. There are wild boar. And bears.'

'Not both in the same wood, there wouldn't be.'

'Get down, get down.'

Kingshaw did. The twigs and dead holly hurt his knees. The wood looked different from here, the leaves seemed higher and much farther away, and the trunks were at an odd angle. It made him sick to look up at them, sideways. The sweet, rotten smell of the leaf-mould came up between his knees, and under the palms of his hands as he pressed them down. He saw a lot of insects, spiders, and shiny, segmented beetles, going in and out of the twigs. There was moss on them, too. Some of it was pinkish, and fronded like seaweed. It felt slimy.

Suddenly, Hooper dropped down on his stomach and lay, his feet almost in Kingshaw's face. He squinted through the bushes.

'There it is!'

Kingshaw wriggled forwards. The deer was some way ahead, poised for flight. Its neck looked taut enough to snap.

'There must be more,' Hooper said. 'They go down to the water I think.'

'What water?'

'Well, there's a stream or something, isn't there? There might even be a river.'

'I don't know.'

'Of course, there always is, in woods.'

'Oh.'

Hooper stood up again and crept on, still following the deer. The ground began to slope downwards very slightly now, and although the clearings were much wider, the foliage got more tangled, in some places there were nettles and clinging ivy, as high as their knees. It felt damp here. When Kingshaw pulled his foot up, he heard a slight, sucking noise. It was still very warm. There seemed to be scarcely any air at all. Kingshaw wiped the sweat off his face.

'I want to stop. I'm too hot in this jumper.'

At once, he wondered why he had felt the need to say it at all. He was alone, he was not *with* Hooper, Hooper had just tagged along and started all this hunting stuff, he didn't have to tell him what he wanted to do. But he realized that he had accepted Hooper's presence now, that he was even glad of it, because they were so far inside the wood. But he was angry with himself for acknowledging Hooper's leadership. He tried to think of how he could get in front again himself.

As he pulled his sweater off he caught sight of his watch. It was gone eight, they had been in the wood for more than two hours. The thought frightened him.

Hooper was standing a couple of yards away, scraping at the leaf-mould with his toe.

'Come *on*, Kingshaw.'

'I don't want to play this game now.'

Hooper's face puckered with scorn. 'What *game*? We're tracking deer, aren't we? I am, anyway. You can do what you like.'

'I want to go. It's about time I was getting out.'

'Out where?'

'Of here. I'm going through the fields behind the wood, and then . . .'

'Then what?'

'Never mind. Nowhere. You'll have to go back, though.'

Hooper shook his head.

'I'm off.'

Kingshaw had stuffed his sweater inside the satchel. Behind him were the bushes, through which they had just come. He went straight on.

'Where are you going?'

'I told you, I've got to go out of here now.'

'Home?'

'Mind your own business. No.'

'Out the other side of the wood, then?'

'Yes.'

'That's not the way.'

'It is.'

'It's not, we were over there. We turned round.'

Kingshaw hesitated. There were clumps of undergrowth all round. He tried to get his bearings. If he went into that clearing to his left, then he would be heading out of Hang Wood. He must be almost on the edge, by now. He walked on, for some way. After a bit, he heard Hooper coming behind him.

The clearing narrowed, but there were none of the tangled bushes here, it was possible to walk upright. The branches of the trees locked closely together, overhead. It was very dim. Kingshaw stopped. It went on being dark for as far as he could see. If it were near the edge of the wood, it would be getting light.

He turned round slowly. But it was the same. Everywhere looked the same.

'What's the matter now?'

Kingshaw heard, for the first time, a note of fear in Hooper's voice, and knew that he was leader, again, now.

'What have you stopped for?'

Very deliberately, Kingshaw inserted his forefingers under the string, and pulled the satchel off his back. He untied his anorak from it, and spread it out on the ground, and then sat down. Hooper stood above him, his eyes flicking about nervously, his face as pale as his limbs in the dim light.

Kingshaw said, 'We're lost. We'd better stay here and think what to do.'

Hooper crumpled. He knelt down on the ground some way off, and began to poke restlessly about among the foliage, his head bent. 'It's your fault,' he said, 'your bloody stupid fault, Kingshaw. You should have done what I said.'

'Oh, shut up.'

There was a sudden screeching cry, and a great flapping of wings, like wooden clappers. Kingshaw looked up. Two jays came flying straight through the wood, their wings whirring on the air. When they had gone, it went very still again at once, and it seemed darker, too. Then, a faint breeze came through the wood towards them, and passed, just stirring the warm air. Silence again. A blackbird began to sing, a loud, bright, warning song. Hooper looked up in alarm. From somewhere, far away, came the first rumble of thunder.

Chapter Seven

'It was thunder,' Hooper said, after several minutes of silence.

'Yes. If there's going to be a proper storm we'll have to shelter. There'll be rain.'

Kingshaw noticed that Hooper was looking across at him, as he spoke, his face queer and stiff. When he replied, his mouth pursed up, as though he were sucking something sour.

'I'm always sick,' he said, in an odd voice, 'in thunderstorms, I hate them. I can't ever be out in them.'

The dark pupils of his eyes had gone small. Kingshaw thought, he is scared, dead scared. I've never seen him scared once before, but now he is.

If he had been vindictive, this was his chance with Hooper. But he was not. He did not much care, one way or the other, so long as he was left alone himself.

'I should think we're safe enough here.'

'We're under trees. You shouldn't ever be under trees, it's the most dangerous thing of all.'

'That's when it's just one tree by itself, in a field or something. This is all right, it's different.'

'Why is it?'

'I don't know. The trees are closer together, I suppose. It just *is* different.'

The thunder rumbled again, not far away.

'I hate it, it makes me be sick.'

'You can be sick then, can't you? It won't matter.'

'Kingshaw, why can't we run for it? If we run we could get out, it mightn't start really properly storming till we get home.'

'Of course it would, we've come miles, haven't we? Anyway, for one, we don't know how to get out, do we? So how can we run home, stupid?'

'We could try, we can just go back the way we came.'

'But we don't know which way that is. Anyway, I'm not going back home, am I? You can do what you want, you can go.'

'I'm not being by myself in thunder.'

Hooper's voice had risen in panic. Whatever self-respect he might have had was gone, he did not care if Kingshaw saw that he was afraid – he *wanted* him to know, in fact, he wanted to be protected.

Kingshaw did not feel sorry for him at all. He was detached. But he wouldn't leave Hooper, he knew that he would have to take charge of things.

There was a feeling of tension inside the wood, as the sky darkened. Every slight movement of the birds sounded very clearly, even if it was far away. Kingshaw was hot. He wanted the storm to break, he wanted rain and coolness. There was something unpleasant about this waiting, he felt everything around him to be holding back some kind of violence. But he was not afraid at all. He felt nothing. His brain was very clear and he could think everything out, he knew what they had better do. He remembered his mother. Perhaps they were in London, by now. He imagined her, clipping along in her high-heeled shoes and the smart green costume, at Mr Hooper's side. But that didn't matter, now, they didn't matter, he was going away, it was going to be all right.

The wood had made everything seem far off, not only removed in distance but in time, too. Here, he felt that he was shut away from all other people, from towns and cities and school and home. The wood had already changed him, enlarged his experience to a point where he felt that he was on the brink of discovering some secret, of whose existence, even, that other world did not know.

There was a great crash of thunder almost overhead, and a tearing noise, as though the sky had been ripped open. Hooper leaped to his feet, and looked about him, wild with terror.

'Come on,' Kingshaw said, matter-of-factly, 'we'd better make a shelter.' He unzipped his anorak, and carried it over to one of the bushes. Hooper watched it, trembling slightly, rooted where he stood. Lightning came, now, making the tree trunks white as it forked down.

Kingshaw draped his anorak carefully over the top of the bushes, spreading it out as much as possible. The bushes were very thick. He got down and crawled underneath.

'Come on,' he said, 'it's all right here, we might stay dry.'

Hooper hesitated, and then came in beside him, crawling on his hands and knees. He went right back into the farthest corner, where it was dark, and curled up tightly, his hands held up towards his face. When the thunder boomed through the wood again, he stuffed his fingers in his ears, and ducked down.

'It's O.K.,' Kingshaw said, 'It's only a din.'

Lightning flickered on the eyes of a bird, perched up somewhere in the branches ahead, and for a second, they shone yellow-green, like torches. The thunder came right on top of the lightning.

'Oh God, Oh God.'

Hooper was completely beside himself, wrapped up in his fear, oblivious of everything except the storm, and his terror of it. Kingshaw remembered how he himself had been, the day the crow had come after him. It must feel like that. He had wanted to tear his way out of himself, he had been so afraid.

'Look, it won't last long, it'll go in a bit,' he said, in a rush of embarrassed kindness. But Hooper could not hear him, he was hunched forward, his neck bent over, and his face buried in his knees.

The rain came down slowly at first, in great, flat drops on to the leaves. But then it was a violent downpour, Kingshaw felt it coming through the bush. The anorak covered hardly any space at all. He looked out and saw the water in a great, silvery sheet, making huge puddles on the floor of the clearing.

After a long time, it began to steady, and fell like needles, but the thunder and lightning came simultaneously again, so loudly that Kingshaw himself jumped in alarm. It sounded like a bomb landing just behind the bush, and the whole wood lit up for a long, slow second, in green-white light. Hooper whimpered, and rocked himself a little, backwards and forwards.

Kingshaw began to wonder what would happen afterwards, and whether Hooper would be ashamed. He thought, now he won't be able to frighten me, he won't be leader any more.

It seemed a long time before the light came creeping back into the wood. The thunder continued to roll slowly, on and on, in the distance. Kingshaw put a hand up to his hair. It was very wet. His clothes were wet, too.

Then, abruptly, sun filled the clearing, it was like a curtain being drawn back in front of a brightly lit stage. Fine steam began to rise up from the sodden ground, and the tree trunks, and the smell of it came thickly into Kingshaw's nostrils. Beads of rain glittered on the bushes.

He crawled out and examined the anorak. It was sagging down in the middle with a great pool of water. He turned it up, and some of the water spilled through the bushes, on to Hooper.

'It's stopped,' Kingshaw said.

He walked off a little way. The ground was spongy, and the wet foliage soaked the bottoms of his jeans again. He stood in the sunlight. High up, small chinks of blue sky showed between the leaves.

'Come on, Hooper, it's O.K.'

The birds were singing again, and there were soft plopping and rustling sounds, as raindrops rolled off and dropped down through the trees.

Kingshaw rubbed his legs. He had been cramped underneath the bush. For ages, Hooper wouldn't come out, though he had taken his hands away from his ears now, and lifted up his head. He sat, straining to hear where the storm was.

It was then that Kingshaw heard the water. Not rain, but running water, somewhere away on his right, beyond the point where the ground began to slope. He turned his head in that direction. It must be a stream, moving fast after the rain. His mouth puckered, with remembered thirst.

He went back over to the bush, and hauled out the satchel. The leather was wet, but when he looked inside, everything was quite dry.

'There's a stream or something,' he said to Hooper. 'I can hear it down there. I'm going to try and find it.'

Hooper looked up at him directly, for the first time since the storm had begun.

'What for?'

'I'm thirsty.'

'So am I.'

'You said you'd brought a drink.'

'I never did.'

'You did so, you said it was stupid not to.'

Hooper said nothing, only began to get to his feet slowly. He came out from under the bush, walked away a yard, and turned his back on Kingshaw, unzipping his jeans and peeing into the bracken. Kingshaw watched him. It went on for a long time. Kingshaw thought, he was scared as scared. Then Hooper said, 'I didn't bring a drink because I knew there was a stream.'

'Liar, you've never been in here before, you don't know anything about it.'

'Oh, yes I do.'

Kingshaw let it drop. He thought that the storm had changed things, given him a hold over Hooper. He had only to look at him, now.

But he had forgotten the sort of person Hooper was. Now, he walked out into the middle of the clearing, and looked briefly around. Then he said, 'Right, I can hear it, it's over there. I'll go first because I'm leader.'

Dumbly, Kingshaw followed.

There was a narrow track, down between the bushes. The ground did not slope very steeply. It had seemed cooler after the rain, but as they went on and on, getting deeper into the trees, the air felt warm and close again, heavy with moisture. The earth was still spongy, and it was very hard work, walking, because of that, and the wet foliage clinging about their ankles. But the running sound of the water got nearer.

Kingshaw was hungry, as well as thirsty, now, he wanted to stop and open the satchel, so he could eat a piece of chocolate. But then, he felt his foot come up against something in the grass. He bent down. Ahead of him, Hooper stopped, and half-turned.

'What's the matter with you? Come on.'

'I've found something.'

'What?'

Kingshaw did not answer. He felt about him, and his hand moved over soft, wet fur. He parted the grass.

The rabbit was dead. Hooper came back and stood over him, and then crouched down.

'What is it?'

'A rabbit.' Kingshaw ran his finger lightly over the cold neck.

'It's been shot.'

'Where? There's no blood.'

'No.'

The animal's ears stood up stiffly, alert, as though it had died listening, but the eyes were glazed, blank and distant, like the eyes of a fish on a slab.

'You can't *do* anything with it, can you?'

'No.'

'Come on, then. I thought you were thirsty.'

Kingshaw ignored him. He picked up the rabbit cautiously. It felt quite

72

heavy, and rather loose, as though there were nothing holding its limbs together, inside.

'Haven't you ever touched a dead thing before?'

'No. Well – only birds. Nothing big.'

'That isn't big!'

'It is. I mean, I've never touched an *animal* that was dead.'

'Haven't you ever seen a dead person, either?'

Kingshaw looked up nervously. 'No.'

'Not even your father? Didn't they take you to look at him in his coffin?'

'No.'

'I saw my grandfather dead. That wasn't long ago.'

'Oh.' Kingshaw had no way of telling if this were true. He moved his fingers about in the rabbit's wet fur.

'Oh, chuck it away, Kingshaw.'

But he was reluctant. He liked the feel of it. He had not known how it would be to hold a dead thing. Now he knew. He nursed it to him. Hooper said, 'It's only dead. Dead things are finished, they don't matter.'

'Yes, they do. Well – dead people do, anyway.'

'Of course they don't. There's no difference.'

'There is, there is.'

'*How* is there?'

'Because . . . because it's human bodies.'

'Humans are only animals.'

'Yes – only . . . only they're not. They're different.'

Hooper sighed. 'Look, when you're breathing, you're alive aren't you? Everything is. And when you stop breathing, your heart stops, and then you're dead.'

Kingshaw hesitated, worried about it, uncertain how to argue. Hooper's eyes opened very wide. 'I suppose you don't believe all that guff about souls and ghosts and everything, do you?'

'Not ghosts . . .'

'When you're dead you're dead, you're finished.'

'No.'

'Look . . . you can *see*.' Hooper poked his finger at the rabbit. Its head flopped heavily sideways.

'It's dead,' he said.

Kingshaw stared at it miserably. He could not think clearly. What Hooper said must be true, and yet he knew that it was not true.

'If you believe all that about souls, you believe in ghosts and spooks.'

'No, I don't.'

'Ghosts are supposed to be people, after they're dead, aren't they?'

'I don't know.'

'Well, they are.'

'You just said that when you were dead you were finished.'

'Oh, I don't believe in any old ghosts. But you do. You've got to, if you believe that other.'

Kingshaw said nothing. But he was still anxious about it.

'So you'd better watch out, hadn't you? But it's all guff, really.'

Looking down at the rabbit again, Kingshaw suddenly noticed a great, mealy wound inside its ear, full of matter and blood and grubs. He flung the body violently away from him. It landed with a soft, hollow slap, in the undergrowth.

When he looked up again, Hooper's eyes were on his, narrowed and mocking. He had paid Kingshaw back for his own terror during the storm. Without saying anything else, he turned and set off again down the track.

In his mind, and in his belly, Kingshaw went on and on thinking about the maggotty wound. The dead rabbit, which had seemed, at first, such a clean thing, was now wholly revolting, defiled and contaminating. He looked down anxiously at the front of his tee-shirt, in case it had left a stain on him.

The next moment, Hooper began to slither forward wildly, flailing out with his arms to try and keep balance.

'Kingshaw, Kingshaw . . . Oh, God . . .'

The track ended, and there was a steepish drop, down between two banks, covered in bracken and fern that came waist high. Underneath, the soil was very wet and slippery, after the rain. Hooper could not stop himself, he was on his hands and knees now, tumbling down through the undergrowth, yelling with fright.

'Kingshaw . . .'

But there was nothing that Kingshaw could do, except go very warily down after Hooper, testing the ground step by step. There was a crash from below, and a shout. At once, birds rose up in alarm from the bushes, and flew off through the wood.

'Are you O.K.?'

Silence.

'Hooper? What have you done?'

Kingshaw let himself slide a few feet down, bending slightly for-wards.

'Hooper? What's happened to you?'

'There's the stream, I've found it, I can see where it goes.'

Furiously, Kingshaw scrabbled down the last few feet, through the soaking wet grass. He tore some skin off the palm of his hand, on an up-ended twig.

Hooper was kneeling down, looking between thick, dark reeds.

'You didn't hurt yourself at all!'

'Oh, no.'

'I thought you were half dead, you made the most awful din. What did you go on yelling and yelling like that for, if you hadn't hurt yourself?'

Hooper shook his head impatiently. 'I thought I was going to. Look, this is the water and it must be going somewhere.'

'Why?'

'It always does. Streams and rivers do. If we just follow it, we'll come out. O.K.?'

'How do you know?'

'It's obvious.'

'I don't think it is, it might not come out, it might just go deeper and deeper into the woods.'

'It won't. You're *thick* Kingshaw, it does come out because we've seen it, haven't we, down under the bridge through the village?'

'It might not be the same.'

'It is.' Hooper stood up. 'Come on, we'll go this way. It isn't any good for drinking here, it's all clogged up with weed,'

'You're filthy. You've got muck all up your legs.'

'So what? Let's get going.'

Kingshaw did not move. It was true that he wanted to get out of the wood just as much as Hooper. But not *with* Hooper. Besides, he wasn't sure if he believed him, about following the stream and being sure to come out of the wood.

But it didn't matter to him what Hooper did, or where he planned to go. Sooner or later, as soon as they found their way out again, Hooper would be bound to go back home. Kingshaw was never going home.

'Look, hurry up, don't *stand* there.'

'I'll do what I like.'

Hooper stopped and looked back at him. He said, 'You'll be by yourself if you stay there. That won't do you any good, will it? You'd die in here, you'd never ever find your way out.'

'Why shouldn't I? I could do it just as well as you.'

'We've got to stick together, it's dangerous if we don't.'

'You got us lost, it was your stupid game.'

'Stuff it. You'd just better follow me.'

Kingshaw was still reluctant. He had a sudden desire to turn and go off in the other direction, to take his chance. But he was not sure if he liked it down here. He wasn't certain how much the presence of the water might change things, and present all kinds of obstacles they had not yet had to cope with. They had learned a little about the woods, when they were up above the stream. Here was different.

It smelled steamy and damp, like a jungle, and there was another smell, too, sweetish and rotten. There was no air. Kingshaw wanted to climb up the bank again, and go on climbing, up and up one of the elm trees until he could see the open sky. They seemed to have been closed in here for hours, for ever. The water moved sluggishly, between the overgrown banks.

'Look, are you coming or not, Kingshaw? I shall go by myself in a minute, I don't care about you.'

Kingshaw knew that he would not. Hooper had been afraid of the thunderstorm. He would never be able to cope with being in the woods alone. He said nothing, but he began to move forward again, slowly.

They followed the stream through the undergrowth for a long way, perhaps two miles, and nothing changed. It was very slippery and muddy underfoot. Nothing living seemed to be down here, there were no birds or butterflies, it was like a dark, damp tunnel. Wild garlic grew around the exposed tree roots, giving off a thick stench.

Suddenly, Hooper stopped dead.

'What is it?'

'Nothing.'

'What have you stopped for?'

'I'm fed up with this.'

'What?'

Kingshaw came up behind him. Ahead, it was the same, a tunnel.

'We're not getting anywhere, it isn't coming out to the open, it's just darker and darker,' Hooper said in a querulous voice. 'I hate it.'

'It was you who wanted to follow the water.'

'Well, now I don't, I've changed my mind.'

'We can't go all the way back.'

'Why can't we?'

'Because that's a stupid thing to do, you never should go back, ever. Besides, there wasn't a way out behind us.'

'How do you know?'

'Because we've *been* there, haven't we?'

'Not all the way we haven't. We could climb back up the bank again.'

'We can do that here.'

'No, it's all briars and stuff. I want to go back.'

'It's miles and miles.'

'I don't care, I want to.'

'Look, I'll go in front, if you're so scared.'

'I don't like it down here, Kingshaw, it's funny. It's creepy.'

'You're a baby. It's bound to lead us somewhere, you said so.'

'Don't keep on saying *you* said, *you* said, the whole time.'

'Well, you did. Mind out.'

Kingshaw pushed roughly past him. He didn't care about Hooper now, he had found a way of talking to him.

As far as he could see, the green tunnel went on. He didn't like it any more than Hooper, but he wasn't going to say so. A bit earlier, he had nearly suggested going back himself, or else climbing up the high bank above the stream. Now, he only wanted to go ahead. He hated making a decision, starting on a plan, and then not finishing. It was a waste. He liked to get to the end of things. Besides, now he had got in front again, now he was leader, he wanted to stay there. Hooper could follow if he wanted.

They went on again. But not for long. There was a bend in the stream, and it ran through a long, low arch of hawthorn bushes. They had to scramble up the sides of the bank here, and hold on to roots and trunks to keep balance, standing sideways and edging along. But then, the bushes ended, and they came out abruptly into a clearing.

Here, the stream was very broad, and it had diverted itself, in between the trees, to form a pool at one end of the clearing. The high banks had been sloping down gradually, and now they came to an end, the water and the ground were level again. It was much lighter, too. The trees were elms, very tall and widely spaced, with the leaves up near the top.

Beyond the pool, the stream flowed on again as far as they could see, and then there was more undergrowth.

'Look, it's like a bathing pool,' Kingshaw said.

'Sort of. A bit small.'

'Do you think somebody dammed it up and made it?'

'I don't know. No, they couldn't have. Hey, look, this bank's got hoof marks all over the mud. The deer must come down here.'

'I told you.'

For a moment, they stood about, feeling that they had made some kind of arrival, but uncertain what to do, now they were here. It did not seem to be any nearer to the edge of the wood, the trees were thick, on all sides around them.

Then the sun came out, and the clearing was full of pale, yellow-green light. The water of the stream and the pond looked completely transparent.

'I know what I'm going to do, I'm going to swim.'

Hooper had pulled the canvas bag off his shoulders, and flung it to one side. Now, he was peeling off his clothes, and tossing them away from him, anywhere, about the grass. Kingshaw watched him. He did not move. He hadn't meant to play about. But once again, Hooper had forgotten everything except the novelty of it, the adventure. He went running, naked, towards the stream, looking like some kind of pale animal, among the trees. The water shot up on either side of him as he jumped in, and then began to splash about, leaping and dancing, and throwing up his arms.

'Come on, Kingshaw, it's great!'

He sent up sheets of spray.

'What's the matter with you? Can't you swim? It's not cold.'

Kingshaw still did not move. He remembered the bright artificial blue of the swimming pool into which the boy called Turville had made him dive.

'Are you *scared*?'

He thought, no, no, because this is different, this is all right. There had been something bad about that place, where everybody stood about and there was a tremendous noise, and he had felt he could have drowned to death in front of them all and they would have gone on, standing about, laughing and talking, taking no notice. He felt suddenly much older, and overwhelmingly strong and powerful, he could do anything at all. He began to take off his own clothes, though with less abandon than Hooper. He made a careful pile of them on top of his satchel.

It felt peculiar, having nothing on, and being outside. He looked down at himself, and curled up his toes, feeling the cold leaves mulching between them. Hooper was watching, waiting for him impatiently, and still beating about in the water. He began to whoop like a wild Indian.

For a moment, Kingshaw stood on the bank, looking down. Then, a great surge of excitement came over him, he felt again the enormous importance of being who he was, and standing where he was, in the middle of the wood. He put his finger inside his mouth, yelling in answer to Hooper, and then gave a tremendous leap into the stream.

It was curiously warm, lapping in and out between his legs and over his stomach. For a while, he simply stood, feeling it and shivering with pleasure. Then he put his head down and began to swim. He could open his eyes under water. It was very dim and green-blue. There were fish. He saw Hooper's legs, waving like the fronds of a sea anemone. He lunged forward.

They stayed in the water for ages. Kingshaw thought, I never want to leave it, this is the best feeling in the world. They washed the mud off themselves, from when they had fallen down the bank, and then raced about, lifting their knees very high, splashing and yelling. In the pool part, the water was quite deep. Kingshaw swam under the surface, and came bounding up at intervals, like a porpoise, showering Hooper with water.

In the end, the sun went in. Hooper was sitting on the bank, examining his toe-nail. The farther trees looked shadowy, and almost black, and the stream was suddenly opaque, eddying about Kingshaw's thighs. He shivered.

'It's broken,' Hooper said, 'I've bashed it on a stone.'

'Is it bleeding?'

'No, but it looks funny. Sort of spongy underneath, where the nail's come off. Pink.'

'Do you want a sticking plaster?'

'Do you want your head looking at?'

'What for? I've got some, haven't I?'

'Plasters?'

'There's a whole tin. Different shaped ones.'

Hooper looked up. 'O.K., then,' he said casually.

Kingshaw walked slowly towards the bank, and hauled himself up.

Hooper said, 'Don't you look queer?'

Kingshaw hesitated, still on his hands and knees, dripping.

'Your arms and legs sort of dangle.'

'So do yours, then. Everybody's do.'

'Not like that. You look like a puppet, when all the strings have gone loose.'

Kingshaw flushed. Without looking at Hooper again, he went towards the pile of clothes. His teeth were chattering, and the tops of his arms were bluish, and goose-pimpled.

'Oh, hell, there isn't anything to get dry on,' he said wearily.

Hooper was standing up on the bank, now, though still looking down at his toe.

'I'm cold.'

'We could light a fire,' Kingshaw said, 'I've got matches.'

'No, it'd be dangerous.'

'Why? We could get stones, and build a sort of hearth. There are plenty of stones under the water. It's pretty damp down here, as well, you couldn't set the trees alight or anything. We could cook something, then.'

'What could we? I've only got biscuits and some tomatoes. And a bag of mints. You can't cook any of those.'

'The tomatoes you can. We could catch something, as well. Hunt.'

'I thought that was supposed to be a stupid game.'

'It isn't a *game*, is it? We want a fire because we're cold, and when you have a fire, you cook things. I'm hungry.'

'What do you think we can find to cook, then? It's not so easy.'

'Plenty of things.'

'*What?* Have you ever made a fire outside before?'

'No. But it's obvious how you do it, you just light it. Look, you'd better put your clothes on if you don't want to get frozen stiff.'

Kingshaw rolled up his own pants into a ball and rubbed them quickly over himself, to take off some of the wetness. He was shivering violently now, and he felt a bit sick. His jeans stuck uncomfortably to his legs as he pulled them up. When they were zipped, he bent down and rolled the bottoms up as far as they would go.

'Look, you do the same, and we can wade in for the stones,' he told Hooper.

It had been all right in the water. But he was suddenly afraid, now, that he had played the fool too much. Hooper still thought it was all a game, he kept forgetting about the storm and how frightened he'd been, forgetting that they were lost, and why they had come here in the first place. Somebody had to concentrate, Kingshaw thought. And it mattered to him much more, getting out of the wood soon.

But he was enjoying himself, telling Hooper what to do. A day ago, earlier this morning, even, he had had no idea how to go about it, was not even sure if he wanted to. Now, he thought, I know what Hooper is *really* like. He is a baby. And stupid. And a bully. Kingshaw felt much older, and different, too, more responsible.

Hooper was behind him, lifting up a flat stone. Kingshaw said, 'Hurry *up*.' There was a silence. At once, he knew that he had pushed his luck. He looked back. Hooper was watching him, the huge stone held between his hands, dripping water. There was the old, cunning expression on his face.

'You needn't try and tell me what to do, Kingshaw.'

'Pack it in, we've got this fire to build, that's all.'

'I haven't got to do anything you say.'

Kingshaw dropped his own stone, in silence, bent down, and began to scrape out a hollow in the ground. Hooper came, with very slow, measured steps, up from the bank of the stream.

'You keep forgetting things, don't you?' he said.

'We need a lot more stones than this, big ones. About twenty I should think. We've got to do it properly.'

'There's a lot I can do that you won't like. *You* know.'

Kingshaw looked up in exasperation, and leaned back on his heels. 'Look, do you want to get this fire built or not, Hooper?'

'Don't pretend you didn't hear.'

'Oh, stop trying to be so clever. You're all talk, Hooper.'

'*Am* I?'

No, Kingshaw thought, no. Oh, Jesus, I am scared of him, I am.

'You're scared of me. That's why you started running away. You've always been scared of me. Don't try getting cocky.'

Kingshaw got up, without a word, and went back down to the stream for another stone. Hooper's footsteps came behind him.

'I suppose you know what'll happen if we stay here all night,' he said.

'What? Nothing.'

'We'll have to keep the fire going.'

'We might.' Kingshaw lifted up his stone, and again did not look at Hooper.

'There are a lot of moths,' Hooper said softly, 'there always are, in woods. Pretty big ones, as well.'

Kingshaw's stomach clenched. In his nostrils, he could smell the mustiness of the Red Room. Hooper had seen the expression on his face. Now, he moved quietly away, and went back towards the site of the fire.

'I'm not frightened of stupid moths,' Kingshaw yelled after him. 'You don't scare me.'

Hooper glanced round, and smiled.

He can't *do* anything, he can't, there's nothing he can do, Kingshaw told himself. It's only things he says, he's stupid.

But he knew, and Hooper knew, that it was not really a question of doing. Hooper had only to remind Kingshaw, by the expression on his face, that was enough. It was the terror he suffered from remembering, from dreaming his own fear.

He wanted to go wild, with the frustration of it, everything seemed to be against him. Hooper's own fear in the storm had been absolute, and yet it had gone, it might never have happened, Kingshaw knew that he was quite powerless to use it as a weapon. By referring to it, he might manage to annoy Hooper, though he doubted even that, and in any case, he would never know for sure, Hooper kept a bland face. But he could never bring the fear back again, only another storm could do that, or something else quite unpredictable, and over which he himself had no control. Hooper's fear was a straightforward response to an outside situation. But his own was quite different, and Hooper had the measure of it, he had done so from his first day at Warings.

Kingshaw knew that he was the loser. His momentary burst of exultation, and his feeling of superiority over Hooper counted for nothing, they were always short-lived. It was really only a question of which of them walked in front, for a while. Kingshaw was used to lacking any confidence in himself, to knowing that he could do nothing very well. Until now, he had not much cared, he'd got by. Now, he cared, his pride had risen, he could no longer be docile about himself. Everything was unfair.

They were building the fire, twig by twig.

'What time is it?'

Kingshaw took his watch out of the satchel. He had no sense of time, at all.

'Oh – it's late, it's three o'clock.'

Hooper sat down abruptly beside the stones. 'Look, what's going to happen? What are we going to do?'

'Make this fire.'

'But then what?'

'Eat things. I'll catch a fish, I told you. We'll put a stick through it, and it'll cook.'

'I mean *after* that. How are we going to get out?'

'Just go on and on, until we come to the fence. Look, we're bound to come out soon, we *can't* go on for ever.'

'I don't see why not. It's miles and miles.'

'What?'

'This. Barnard's Forest.'

'Don't be stupid, that's not where we are! We're only in Hang Wood.'

'Of course we're not, how can we be? Hang Wood's small. We've been going through here for hours and hours.'

'Well, maybe we're going round in a circle, then. We *can't* be in the forest, anyway.'

'Why can't we? I don't see how you know.'

Kingshaw sighed. 'Because you have to come out of Hang Wood first, I looked at it on the map. You go out and across a sort of field, and *then* you come into the forest.'

'Not if you go the other way.'

'What other way?'

'Not if you go through the part where they join. That's at the very top. There isn't any field there at all, you go straight into the forest, and that's what we've done.'

There was silence. Kingshaw sat down on the ground as well, thinking about it. After a bit, he said, 'Are you sure?'

'Yes.'

'Oh.'

'I thought you'd be bound to know *that*. Anybody'd know that.'

'No.'

We'd be all right if we were just in Hang Wood, that's nothing. But we're not, we lost the path when we were going after the deer.'

'That was your fault.'

'You didn't have to come.'

'But now we might just be going farther and farther inside.'

Hooper was poking the end of a twig about, in the leaves. 'Yes. And we don't know which is the going out way, and which is the going in way.'

'No.'

'There isn't any way of telling, either. We can't find out. We might be anywhere.'

'Yes.'

Hooper's face was ashy white. 'They'll never find us,' he said, his voice rising, 'even if they knew where we were, even if they sent a hundred people, they might never ever find us.'

Kingshaw didn't answer. Suddenly, Hooper threw himself forwards, and began to beat his fists into the ground, tearing convulsively at the leaves and soil with his nails, and making a hoarse, screaming sound, low down in his throat. He drummed his legs harder and harder.

Kingshaw watched him, in alarm. He said, 'Stop it. Pack it in, Hooper, that's a stupid way to go on.'

But Hooper was too far gone to hear him, his screaming got louder, and he started to sob. Kingshaw was unnerved, feeling his own panic coming back. He had to do something, more for his own sake than for Hooper's. He was going to get up and run away, anywhere, into the trees, but he stopped himself, he was bound to get lost, and besides, he thought he ought to stay with Hooper. In the end, he stood up, leaned over him, and caught hold of his legs.

'Stop it! Shut up, shut up, shut up!' He rammed the legs forwards, banging them on the ground again and again. It made no difference, Hooper went on screaming and flailing about hysterically. His voice echoed all round the clearing, very high and hollow.

Desperately, Kingshaw pushed him over hard, on to his back, and slapped him again and again across the face. 'Shut up, shut up, Hooper. Oh God, will you stop doing that, *stop* it.'

Hooper stopped. He lay on his back, his knees bent right up towards his stomach. The wood was absolutely silent. Kingshaw moved away slowly. He could feel his heart racing. He had never touched Hooper before. He didn't like it.

For a moment, he thought that Hooper might start again, or else that he might get up and begin to fight. But he did not move at all, not for a long time. The wood was very quiet and the sun had come out again. Then a bird began a strange, whooping call, in the trees above them.

Hooper rolled slowly over on to his stomach again, face pressed into the ground, and began to cry. He went on and on, mewling and snuffling. Kingshaw watched, kicking at a tree root, not knowing what to say. But Hooper seemed to be unaware of him, and in the end, he went and got on with making the fire.

He had dug a round, shallow trench, and placed the stones in a half-circle, like a wall behind it. A pile of dry leaves and then twigs, placed criss-cross, on top of one another, were arranged in the trench, with plenty of spaces in between. Kingshaw found a long, straight stick, and began to peel it, to make a skewer. He sat cross-legged on the ground, with his knife. It was very quiet again, except for Hooper, snivelling, and the sound of the water.

Kingshaw tried not to think about what Hooper had said. In any case, he might be wrong, they mightn't be in the forest at all. Nothing would happen. They hadn't even been here for a whole day, yet, and they had plenty of food. They might be just near the very edge of the wood, for all he could tell. But he decided that, if they had got to stay tonight, then it ought to be here, in the clearing. There was water, and there would be a fire. If it rained, they could go under the bushes. Altogether, he thought it was a good place. He was pleased with himself for thinking things out, and not going to pieces, like Hooper.

Then, he remembered the string. As soon as he did, he couldn't imagine why he had not thought of it before. He laid the peeled stick across the stones, and went to the satchel. There was a movement behind him, as Hooper got uncertainly to his feet. Kingshaw did not look round at him, at first. He examined the string. It was a thick ball, very tightly rolled. There ought to be quite a lot of it.

When he did turn, he saw that Hooper was crouching over and being sick, into the stream. Kingshaw watched nervously. The sick stopped. Hooper wiped his sleeve across his mouth.

'Is it O.K.?' Kingshaw said.

Hooper straightened up, and shrugged. But he went on staring down into the water. Kingshaw walked a few yards nearer to him.

'Look, Hooper, I've thought of something. I'm going to go and find out if we're near the outside, or anything.'

Hooper looked round at once, his eyes wide with alarm. His skin was grey-white, the colour of gone-off milk.

'You can't, you'll get lost.'

'No, I won't. I'll tie string to a tree and then unwind it, as far as I can go. Somebody did that once in history and they got away from a bull. Or something. Anyway, it works. It's pretty long. We might be almost on the outside, you can't tell from here. I'll go in every direction, in turn, and then look around and see if it looks any lighter ahead. Anyway, we'll know where we are a bit more. It's a good idea.'

'I think it's stupid. I thought you said we were going to have a fire and cook something.'

'When I get back we will. You can start the fire now, if you like.'

Hooper looked down into the water. 'I could try and get a fish.'

'O.K.'

'But you'd better not go, all the same, Kingshaw.'

Kingshaw hesitated. He thought, he doesn't want to be by himself. He said, 'It won't take long.'

'Anything could happen. The string might break.'

'I could still get back . . .'

'There might be . . .'

'What? What might there?'

'I don't know. Things.'

'What sort of things?'

'It's a forest, isn't it, there might be anything.'

'Nothing that'd *hurt*. I shouldn't think.'

Hooper knelt down, and began to slip his hand about in the stream, trying to feel a fish. 'O.K. Go on, then, if you're so stupid. You needn't think I care if you get lost.'

Kingshaw said, 'I'll leave the matches for the fire.'

Hooper ignored him.

He went straight ahead, at right angles to the stream and away from it, through the trees. On the edge of the clearing, he tied the string to the branch of a tree, with half a dozen knots. Then he walked on, unwinding it through his fingers.

For as far ahead as he could see, the trees just went on. They got close together, and became mixed up with brambles and undergrowth again, some way off. Here, he was in the lightest part, looking towards the darkness. That couldn't be the outside, then. It was very still. The air was less damp-smelling here, though, and there were more birds, moving about and calling. He turned left, and the clearing was no longer in sight, but the string went lacing back through the trees. Ahead, there were more thick bushes, and he thought he ought not to go through them, in case of getting the string ripped on a branch. There was no sign of the wood coming to an end, in any direction that he could see. He felt closed in, and stifled, with the everlasting dark greenness overhead, shutting out the sky.

A rabbit was on the exposed root of a tree, almost at his feet. Kingshaw stopped. He thought, I could kill a rabbit. We could cook that. He had brought his penknife with him. That was what he would do, if he had really meant what he said about the hunting. When they had run out of the food in the satchel, and if they had still not found a way out, they would *have* to do it.

The rabbit had not seen him. He moved forward a step, hardly breathing. The animal turned its head and looked at him in alarm. He saw how its nostrils quivered and twitched. The eyes were very shiny and translucent. Kingshaw lunged forward suddenly, and fell upon the rabbit, pinning it to the ground. Underneath his hands, its soft, loose body struggled and heaved about, and then went dead still. It felt very warm. He remembered the other rabbit he had touched. Slowly, he eased his hands back, a little at a time, until he had a firm grip on each side of it, and then lifted it up, squeezing a little. The legs and feet scrabbled madly, and he saw that its eyes were bloodshot, rolling with fright. He knew that he would not kill it. It would have been easier for him to kill Hooper.

He bent down and released the rabbit. For a split second, it remained as he left it, paralysed, its fur still bearing the imprint of his hands. Then, it bounded away into the bushes, stirring up the dead leaves.

He turned right, next, and went on as far as the string would take him. There were oak trees here, with enormous trunks, wrinkled and grey like the legs of elephants. In between them, stunted, thin trees, killed for lack of light and space, were overgrown with grubs and fungus like pale suède.

Kingshaw thought, I could just go. I could drop the string, and walk away, on and on.

The idea filled him with excitement. He would have nothing, he would be quite free and alone, without Hooper behind him, and without even the satchel. He was not remotely afraid. All day, he had been learning that it was not so much the physical things, or the threat of physical difficulties, that frightened him. He could cope, he was resourceful. He wanted to be alone in the wood, now, he had discovered a new world.

But there was Hooper. Kingshaw sat down for a moment on the grass, and remembered how he had been sick into the stream. Hooper couldn't cope alone, either with himself, or with anything that might happen to him. He would go mad with terror, he would be like a baby. In the end, he might start wandering about, unable to think sensibly, or plan where he was going. Kingshaw knew he ought not to leave him. For some reason, Hooper had wanted to follow him here. He hadn't liked it, because he wanted to get away. And he was still afraid of Hooper, there were byways of his personality that he knew nothing about. Hooper was devious, never to be relied upon, or trusted.

All the same, Kingshaw felt responsible for him, he had an odd sort of concern, knowing his own strength, now, in ways that mattered, knowing that he was the only one who might get them both safely out of the wood. If he went away alone now, something terrible would happen to Hooper, and it would be his fault.

He got up, and began to retrace his steps, winding the string up again into a ball. It took a long time. He expected that Hooper would have caught a fish, and it would be cooking on the fire. He was very hungry. Something about the whole idea pleased him. Hooper would treat it like a game, in any case, and it seemed like one, suddenly.

He found the clearing again, but at first could not see Hooper. The fire was as he had left it, still unlit. He thought, hell, he's gone off on his own, or something, he'll get lost, I shall have to start looking for him. Hell, hell.

He cupped his hands round his mouth. 'Hooper!'

Then, he saw one foot sticking up above the bank of the stream. He must still be fishing, then.

'You're useless, Hooper, if it'd been me, I'd have caught about ten fish by this time, *more* than ten, you're . . .'

He came to a dead stop.

'Oh God!'

Hooper was lying face down, his legs stuck up over the bank. There was a bit of blood on the water, looking as though it came from his head.

'Oh God, Oh God . . .'

Kingshaw went down on both knees and began to haul frantically at Hooper's legs. He was very heavy, and wedged somehow, he couldn't move him. He slid down the bank rapidly, and into the water, and got his hands under Hooper's head. There was a big swelling on his forehead, where he had bashed it against a stone. That was where the blood was coming from. But it was the stone that had kept his face up above the water, too. Panting, Kingshaw pulled him round clumsily, and managed to get him half on to the bank. He had to hold him, with one hand, to stop him rolling back, while he pulled his legs up. When he climbed out of the water himself, he was sobbing slightly, with the effort of it.

Hooper lay very still on the ground. His face was oddly shiny. But the blood had stopped. Kingshaw had no idea what to do. He thought that Hooper probably hadn't swallowed much water, but he couldn't be sure, and if he had, it ought to be got out of him, somehow. He didn't even know if he was breathing.

Somehow, pushing and shoving, he got him on to his side, and began to rub and push his back, in wide, inexpert circles. He went on and on. Nothing happened. Then, Hooper writhed, pitched over and made a violent noise in his throat. Kingshaw pulled him off his face again, and saw water and vomit begin to come from his mouth and nostrils. Hooper's eyes opened, and shut again.

He had heard of things you ought to do to people, breathe into their mouths or pump their arms up and down, somehow, but he thought that if Hooper was sick he must be breathing. His eyes kept rolling open.

Eventually, he half-dragged, half-lifted him along the ground, up to where the fire was laid. Hooper's shirt, and the top half of his jeans, were soaking wet, and it was almost impossible to get them off at first, he was so inert and heavy. They stuck to his skin, too. In the end, Kingshaw managed it. His own clothes were wet, but he had left the sweater and anorak behind him when he went off exploring into the wood. Now, he pulled the sweater over Hooper's head, and then covered him with the anorak. He didn't know what else he could do. He wanted there to be someone else, to take charge, he was afraid of Hooper dying.

If he could get the fire alight, he thought he would dry himself out eventually, but he was shaking all over, so that he dripped water off his clothes on to the matches at first, as he struck them. When he did get one alight, he lay down and tried breathing into the twigs, to keep them going.

He was certain that Hooper would die. He might only just have fallen in, but on the other hand he might have been there right from the first moment Kingshaw turned his back on the clearing. He blew harder on the fire. It was something to do. He dared not look at Hooper again, and he needed to get himself warm, too.

If Hooper died, it would be his fault. He shouldn't have gone off. Hooper had said earlier that they ought to keep together. 'It's dangerous.' 'Oh, Jesus, Jesus . . .' Kingshaw let out an abrupt sob of panic.

But the fire had caught now, and the flames began to spurt up, green and orange, between the twigs. He had to move back from the smoke.

If Hooper was dead, if Hooper was dead, if . . . He didn't know what would happen, except that he would be on his own. What did he have to come here for anyway, why hadn't he gone on the roads, he would have been there now, nothing would have happened to him, Hooper wouldn't have found him, he would have been safe. It was gone five o'clock. He stared into the livening fire, and tried to stop himself crying.

When he heard Hooper begin to retch, he shot round in terror, it was like hearing the dead.

Hooper was sitting up, and leaning forward. Kingshaw went and crouched down beside him.

'It's O.K., it's O.K.'

Hooper's eyes were open, but for a moment he seemed unable to focus properly.

Kingshaw said, 'Look, there's a fire now, you'd better go near it. It's O.K. You'll be all right, Hooper. Oh, God, I thought you were dead, you looked as if you were dead.'

Hooper drew up his knees, huddling into himself. He said, 'I didn't get a fish, I almost did, Kingshaw, you needn't think I didn't try, only I couldn't keep it, it slipped, I couldn't . . .'

'O.K. Look, it doesn't matter, never mind about the fish. You'd better lie down and go to sleep or something.'

'My head hurts.'

'Well, you bashed it on a stone, that's why. But I had a look at it, I think it's all right.'

'My throat hurts. I want a drink, I want a drink.' Hooper began to shiver again.

'I could bring you some water in my hands . . .'

'There's a cup, I brought a cup. It's in the bag.'

Kingshaw hesitated doubtfully, and then picked up the canvas holdall, from where Hooper had flung it when he first went in to swim.

The cup was small, a tiny one. Kingshaw turned out the contents of the bag on to the grass. There was the food Hooper had told him about before, biscuits, tomatoes and sweets, and some salt in a screw of paper. There was a map of the whole of England, a torch, a propelling pencil and a roll of Sellotape. Kingshaw thought that Hooper must have just taken anything he could find, in his hurry to get out. At the very bottom of the bag, he found three small, white tablets. They were a bit dirty. He smelled them, and then put the tip of his tongue on to the surface. He thought they were probably aspirin.

'Look, I know what, I can make you a hot drink. If I put the mug on top of the fire, the water'll boil. I've found an aspirin you can have.'

'They make me sick.'

'Well, you can't be sick any more than you have already. It's good for you, it'll stop your head hurting. I know, I'll put some of that jelly cube stuff I've got in the water. It'll melt then and be like sugar.'

Elated at his own enterprise, and no longer so afraid, because Hooper was not dead after all, Kingshaw went bounding off, and filled the cup with water. When he came back, he got the pair of socks out of his own satchel, and wound one round the cup handle. Then he balanced it carefully on top of the fire.

Hooper said, 'You were gone ages. Did you find the way out?'

'I'm not sure.' He thought it was better to lie. He was afraid of Hooper going off into a panic again, screaming and throwing himself about.

'You have found it, you *have*. Where are we, Kingshaw?' Kingshaw squatted over the fire, not replying.

'You'd better not try and sneak off, you'd just better not go and find the way out by yourself, that's all. If you do I'll kill you.'

Kingshaw glanced round. He said mildly, 'You won't. I haven't found a way out, if you want to know, I've got no idea where we are, so.'

He turned his attention back to the mug of water.

Chapter Eight

'Kingshaw, it's getting dark.'

'I know.'

'What time is it?'

'You ought to have a watch of your own, I'm fed up with telling you the time.'

'My father's going to give me a new one for this Christmas, he's going to give me a gold watch, anyway, with a thing for the date on, and roman numbers you can see in the dark. It'll cost a lot of money. About fifty pounds, I should think. *More* than fifty pounds.'

'Liar, no watch costs that much.'

'They do, they do. They can cost hundreds and hundreds of pounds, sometimes. You don't know anything about anything.'

'Nobody's father would buy them a watch that cost fifty pounds.'

'My father would, because I'm the most important thing he's got in his whole life, he said. So he'd buy me anything I wanted.'

Kingshaw was silent, impressed by Hooper's self-confidence.

The light had faded and faded, sucking the colour out of the trees and bushes, until everything around them looked pale brown, like an old photograph. There was no wind at all. It was still very warm.

'Anyway, what time *is* it?'

'Gone eight o'clock. Twenty past eight, nearly.'

Kingshaw scratched his hair.

'You've got nits.'

'It's midge bites.'

'If you make the fire a lot bigger they'll go off. Midges don't like fire.'

'No, it's the smoke, it kills them.'

'It doesn't *kill* them, they just don't like it, so they go away.'

'Yes, it does kill them, you can see them dropping in. They get suffocated.'

'The moths will come as well.'

'Stuff it. We've got enough to think about.'

'If one little moth came and crawled on you, you'd pee your pants.'

'I said stuff it.'

'Scaredy-baby.'

'Shut up.'

'*Are* you?'

'What?'

'Scared?'

'What of?' Kingshaw asked warily.

'Anything. Of when it gets dark.'

'No.'

Hooper peered into his face, trying to make out whether or not Kingshaw was lying. He was sitting right up close to the fire.

'That bump's swollen on your head. It's gone all black.'

'That's your fault.'

'Don't be stupid. Does it still hurt?'

Hooper put up a hand and explored it tentatively with his fingers.

'If I press on it, it does.'

'Oh.'

Kingshaw went on scratching at the midge bites.

He had caught a fish himself. At first, he planned to stab it with his penknife, but when he got it out of the water, he couldn't. It might not die straight away, and besides, the blood would get all over him. If fishes had blood. He wasn't sure. They didn't look as if they did.

It was a pretty big one, with brownish bars across its underside. The only thing he could do was leave it on the grass, flailing about, and go away for a bit.

'Where is it?'

'It'll be dead in a minute.'

'You should have cut it open.'

'Why don't *you* then?'

'Because you're looking after me. My head hurts, anyway.'

'Baby.'

'I might have been dead, because you went off and left me, and if I had been dead, you'd have been a murderer, you shouldn't have gone into the wood by yourself.' Hooper had gone on and on, whining about it.

'Oh, shut up, you're not dead, you've only banged yourself.'

'You're a bully.'

Kingshaw stared at him, incensed by the unfairness of the remark, unable to say anything at all to counter it

'You can't just leave a fish and let it suffocate, that's like murder as well, that's awful.'

'Why is it? It's not any different from stabbing it with a penknife.'

'It is, anybody could tell you that. It's crueller. You're a bully.'

Kingshaw walked off to get more wood for the fire. When he did go back to the fish, it was dead. He tried not to think of how it had gone on writhing and lashing about, without any water. He picked it up. It was quite heavy, and glutinous between his hands.

'You'll have to cut its head off now.'

'No, I won't, I'm going to put the stick through it. This is like a barbecue. That's how you do it.'

'What about its insides? You can't eat those parts.'

Kingshaw hesitated a moment. Then said, 'We have to pick off the meat It doesn't matter about the insides, we won't come to them.'

'What if it's poisonous?'

'No fish is poisonous.'

But it had not tasted any good. The skin burned off straight away, but just under the surface the marble-grey flesh was still cold and raw. Hooper had eaten a mouthful, and then spat the rest out on to the grass. Kingshaw ate more. But in the end, the stick caught fire.

'That was vile muck. You're bloody useless, Kingshaw.'

'You couldn't do any better.'

'You're supposed to be looking after me, because I hurt myself.'

'Baby-baby Hooper!'

'You wait, you wait . . .'

Kingshaw had opened the satchel and Hooper's canvas bag, and they ate some biscuits and nearly all the tomatoes.

'Tomorrow we've got to have rations,' Kingshaw said. 'I'll divide all the food up. It won't last for very long.'

'Then what'll happen?'

'We'll have got out by then.'

'What if we don't?'

'We *will* have.'

'I wish we hadn't ever come in here, anyway.'

'*You* didn't have to, you just followed me.'

'It was you that got us lost.'

'No, it was not, so, it was you that started running about like a stupid fool.'

The light went, all of a sudden. One minute, Kingshaw looked up and he could still see beige chinks of sky, far above, and the next minute, he could not. The fire spurted.

'They'll be coming home now,' Hooper said, 'they'll be on the train.'

'I suppose so.'

'Soon, they'll start looking for us.'

'No, they won't. Not tonight, anyway.'

'Of course they will. Why won't they?'

'Because how will they know we're not in bed? If they don't get back till late they won't even bother to look.'

'There's Mrs Boland and she'll tell them.'

'No, she goes at four o'clock. She'd think we'd just gone for a picnic or something, she never bothers. Nobody will know.'

'Your mother goes upstairs to see you, I know, because I hear her. She has to kiss you good-night like a little baby.'

'Boil your head. She doesn't always come.'

'Yes, she does, then. Kiss, kiss, kiss. Oh, there, my little darling, dear little baby-boy, Mummy loves her little baby-boy, Mummy goes cuddle, cuddle, cuddle, every night, little diddums baby – that's what.'

'Just because you haven't got a mother at all.'

But Hooper was unmoved. 'I wouldn't want one.'

'That's a stupid thing to say.'

'Fathers are better. Anybody who hasn't got a father is useless.' Kingshaw stood up and went nearer to the fire. Hooper looked at him. Kingshaw was holding a long, thick stick in his right hand. For a moment, neither of them moved. He saw Hooper's eyes widen.

'You'd better not try and hit me.'

Kingshaw looked down at him scornfully, and then threw the stick on to the fire. The flames leaped up, throwing a shadow behind him, on to the grass.

'If you don't want to catch fire, you'd better move back out of the way.'

Hooper only went on, staring into the blaze. He said casually, 'Has your mother gone after a lot of people?'

'What do you mean?'

'I mean like she's gone after my father.'

Kingshaw felt the blood coming up into his face. He seemed to be going hotter and hotter, right inside himself. He thought, I was stupid, I could have bashed him with that stick, bashed and bashed his head in.

Now, Hooper was leaning on his elbow, looking up, his face prideful, in the flickering light from the bonfire. Gloating.

'That's why you came here. You didn't think it was for anything else, did you? She wants to be married to my father. He's rich.'

'Liar, liar, liar. Your father isn't anything, she doesn't even *like* your father. She hates him.'

Hooper smiled. 'There are things I see that you don't.'

'What? What things?'

'Never mind. But you've got to believe me.'

'Your father's nothing.'

'Look, it's all right, Kingshaw, it's only what ladies do. If she hasn't got a husband, she's got to find one.'

'Why has she?'

'Well, because he'd give her money and a house and things, that's what always happens.'

Kingshaw walked slowly away from the fire. He couldn't go on answering back, having a stupid argument. Hooper always wanted to keep up for hours. But it was all true, he could see that.

He hated his mother more than anybody, more even than Hooper, now. He had a terrible twisted-up feeling in his belly, because of it. Now, Hooper knew. 'There are things I see that you don't.'

There wasn't anything he could do. Except get away. It was his father's fault, really, because his dying had been the start of it all, the not having enough money, and living in other people's houses. Even at school, he couldn't forget it. People had found out that he was a G.B.B. – a Governor's Bequest Boy, which meant he didn't pay fees any more. His mother made things worse. She came on speech day and sports day, all got up with earrings and awful, slippery-looking dresses, and started putting on lipstick where everybody could see. Brace had said, 'Kingshaw's mother's an old tart.'

He wished she was dead, instead of his father.

The darkness was as thick as felt, all around him, he didn't dare look ahead, between the trees. Something would happen now, because of what he'd thought about his mother. If you wished people dead, they heard you, somehow, and then it happened. He didn't know what. But later, he looked down and saw the wart on his left hand, by the light of the fire. That proved it.

Hooper was asleep. He lay with his legs all pulled up and his thumb in his mouth. Because of the bang on his head, Kingshaw had given him the anorak, to roll up for a pillow.

He felt protective towards Hooper, and patient with him, now, since finding him in the stream. He had become more important, somehow, because he had been so near to dying. He might easily have died, if the water had come up over his face, or if he had bashed his head much harder. Perhaps he might still die. People caught pneumonia from having been in water. Or something might have happened inside his head, from the bump. There was no way of telling.

Kingshaw thought now that whatever Hooper said about his mother didn't much matter. Hooper was a nuisance, always arguing and being stupid, like a baby, or else trying to say and do things that would scare him. None of it mattered any more, because they were both lost. He was stuck with Hooper. There was nobody else.

Hooper stirred on the ground, moving his legs up and down rhythmically. The thumb was still tight-fitted into his mouth. Kingshaw watched him. Everything else, their time at Warings, the Red Room, his mother and Mr Hooper, his hatred, all that seemed years and years ago, he could scarcely remember it. Nothing that he had ever known, outside of the wood, seemed real.

The fire was dying down, burning blood-red, underneath. Then, the noises began. A long way off, a fox began to howl. Kingshaw thought it sounded like wolves. Well, foxes were like wolves, only not so dangerous. When the howling came again, it was answered by some barks, close by.

Eyes, he thought, you can see their eyes. He looked around him fearfully. It was completely dark. There was nothing. But things moved, suddenly, there were odd, dropping, rustling, scuttering noises, movements in the water. Twigs cracked. Only Hooper slept, turning over and whimpering, now and then.

Kingshaw wished he had a blanket to hide his head under. He could lie down and close his eyes until they ached, but it wouldn't be the same, because his skin felt exposed, and he had only to half-open the lids, to see into the darkness. A blanket would have muffled anything, made him feel safe. Whatever came, then, he needn't know about it.

The woods crept and stirred. Kingshaw felt himself holding his breath. Every so often he glanced round, over his shoulder. The fire cast shadows, and odd flickers, into the darkness. Occasionally it shifted, and the twigs collapsed into soft, ashy heaps.

He lay down again, and took his arms out of the sleeves of his sweater. He could pull it up, then, right over his face. But that was no good, he couldn't breathe. He lay for a moment, and smelled his own, close, hot smell, not hearing anything. Then, he had to pull his head out, and gulp in the warm night air. He folded his arms instead, pressed his face down into one, and covered his ears over with the other. The fox howled again. He could still hear everything. An owl came, with an ominous, swift whirring of its wings, down on to something in the grass. Earlier, they had watched a sparrowhawk overtake a small bird, in mid-air, reaching out and pulling it back with its claws, and then gripping it to death as it flew on. Its small eye glinted yellow. Afterwards the wood had gone very still.

Kingshaw felt suddenly cold and dead, inside himself. He wanted to cry. There was nobody to go to, nobody to tell. Hooper had to be looked after. There seemed no chance at all of their either getting out by themselves, or of being found. They would die. He jerked up anxiously, afraid the fire might go out. They hadn't many matches.

But there was another thought, about his mother and Mr Hooper. They might not want either of us back. So they might just leave us. Hooper's father had said, you are the most important thing in my whole life, to Hooper. But you couldn't tell. People changed. Kingshaw thought that there was no hope for themselves at all.

The owl began hooting again. It was a long time before he fell asleep.

When he woke again, it was still dark. He sat bolt upright even before he opened his eyes, heart racing. He knew at once where he was. Why had he woken? It was very warm and very quiet, in the clearing. The fire had died right down to a dark-red glow. Kingshaw got up stiffly and began to swing his arms about, to get rid of the cramp. Then he heard Hooper.

He was lying on his side, but now he flung himself over hard on to his back, and began to talk in an incoherent, moaning sort of way, on and on. He was turning his head about from side to side, on the ground.

'Don't, don't, don't, don't, don't, it isn't fair, it isn't, oh . . . don't, don't. I've got to, it isn't fair, I've got the blazer. Oh, don't, don't . . . Mummy! Mummy! Mummy! . . .' His voice rose suddenly to a scream, and he sat up, still asleep, drumming his legs. His eyes were screwed tight shut. 'Mummy! Mummy! Mummy! . . .'

Kingshaw went over and knelt beside him.

'Wake up,' he said, hesitantly, and then much louder, 'It's O.K. Wake up, Hooper, you'd better wake up. It's O.K. Look, we're only in the wood, it's only me. *Wake up*, Hooper.'

Hooper went on screaming. His face and neck were flushed. Kingshaw was terrified, as he heard his voice echoing round among the trees and far away, into the forest.

'Don't, don't, don't, don't, don't . . .'

Desperately, he reached forward and hit Hooper twice across the face with the palm of his hand. 'Shut up!' It made a sharp noise. He thought, I am always hitting him. At once he stood up, and backed away a little, alarmed by what he had done.

Hooper had stopped. His eyes were open and he looked around wildly for a moment, then he began to cry. Kingshaw moved up to him again.

'Listen, it's all right, I'm awake as well.'

Hooper looked at him, uncertainly, as if puzzled. Then he lay down again, and put his hand up to his eyes.

'I'm hot. My head hurts. I'm hot as hell.' The tears squeezed out between his fingers. He began to struggle to take off his jumper.

'You'd better not do that.'

'I'm boiling hot, I'm all sweating.'

'Yes, but it's night, you might catch cold.'

Hooper whimpered.

'There's one of those aspirins left,' Kingshaw said, 'I'll get you some water. It'll probably make you feel better again. You might go to sleep.'

Hooper did not answer. Kingshaw found the tin mug, and walked through the darkness towards the stream. He knelt down. It was beautifully cool here, and the grass smelled sweet and damp. The noise of the water sounded comforting. He lay full length and put his face on to the grass, closing his eyes. It was cool. In the trees, the owl hooted, but it didn't frighten him now. Everything went still.

'Kingshaw!' Hooper's voice was whiny, with fear.

'O.K.'

He reached out the cup and filled it, and drank some water himself, then splashed the remainder over his face and hair. He wished he could lie down in the stream, just lie and lie, with the water moving over him.

He took the cup back, found the last aspirin in the canvas bag, and gave it to Hooper. Then he made up the fire. The wood he had gathered the previous afternoon was almost gone.

'I'm hot,' Hooper said again.

'I suppose you've got a temperature, that's why.'

'I had tonsilitis, last winter. At school. I had a very bad temperature, then.' He was dipping his fingers into the mug and then wiping them over his face.

'You'll be O.K.,' Kingshaw said. Though he did not know.

The fire had gone black, because the new twigs were not yet alight underneath. Kingshaw sat by it, and heard Hooper's voice but couldn't see him. He said, 'If you're still ill tomorrow, we'll have to stay here.'

'We can't.'

'There's no good wandering about trying to find a way out, that'd be stupid.'

Hooper sniffed.

'Anyway, I expect they'll come for us. We ought to stay in the same place, so they can find us.'

'They'll never find us. It's miles and miles big, this forest, it's huge. They'd look for ever.'

'They'll bring dogs.'

'What sort of dogs?'

'Police dogs.'

'Will they get the *police?*'

'They might.'

Privately, Kingshaw remembered what he had decided yesterday. That his mother and Mr Hooper might not want to find them at all. He still believed it.

'You'll get into trouble when they do come,' Hooper said, 'because it's your fault.'

Kingshaw sighed. A breeze set up a whispering movement through the trees, but there was no coolness. When it died down, there was no air, no sound.

Hooper said, 'What will you do?'

'When?'

'When they come for us. Will you run away again?'

'I don't know. I haven't thought about that yet.'

'They might take you and put you in one of those boys' prison places.'

'What for? I haven't done anything.'

'You've run away.'

'Well, anybody can run away, there's nothing to stop you.'

'No, you're not allowed to, they make you come back. And you got us lost.'

'Not on purpose I didn't.'

'You made me follow you.'

Kingshaw stood up, furious; 'I bloody well didn't, you're a liar. You'd just better not say that, Hooper.'

'I will.'

'They won't believe you. It was you that followed me, I didn't want you, I never wanted to have anything to do with you.' He almost wept with frustration, seeing that Hooper might say anything, might so easily make himself believed. It was ludicrous that he could be accused of leading him away, ludicrous, but entirely possible.

'I ran away by myself,' Kingshaw said, 'and you're a copy-cat, you wanted to come, just to be in on something, just to see what I did.'

'No, I did not. Anyway, I don't like it here, I want to go home. I don't want to be lost.'

'Oh, pack it in, great blubbing baby. You think you're so clever, bossing everyone about. You're just a baby yourself.'

'I want to go home.'

Kingshaw went and stood over him, exasperated almost beyond bearing. But he said, trying to be kind, 'Listen, it's stupid to go on and on arguing. And it won't do any good to blub, either. It doesn't matter how we *got* here, we are here, and we're lost, so we'd better stay till someone comes. You're only feeling frightened because of being ill. It's what happens when you get a temperature.'

'I might die.'

'You won't.'

'I could. What if I did. What'll happen, Kingshaw?'

Kingshaw had already thought of it. Of their both dying. But the moment Hooper spoke the words out loud, it sounded crazy.

'Look, don't be stupid. You only banged your head and got wet, and that isn't going to make you die.'

'I don't feel very well. I'm all shivery. I'm cold.'

'Well, you can have my jumper then.' He stripped it off quickly, and threw it down.

'It smells,' Hooper said, 'it smells of you.'

'Put it on. Then put the anorak on top of it. I'm not cold. I can go by the fire.'

He could see Hooper shivering. His face had gone dead white, and his eyes were very bright, staring at him, from dark sockets. 'Kingshaw . . .'

'What?'

'Don't go away.'

'I told you, we're going to stay here.'

'But you might change your mind. You won't, will you? You won't go and try to find the way out again, will you?'

'No. Not now, anyway.'

'I mean never. I don't want to be by myself.'

'In the morning I might. I could have a look in the other direction, with the string.'

'No, I don't want you to. Look, you're not to leave me by myself.'

'You'd be O.K.'

'No, no, no! You've got to stay here, you've got to. I'll tell them you went away and left me by myself.'

'All right then.'

'What?'

'I won't go.'

'Promise.'

'O.K.'

'I don't like it, I wish I hadn't come after you now.'

'Well you did.'

'You're not to go away and leave me.'

'I've said no.'

'If you did, I'd hear you.'

'I *won't*. You are a baby.'

'I'll lie awake and watch you, I'll keep my eyes open, you couldn't go, without me seeing you.'

'I said I *won't*, I won't, I won't. Now shut up whining.'

'You have got to say, I promise. Go on.'

Kingshaw felt his patience breaking. He had already promised.

'You've got to *say* it, or else it doesn't count. Go on, go on.'

Kingshaw looked over at him with sudden interest. He knew that Hooper was feeling ill. Frightened. Not himself. He had never once been like this at the house. All the same.

'Are you always scaredy? At school are you?'

'No, I'm not, I'm not ever. I'm only telling you what to do, that's all.'

'You are scared. You're scared now.'

'So are you, then.'

'But I wouldn't go on whining, like you. Scaredy Hooper.'

'I'm not. I hate you.'

Kingshaw poked a long stick farther into the fire. He didn't know why he suddenly wanted to taunt Hooper, to see how far he could go, what he could make him do. He already had the upper hand, for the time being at least. But he had to prove it to himself. He was embarrassed by Hooper's sudden way of whining and pleading with him.

But now, Hooper said in a low voice, 'If you sneak away and then they come here, and they find me, and then they go and find you, I'll kill you, I'll . . .'

'What, then?'

'Never mind. You wait.'

'Can't scare me.'

'I can. I did. That's why you ran away.'

'Balls.'

'It is, it is. You cried when you saw a crow, anyway, a stupid old bird! Cry baby, cry.'

'Stuff it.'

'If you run away . . .'

'Oh, Jesus, I've told you, haven't I, I'm not *going* to run away.'

'Well you've got to *promise*, then.'

Kingshaw leaped up, maddened by Hooper's voice, going on and on. He stood over him, yelling. 'Shut up, Hooper, *shut up*. I'll kick you, I'll bash your head in, if you don't shut up, you needn't think I won't.'

Hooper cringed back suddenly, caught by surprise. He half got to his knees, trying to move away. Kingshaw straddled him.

'Are you going to shut up now?'

'Yes. I . . .'

'If you say anything else at all, I'll kick you. I could hurt you because you're ill, I'd win easily. Now shut up.'

'You won't, you mustn't . . .' Hooper began to cry again, loudly, out of fear.

Kingshaw watched him for a second, wanting to beat him. Then, abruptly, he turned and walked away. He was frightened by what he had done, and of the voice that had come out of himself. He had been ready to kick and punch Hooper, anything to stop him from whining and nagging and blaming. His own violence astounded him.

He wandered off a little way into the clearing, kicking his feet against the tree roots, stirring up the leaves. Not far away, some animal grunted, and then yelped out a warning.

After a bit, he went slowly back and lay down again beside the fire, staring into its red heart until his eyes smarted. He felt oddly numb, but himself again, calm. He wouldn't touch Hooper now. The fire sputtered and glowed. He felt safe with it. That and the water. He wasn't comfortable, though, because he'd given Hooper all the extra clothes, and twigs and dry bits of leaf were sticking into him, through his shirt and jeans.

He said, 'Hooper?'

Silence.

'Are you O.K.?'

'Shut up.'

Kingshaw hesitated. He was ashamed of himself. He remembered how Hooper had screamed out 'Mummy, Mummy'. That had surprised him more than anything.

'I wouldn't really have hit you.'

He knew he was letting whatever advantage he might have won leak away again, playing back into Hooper's hands. But he thought that whatever happened he had something, an inner strength or resolution that Hooper lacked. It would carry him through things. He felt that he no longer needed to run away, at least as far as Hooper was concerned. Their roles had not been reversed, but still, something had changed. Kingshaw felt aware of himself, and of his own resources.

Aloud, he said, 'Look, you needn't worry, Hooper, we've both got to stay here till they come for us.'

Hooper lay absolutely still, beyond him in the darkness. But Kingshaw could feel him, listening.

He tried not to think what would happen if nobody did come for them.

Chapter Nine

They came. It was late the next morning.

Both of them had been awake for hours since dawn. As the light filled out, the birds started chattering above their heads, and all round them, every bush was thick with birds. They had been there all night, then, still, silent.

Kingshaw thought, it is a whole day. But it might have been a year, five years. Everything outside the wood had receded until he no longer believed in it.

He looked over at Hooper. He was awake, lying on his back with his eyes open.

'I'd better get some sticks. The fire'll go out.'

'Let it.'

'No, there's only half a box of matches. We don't know how long we'll have to be here. We mustn't waste anything.'

Hooper sat up, and then stood, a bit uncertainly. He said, 'I feel O.K. now. I don't feel so funny.'

'It's gone all greeny-brown, though – where you fell.'

Hooper put up his hand and explored it.

'It's not swollen.'

'No. I'll get the sticks.'

There had been no mist this morning. The early light came filtering palely through the wood, making the tree trunks like watered silk. At first it was grey, then faintly yellow, then golden, and the floor of the woods was rust-coloured, where the dead leaves lay.

Kingshaw stepped about, picking up sticks, hearing the birds chirruping. All through the night, the woods had felt secretive, things had lurked and hovered, eyes had watched, there was something fearful in them, an air of suppression.

Now, everything was revealed by the sun, birds and insects scuttered about, the whole place was alive. Kingshaw breathed easily, full of relief.

*

'I'm going to swim,' he said later. They had eaten tomatoes and biscuits for breakfast. Hooper was lying flat on the ground in a lozenge of sunlight. His clothes looked crumpled. Just ahead of him, below a bush, a thrush was banging a snail down on to a flat stone to smash the shell. Hooper watched it intently.

'You'd better not come in the water, though. You might have got a cold from yesterday.'

'I'm all right.'

'Well . . .'

'Anyway, I don't feel like swimming. In a minute, I'm going to get a biscuit and see if this bird'll come for crumbs.'

'It won't.'

'Why won't it?'

'Because it's wild. Not like in the garden.'

'Don't be stupid. All birds are wild, they're all the same.'

'It won't come nearer if you're there.'

'We'll see.'

'It's a waste of food. We need to save it all.'

'I'm only giving it crumbs. Anyway, you mind your own business, Kingshaw.'

But Hooper spoke mildly, his attention fixed on the bird.

Kingshaw took off his clothes, and went and lay down in the shallowest part of the stream. The stones were cold against his buttocks and shoulders, but not sharp. The water moved over and over him, parting and coming together again. He opened his legs wide and then closed them, like scissors. The sunlight was limey-yellow, coming through the leaves above. They fidgeted gently the whole time. A black and white bird flew up, parting them, going off into the open sky.

Kingshaw closed his eyes. He didn't want to swim, not to move at all. He thought, this is all right, this is all right. Hooper was still watching the thrush. It had got the snail out of the broken shell, now.

All round them, the wood pigeons called.

It was then that he heard the first shout. A dog barked. It was far away, at first, but they got nearer very quickly. None of it seemed to take long. Crash, crash, crash they came, through the undergrowth. Someone shouted again. They were almost in the clearing, but Kingshaw couldn't tell what any of them had said. The dog barked again.

He opened his eyes, and saw Hooper, sitting up, looking at him.

'Someone's coming.'

Kingshaw did not answer, did not move, only closed his eyes again and lay, letting the water sift over his naked body. He thought, I don't want them to come, I don't want them to find us. Not now. This is all right. I want to stay here.

He didn't even mind Hooper, now. Not in the wood. It was another world. If they couldn't have found their way out, then they would either die, or survive. But this was what he had wanted. To get away, change things. Now, someone was coming, they would be taken back to the house.

For a second, he dreaded it. Then, he remembered everything that had happened with Hooper, since yesterday morning. Things *had* changed. Perhaps it would be all right.

There was another shout. When he opened his eyes again, his view of the tree-tops and the sunlight was blocked, by a man's head.

Chapter Ten

'It was Kingshaw, it was Kingshaw, he pushed me in the water.'

Kingshaw whipped round, astounded by the coolness of Hooper's treachery.

'You liar, I didn't, I didn't, I wasn't even there, I never touched you. You fell in.'

'He punched me in the back.'

'Liar, liar, liar!'

'Charles, how *can* you speak like that, how can you be so naughty?'

'I didn't *touch* him.'

'Then why ever should Edmund say that you did? I am quite sure he would have no reason to tell an untruth.'

'Oh yes, he would, he's a sneaky little liar, he'd say anything. Well I didn't touch him.'

'Oh, what a way to speak! You make me so ashamed of you.'

They were in the breakfast room. Beyond the open window, the garden lay in the heat of the early afternoon sun, full of bees and vivid flowers. Kingshaw wanted to get out there, on his own.

'I might have been killed, mightn't I? Hitting my head on a stone like that. I might have been dead.'

'No, dear, I don't think that would really have happened, you're not to worry about it. But you have had a very nasty fright.'

'He sat on me and bashed me, as well, after I'd done it. He went on and on.'

Kingshaw watched his mother bending over Hooper examining the bruise. He thought, I hate you, I hate you both. Hooper wouldn't look up at him.

He began to say, 'He was trying to catch a fish with his hands, and he slipped, he just fell in and bashed his head, that's all. I wasn't even there . . .'

But he let his voice tail off. It was useless. Nobody spoke. His mother and Mr Hooper stood, making a pair beside the kitchen table and looking at him with blank faces. Kingshaw turned away. Whatever they believed didn't matter. It was his fault, they said, all of it, he was the one who'd gone off first, he had chosen to go into the wood. Hooper had only followed, none of it was his fault. They hadn't even bothered to ask why. A bit of an adventure, they said, an expedition, silliness. He could not explain that he had wanted to go right away for ever.

Now, he wandered towards the door.

'Charles, you are to stay here, you are not to go out.'

He hesitated.

'You must get a book and go to your bedroom.'

'What for? There isn't anything wrong with me.'

'And do you not think that it might be because you have *done* something wrong?'

'I haven't, I haven't, it's not fair. I didn't *touch* him.'

'Oh, we are not talking about that now. I was thinking that it was very naughty of you to go off in that way at all, leading Edmund into trouble.'

'He didn't have to come, I didn't want him.'

'And besides that, you have had a very nasty fright.'

'No, I haven't.'

'Now there is no need to answer back and be silly, even if you think you are trying to be brave. I think I know what is best for you.'

'I'm O.K.'

'Don't say O.K., Charles, how often must I ask you that? Now, I have said that I want you to go to your bedroom, dear. I don't quite like this way you have, of arguing and answering back. You are only eleven years old, after all. And especially not in front of Mr Hooper.'

'I don't see why I can't go out.'

'Because you cannot be trusted, can you? There is no knowing what might happen next. I am very upset, you have no idea of how we both feel today, after such a terrible experience, coming home and finding you gone like that. Well, you must stay indoors and rest.'

Mr Hooper coughed. 'Perhaps a game . . .' he said tentatively, 'perhaps the draughts board . . . I think they might go into the sitting room and play a quiet game, something of that sort.'

'Oh, rot!'

'Charles!'

'I'm not playing stupid draughts. I'm not playing anything with him.'

'Charles, I will *not* have you speaking in that way. Now please apologize to Mr Hooper. And to Edmund. That is so silly, when he is your special friend.'

Kingshaw wanted to scream into both their faces, shout and shout to make them understand. He said, 'If you want to know what I wish, I wish he had split his head open on that rotten stone, I wish I hadn't come and found him in time, because then he'd be dead. I wish he *were* dead.'

Mrs Helena Kingshaw sat down abruptly on the kitchen chair, a little moaning noise came from her lips.

Kingshaw was terrified of what he had said.

'I told you, I told you, he pushed me in, he *wanted* me to get hurt.'

'I didn't touch you, Hooper, and you know, so stuff it.'

'He kept on punching me all the time, as well, he kicked and punched me.'

'Liar, liar, sodding little liar!' Kingshaw lunged at him.

'*Now* . . .'

Mr Hooper held him back. His hand was very thin, with long, bony fingers digging into Kingshaw's forearm.

'This is a bad way to behave, a very bad way,' he said, 'I wonder you are not both very ashamed of yourselves.'

'He's a bully, anyway,' Hooper made a babyish face.

Kingshaw pulled himself out of Mr Hooper's grasp. He was almost in tears, it was like having a wall in front of him which he must batter down. He could not say, I looked after him, I got him out of the stream and made him sick up the water he'd swallowed, I made him a drink and gave him my sweater and everything, I was afraid he was dead, I said, it's O.K., it's all right, Hooper, you needn't get scared. When he fell I wasn't even there, I never touched him, not even the time I stood over him and wanted to hit him to make him shut up. I didn't touch him. None of it was like that.

But he said nothing. He didn't understand himself, now, looking at Hooper as he sat on the chair in the breakfast room. He had put up with him until he could no longer bear it. Now, he would have killed him.

He saw that they did not really know him, not any of them, they had been completely unaware of everything he thought and felt, quite ready to believe Hooper's lies and complaints. To Kingshaw, the lies were so crazy, so blatantly unlikely, he thought anybody must see through them.

But they did not, they knew so little of him that they would believe anything. Kingshaw felt himself more than ever removed from them, locked up in himself. You thought they knew you, and saw all the reasons why, but not even his mother knew. When she looked at him, she saw some other person. She didn't know what was inside his head, she had never known anything at all that was true about him.

Hooper was bad. He knew that now. There couldn't be any kind of truce between them, after all. Kingshaw felt suddenly weak with tiredness.

'They had better both go upstairs.'

Mrs Helena Kingshaw blew her nose.

'I feel that is much the best thing. They are over-tired and hysterical. But of course, if you disagree . . .'

'No, no. Oh, I am sorry, I cannot think clearly, my head is aching. I cannot apologize enough for Charles, I cannot understand . . .'

'Yes, yes. Now it is quite all right.'

'Oh, you are so kind to us! If Charles does not understand how fortunate we are – well, he is only a child, after all, there is not . . . But I do, I . . .'

Kingshaw thought, shut up, shut up, shut up. He wanted to shake her, to stop the crying, and that way of speaking to Mr Hooper. He was sick with shame at her.

'Now you will both go to your rooms, please. We have had quite enough, I think, quite enough. Edmund . . .'

'I want an aspirin. My head hurts again.'

'You shall have one, dear.' Mrs Helena Kingshaw jumped up. I shall not make a favourite of my own child, she thought, especially when all the blame for this lies with him.

'Yes, I will put your aspirin in a nice drink and then you won't taste it.'

'Baby,' Kingshaw said furiously. 'There's nothing wrong with him anyway. You should have seen him in the thunderstorm. He cried and blubbed, he was scared as anything – he *peed* with fright.'

'Charles, dear . . .' His mother turned round from the sink, a little smile on her mouth, 'Charles, I am very surprised at you, and just a little ashamed, I must say. You are being very vulgar and very unkind. I should have hoped you were big enough now, to understand that sometimes people *are* afraid of things, and that it is not their fault. It isn't always the people who have no fears at all, who are the bravest, you know. A thunderstorm can be a very nasty thing.'

'I'm sick,' Hooper said primly, 'in storms. I always have been sick. At school I'm allowed to go out of form and lie down, if it thunders.'

'Stupid baby.'

'Charles . . .'

'Blubbing at a little bit of old thunder like a baby.'

'I shall be very angry in a moment. We have had too much of that horrid way of talking. You had better go to your room, as Mr Hooper has told you.'

Kingshaw turned away in disgust. As he passed, Hooper kicked out hard at his ankle. In spite of the pain that shot up his leg, Kingshaw scarcely hesitated. Hooper was watching him intently, under his lashes.

Mr Hooper stood back, smoothing his hair, very tall and thin and grey, like some sort of terrible bird. Kingshaw thought he would like to spit great gobbets of phlegm into his face. He rolled saliva speculatively round in his mouth.

As he shut the door behind him, he heard his mother's voice, beginning to apologize.

He had never been sent to his room before. The way he was behaving was entirely new to him. It made him feel odd, not like himself. But it was necessary, he felt he had somehow to defend himself against all of them. He had seen at once, from the moment they had been brought back into this house, that with Hooper nothing was different. He would wait for his chance.

Kingshaw felt trapped. Hooper won and went on winning, there was no escape. He had gone away but Hooper had come after him, clung to him, made him return.

He walked slowly up the wooden staircase, smelling the smell of this house again. The nearer he got to his bedroom, the more afraid he felt. Everything that had happened inside the wood was beginning to seem unreal, the validity of it was being sapped away. The house was taking over again, and dictating to him about what he must feel and do. He remembered the first day of getting here, and the note that Hooper had thrown down to him, the way his mother had looked at Mr Hooper, as they shook hands. He had known then.

His legs ached. The sleep in the wood last night hadn't been very good sleep. He kicked off his shoes and lay on the bed. From outside, through the open window, he heard the voice of Mr Hooper, and then his mother, the chink of a teaspoon against a cup. The sounds carried sharply, through the hot summer afternoon. The two of them seemed to be closer together, since yesterday, partly because they had been to London together, but also, Kingshaw decided, because of his own going away. When they looked at him, the expression in their eyes was the same.

'Now I have brought you a drink. Get into bed properly, please.'

It was very hot, very still. He had the window wide open and the sheets and blankets thrown back. Mrs Helena Kingshaw drew the curtains across, the bracelets slipping and chinking down her arm, from elbow to wrist. He thought, she will marry Mr Hooper.

'I have come to have a little talk with you dear. I think it is quite time, don't you?'

Kingshaw bent his head and pushed his face into the mug of Ovaltine. Steam came up in a round ring, about his nose and mouth.

'Pull up the bedcovers, Charles.'

'I'm too hot.'

'Well you cannot sleep like that, it would be very silly.'

'Why would it?'

'Because you would catch a chill, dear, wouldn't you? The temperature drops in the middle of the night, when you are asleep.'

'Last night I slept outside without any sheets or blankets or anything, I didn't even have a jumper. I was all right then.'

'I think we shall have to wait and see about that. I have been very worried in case that nasty cough of yours comes back.'

She was sitting right up to him on the bed. He could feel her weight, the shape of her thighs, if he stretched his foot out. He moved away a little.

'Was it very frightening, darling?'

'No, it wasn't frightening at all. It was great.'

'Oh, I am sure that you were a little bit afraid, all alone in that wood!'

'Hooper was. He kept on blubbing.'

'That *is* a nasty word.'

He looked away from her, out of the window.

'I think there must be a lot you haven't told me.'

Silence.

'Don't you think you should be a little bit sorry?'

'What for?'

'I was so *worried* about you, darling.'

'Oh.'

'Yes, it is all very well for you to say oh, in that way, but you cannot think how it was! You are not usually so inconsiderate, Charles. And Mr Hooper was worried, too.'

'Oh.'

'Yes, he was really *so* concerned, and not only about Edmund. I think he has grown quite fond of you.'

Kingshaw felt his stomach contract.

'He has been so kind to us, darling. You must try very hard not to be ungrateful, or impolite to him. It is only a question of a little thought before speaking.'

Outside in the trees, an owl hooted.

'I don't think you quite realize where we would be, if it were not for Mr Hooper's kindness.'

'We'd just be somewhere else, wouldn't we? In somebody else's house.'

'Oh, it is not quite so straightforward as that – not by any means. But you are too young to understand.'

Kingshaw thought about the wood again. He would have liked to be there, lying down in the stream without his clothes on.

'Oh, whatever made you do such a silly thing? Going off so far and then into those woods, without telling anyone?' He shrugged.

'I can hardly understand you, Charles. You were always such a nervous child, you used to be frightened of the dark when you were a little boy, I had to leave a lamp on, beside your bed.'

'That was ages ago, that was when I was a baby.'

'Oh, not such a baby as all that . . .'

'It was before I went to school. I'm not frightened of anything now.'

He wondered if she believed him. He did not know what she thought.

'Thank you for my drink.'

He wanted her to go.

'Charles, I *do* so hope we are going to be happy, dear. *I* am happy, now.'

Kingshaw stared up at her. There was green powder in the wrinkles along her eyelids. He hated it.

'Is something the matter? Are *you* all right here?'

'Yes, thanks.'

'You would tell Mummy, wouldn't you? It is probably such a tiny thing bothering you, we could clear it up at once, and everything would be quite all right again. I hope you don't think that you are too big, now, to come and tell me things.'

'I'm all *right*.'

'I do know that perhaps Edmund is not quite like all your other friends, but he is . . .'

Kingshaw said passionately, 'I hate him, I've told you. I hate Hooper.'

'Oh, that is a wicked, wicked way to talk, whatever can you be thinking about? Whatever can poor Edmund have done to you?'

He could never begin to tell her. Did not want to. He rubbed and twisted the edge of the sheet between his fingers, willing her to go away. She said, 'Now, there is something I think I will tell . . .' But she stopped.

'What? What's going to happen?'

'No, no, I shall not tell you, after all, not until tomorrow. It is much too late, you have had a very exhausting day.'

'You've got to tell me, you've *got* to. I want to know now.' Kingshaw sat up in bed, sensing some terrible new secret.

'Mr Hooper and I have been talking such a lot about the two of you, and making some exciting new plans . . . Mr Hooper has been very, very kind to us, Charles. But there . . . I have quite made up my mind now, I shall not say anything more about it, you are much too tired already.'

'I'm not tired, I'm not.'

'Don't contradict me like that, dear. When everything is settled you shall know, it will all be a lovely surprise.'

Mrs Helena Kingshaw got up, straightened the bedclothes, and then leaned over her son. The green bead necklace touched coldly against his face.

When she had gone, he got up and went to the window. The moon was forming the yew trees into weird shapes.

He thought, they will be getting married. It's what Hooper said. We shall have to live here for ever and ever, Hooper will be my brother. That is their secret.

He stood for a long time, in the darkness. It was very hot. He remembered the close, damp, soily smell of inside the wood, the way things had moved and rustled. He thought, people are no good, then, people can never help me. There are only things and places. There is the wood. Terrifying and safe.

He went back to bed.

Chapter Eleven

Mr Joseph Hooper wiped the marmalade from around his small mouth, with a napkin.

Kingshaw looked at them all, sitting at the table. He thought, now they are going to say it, now I shall know. His mother fiddled with the sugar bowl, a blithe expression on her face. He saw her glance towards Mr Hooper. Mr Hooper glanced back. Kingshaw thought, he will have to be my father.

Mr Hooper said, 'Well now, here is a happy piece of news for a summer morning. I have a great surprise for you, Charles. *Next* term, you will not go back to St Vincent's, you will be going off to school with Edmund!'

He only knew that he had to run, to get away from Hooper. The house was no good. He ran up and up, and along every corridor, and whichever room he chose, he dared not stay there, Hooper would find him. He stood on the dark landing outside the attic, his chest hurting with trying to get his breath. More than anything else, he wanted to go back into the wood, now, deeper and deeper, with all the branches of the trees closing back together behind him, to conceal himself. He wanted to find the stream.

But he would never reach the wood. Hooper would come after him, over the fields, crashing through the undergrowth, hunting him down.

Footsteps on the stairs. Kingshaw began to run.

He had seen the shed before, lots of times, through a gap in the tall hedge that ran round the garden of Warings. There was an allotment, which nobody looked after, and nettles grew, waist-high. At the very bottom, in one corner, was the shed.

Kingshaw ran down the drive, between the rhododendrons, and turned left. A little way along the lane, he stopped and waited. It was very warm. He heard the sound of a tractor up on Dover's Hill. Nothing else. After a moment longer, he began to retrace his steps, keeping close to the bushes, until he came to the broken wire fence at the entrance to the allotment.

There was no sun, only a mass of thick grey cloud, lowering over the countryside, and still, close, thundery air.

The door of the shed was shut, and there was a padlock. But when Kingshaw touched it, his fingers came away brown with powdery rust, and the padlock dropped open.

He wanted to cry with the relief of having escaped from Hooper. He had found a place, he was by himself. He had never dared to come here alone before.

He remembered how they had looked, the three of them sitting at the breakfast table, how Hooper had stirred his spoon around and around in the teacup, bland-faced, knowing.

'You will be going to school with Edmund.'

Kingshaw walked forward very cautiously into the shed, smelling his way like an animal.

It was airless and very dark. When the door swung open, a scissor of daylight fell on to the concrete floor, showing clumps of trodden-down straw, and mud. Kingshaw took another step inside, looking anxiously round him. Nothing. Nobody. A pile of old sacks in one corner. He went slowly over to them, and sat down. He was shivering a little.

Seconds later, the door slammed shut. Kingshaw leaped up and ran forward, but as he put his hand out to the door, he heard the click of the padlock. After that, silence.

For a moment or two, he waited. Then he said, 'Hooper?'

Silence.

'Look, I know it's you.'

Silence.

He raised his voice. 'I can get out of here, you needn't think I'm bothered if you've locked the stupid door. I know a way to get out any time I like.'

Silence.

If Hooper had locked him in, then he had been watching out of a window, and then followed him. He was cunning, he could do anything. Yet he had seen and heard nothing, and he had kept on looking back.

He thought, perhaps it isn't Hooper.

The allotment led towards a thick hedge, and then into the fields. It was right away from the village, there never seemed to be anyone about up here. But now there might be. Last year, someone had been strangled to death twenty miles away. Hooper had told him that. Twenty miles wasn't far.

He imagined tramps and murderers, and the cowman at Barr Farm, with bad teeth and hands like raw red meat. Anybody might have been hanging about behind the shed, and locked him in. Later, they might come back.

Sometimes, they were not allowed to see the newspapers, at school, because of things like murder trial reports, but they had them all in the Senior Library, and Lower School boys got sent in there, on messages. If you began to read something, your eyes went on and on, you couldn't stop them until you knew every terrible thing about it, and then you had thoughts and nightmares, you could never return to the time of not-knowing.

He remembered that he was not going back to his own school. That was all finished. He went about the building in his mind, thinking about the smells inside all the rooms. Perhaps he didn't mind so much about the people, except for Devereux and Lynch. And Mr Gardner. People didn't matter. But he couldn't separate any part of it, now, it was the whole of his existence there, that jelled together in his mind, time and place and people, and the way he felt about them.

He was still standing by the door of the hut. Somebody had used it for animals, once. It smelled faintly of pig muck, and old, dried hen pellets. The walls and roof were made of corrugated metal, bolted together. There was no window, no light at all from anywhere, except for a thin line beneath the door. Kingshaw put out his hands and began to grope his way slowly round until he came to the corner with the sacks. He sat down.

Perhaps they wouldn't wait until night before they came back. Anybody could walk down the allotment and into the shed, and never be seen. They could do anything to him, in here, choke him, or hit him with an axe, or hang him, or stab him, they could get a saw and saw off both his feet and then leave him to bleed. Kingshaw stuffed his fist into his mouth, in terror. Somebody had done that, he'd read it in one of the blood-bath books Ickden had had, last term. Ickden lent them out, at 2d. for four days. Kingshaw had read it in the bogs, and wished that he could stop himself and dreaded the nights that came after.

Now, he said to himself, it's Hooper, it's Hooper, there's nobody else it could be. Hooper would be creeping through the grass, back up to the house. Then, he would just wait. Hours and hours, all day, maybe, wait until he decided it was time to let him out.

Kingshaw said aloud, 'I'm not scared of being by myself in the bloody dark.' His voice echoed.

But it was not the dark, only the thoughts which passed through his head, the pictures in front of his eyes. He remembered why he had come here, remembered Mr Hooper's face, smiling at him, that morning, over the breakfast table. 'You will be going to school with Edmund.' He knew nothing about the place, except its name. It was called Drummonds. They were the ones who knew.

The sacks at the bottom of the pile were damp, and now the damp was coming through. Kingshaw stood up. His jeans felt wet, over his behind. He went back towards the door, and lay down on his side, trying to see out. But the crack was much thinner than he'd thought, now he got down to it, he could see nothing except a faint greyness. He stayed there, pressing his ear to the cold concrete floor of the hut, and straining for the sound of movement, for footsteps. There was nothing.

Then, minutes later, the faint sound of a truck, going down the lane. Kingshaw leaped up, and began to pound and beat upon the door, and then on the corrugated walls, until they crashed and rang in his ears, to scream and yell to be let out, he thought Oh God, God, God, please let somebody come, please let somebody come down the lane, or into the garden, please, Oh God, God, God, God . . .

He gave up. The palms of his hand were hot and throbbing, and the skin had come off one of his knuckles. He sucked at the loose edge, tasting blood. Silence.

Hooper might have decided to leave him in the shed for ever. There was nothing and nobody who could stop him, nothing that he would not be capable of.

Eventually, Kingshaw crawled on his hands and knees back over the concrete and the mucky straw, on to the sacks. He pulled out the bottom ones, which were the dampest, and started to spread the others over the floor. He meant to lie down. He could see nothing at all, only feel clumsily at what he was doing. Then, something ran out of the sacks over his hands. He screamed, and began to beat them desperately against his

122

trousers, terrified of what it might be. In the end, he was certain that it had gone. His fingers, when he opened them out again, were slimy and sticky.

He retched, and then began to vomit, all over the sacks, the sick coming down his nose and choking him. It tasted bitter. He bent forwards, holding his stomach. When it finished, he wiped his mouth on the sleeve of his shirt. He was shivering again.

There were no more sacks, only a pile of the straw, matted up in the corner nearest the door. Kingshaw groped his way to it. When he lay down, he pulled his knees tight up to his belly. He wanted to cry and couldn't. He put his hands up over his eyes, and behind the closed lids, green and red patterns heaved about, pricked out with the fine, bright points of stars.

In the end, he slept.

There was a Punch and Judy show. The squawky puppet voices sounded very loudly in his ears, shouting something to him, but he couldn't make out any of the words.

The beach was very small, with high cliffs curving round in front, and the sea behind. The tide was coming in, creeping nearer and nearer to them, as they sat in front of the puppets.

The Punch and Judy stall was made of striped canvas, red and white, with a frill round the little square stage. It was dark inside there, like an open mouth.

Kingshaw was in the middle of them all, pressed in by the arms and legs and backs of the others, smelling the boys' smell, of hair and grey woollen jerseys. There were crowds of them, thousands of boys, as far as he could see, and more kept arriving, sitting down and pushing in, tighter and tighter. He couldn't move anything except his eyes, and his fingers.

The sand of the beach was very white, cold and grainy, like sago, like the dust on the surface of the moon, and it was night, too, it was dead and cold and black. Only the puppets were lit up, so that you had to look at them.

Devereux was next to him, arms clasped tight around his knees. Kingshaw kept nudging and pushing against him, trying to get him to look or speak, but he only stared straight ahead, mesmerized by the puppets. He saw that they had real, human heads, above the billowing cloth bodies, and when the beating part began, Punch's skull broke open and poured blood, and the voice of the Judy puppet began to shriek and shriek, as the body throbbed up and down, and the shriek turned into the caawing of a crow, the puppet stage was full of hooded crows which began to take off, one by one, and circle above the heads of the boys, crowded together on the cold sand.

'Kingshaw . . . Kingshaw . . . Kingshaw . . . Kingshaw . . . Kingshaw . . .'

The voice came from far away. Kingshaw was rocking to and fro on the floor, holding his arms up over his head to keep out the dreadful caawing of the crows, and the sight of the puppet faces.

'Kingshaw . . . Kingshaw . . . Kingshaw . . .' A long whisper, from far off, down a tunnel.

'Kingshaw . . .'

He came awake, bolt upright, opening his eyes into total darkness. Jesus God . . . He remembered where he was.

'Kingshaw . . .'

The voice was somewhere at the back of the shed, detached and peculiarly muffled behind the tin walls. There was a faint scrabbling sound, up near the roof.

'Kingshaw . . .'

Hooper. Kingshaw got up slowly. But he did not go any nearer to the voice.

'What are you doing?'

He waited, silent, scarcely breathing.

'Kingshaw?'

'Bastard . . .'

Pause. More scrabbling. Hooper was at the back of the shed somewhere. He laughed.

'Aren't you scaredy, all by yourself in the dark, dark, dark . . .?'

'No.'

'Liar.'

'I can get out if I want.'

'How?'

'You'll see.'

'I'm not stupid, there isn't any way out of there except the door, and that's locked, and I've got the key.'

Kingshaw felt his head begin to swim round. He was terrified again, and he began to scream out like a cornered animal.

'Bastard, bastard, bastard, bastard . . .' His voice rose.

Hooper waited till he stopped. The walls echoed and rang. Then he said, 'I told you you couldn't get out.'

'What have you locked me in for, anyway? I haven't done anything to you.'

'Yes, you have.'

'*What?*'

'Lots of things.'

'I haven't, I haven't, I never touched you.' He was still bewildered by the monstrous unfairness of it all, by the truce he had thought was between them being flung back into his face so violently. The time they had spent in the wood might never have been.

Hooper said, 'Maybe I put you in here just because I felt like it. I wanted to. It's about time someone taught you a lesson, Kingshaw. Maybe I want to make you go away.'

'Look, I bloody well don't like being here, Hooper, you needn't think I want to live in your stinking house and go to your rotten school.'

'You'd better not say that again.'

Kingshaw felt his way through the darkness, towards where the voice was coming from. He said desperately, '*You're* the one that does things, you're the one who tells lies . . .'

'I've got the key.'

'I don't care. They'll only come and look for me.'

'They wouldn't know where to start, they don't know about this place.'

'They'd find me in the end.'

'I'll tell them you've gone back to the wood.'

Kingshaw thought that there seemed to be no hope at all for him. He knelt down, and felt about carefully on the floor. But it was only concrete, cold and damp. He sat, hunching up his knees. Whatever happened, however long it lasted, he wouldn't ask Hooper to let him out, he wouldn't do anything at all, now, except sit here. The only thing that seemed to matter was that he should not give in.

'You're coming to school with me,' Hooper's voice went up and down in a sing-song.

Kingshaw was silent.

'You'll be in my dorm.'

'I might not.'

'Yes, you will, you'll be new. They'll put you in there because you've come with me and you live with us, they'll think it's what you want.'

'I don't care.'

'I'm Head of Dorm for next term.'

Kingshaw went cold. He knew that it was sure to be true, and that it would be the worst of all things that were coming. Hooper had power now, here. He would have power there, too, then.

'I can do what I like, and the others have got to do what I say. I can make anybody do anything to you.'

Kingshaw stuffed his ears with his fingers, and tried to stop hearing, his heart thumping and thumping. But the voice still came through faintly, like the voices of the Punch and Judy puppets. He felt himself slipping backwards, into the appalling dream.

'I've got a lot of friends. You see, you wait . . .'

'Shut up, shut up, shut up . . .' But he only whispered it to himself, desperate that Hooper should not hear and triumph.

'They put baby new boys down in the cellar.'

Kingshaw raised his head. 'I'll be older than the new boys. It won't be the same.'

'Yes, it will. I said *baby* new boys and you're a baby. Mummy's little baby-boy. You needn't think they won't know *that*.'

Kingshaw said quietly, 'I can tell them about the thunderstorm.'

'It wouldn't matter what you'd say, because nobody'd believe you.'

'Why? Why wouldn't they? They'd believe me because it's true.'

Hooper laughed again. 'You'll be new. Nobody ever listens to what newers say, didn't you know that? Newers aren't allowed to speak until they're spoken to.'

Kingshaw did not answer. At his own school, newers were special. He had been seven when he'd first gone there, and when you were one of the youngest, everybody was made to be kind to you, you had chocolate biscuits at tea and a story at bed-time, everybody looked after you.

There was a sudden slithering noise along the roof of the shed, and then a thud. When Hooper spoke next time, his voice came from near the ground.

'I saw you running over here. I see everything.'

'Nosey-face.'

'There isn't anything at all you can do, Kingshaw, because I'll always see you.'

'Think I care?'

A pause. Then, 'In science, they make you cut up dead moths.'

Kingshaw's throat contracted. He swallowed hard. 'Liar.'

'All right, then, wait and see. It'll make you cry and everybody'll laugh at you.'

He wanted to stop Hooper from telling him anything else, his mind was working and working terrifyingly, on everything he had said, as he sat in the darkness. But there wasn't any way to do it, and he stiffened his muscles, forcing himself not to scream out in fear and rage and misery, not to say, Oh please, don't, please, please, Oh God, I don't want to go anywhere with you, I'm scared, I'm scared, I want to get out of this bloody, bloody shed.

'I'm going away now,' Hooper said.

Kingshaw dug his nails hard into the palms of his hands. He thought, let me out, let me out, let me out, God . . .

'Kingshaw?'

'Do what you like.'

'A rat might be in there.'

'There isn't.'

'It might be. How do you know? You can't see.'

'They make a noise, they scratch about. There isn't anything.'

'Moths don't, though. There might be a lot of moths. Or there could be a bat, hanging upside down from the ceiling, and in a minute I'll bang and bang until it falls down on your head. It'd make you go mad.'

Kingshaw felt the sobs of terror rising into his throat, squeezing the muscles until they ached. He forced himself to swallow and swallow them down. He began to whisper to himself, to chant: 'I'll kill you, Hooper, I'll kill you, I'll kill you, I'll kill you, I'll kill you.' All of a sudden, he screamed it out loud, and the noise of his own scream frightened him more than anything.

For a long time, there was no more sound at all, inside or outside the shed. Kingshaw began to weep, quite silently, not bothering to wipe the tears from off his face. In a minute, Hooper would start again, cry-baby, cry-baby, cry-baby, cry, blubbing for his Mummy, little scaredy-custard, cry-baby, baby, baby, baby . . . He did not care, now. He went on weeping, for a long time.

But Hooper must have gone. Kingshaw called out, in the end, and there was no reply, no movement.

He dared not stand up, or crawl back towards the light under the door, now, because of what there might be in the shed, rats, or moths, or a bat in the ceiling. It was silent. After a while, he began to cry again, because there was nothing else to do, no other comfort.

What he heard first were the footsteps, running towards him through the grass outside, and then a bump, and the click of the padlock. The door of the shed swung open.

Hooper shouted out to him, already running off again, 'It's lunchtime, and you're late, you'd just better hurry up, stupid face, we've got to go somewhere with my father.'

Nettles and sorrel crashed down under his plunging feet, as he went.

Kingshaw got up. His legs were numb and stiff from the concrete floor. He wiped his face on his sleeve.

In the house, Hooper washed his hands at the kitchen tap. He said, 'We were being bandits,' in reply to Mrs Helena Kingshaw's gay question.

Outside, great, flat spots of rain began to fall heavily, one by one, like sweat from the sky, as Kingshaw walked back, very slowly, across the allotment.

Chapter Twelve

Mrs Helena Kingshaw ran her hands lightly over the soft dresses in her wardrobe. She thought, we are all going out in the same car together, it will be just as though we are one family. For he had said, 'Today shall be a holiday,' had told her firmly that she must rest and relax, and she had given way, after only a little, formal protest. She enjoyed being treated in that way by Mr Hooper.

The rain had come to nothing.

The road wound up and up, narrowly, between high ferny banks, and the trees arched together overhead. Kingshaw waited, holding his breath until there should be an end to the long, green tunnel, and they would come out into the open, where there would be air and sky. He wanted to run and fling his arms about. They were going to Leydell Castle.

But as soon as the road reached a peak, it began to drop again, down and down, there was no break in the roof of trees. Kingshaw and Hooper sat apart and silent on the back seat of the Rover car. Kingshaw stared at the wart on his left hand. He thought, I shall never see Broughton-Smith again, in the whole of my life.

The road forked to the left, and the trees parted.

First, there was the castle ruin, and beside it, a lake. Around the lake ran a gravel path, and around that was simply close-cut grass, in a huge arc. Slopes rose up behind and to each side, thick with conifers. The clouds were still low and misty, pressing in upon them.

Mr Hooper switched off the engine of the car and it was very quiet, suddenly.

'Now I have brought maps and guide books,' he said, turning a little in his seat, towards Mrs Helena Kingshaw. 'I am not a man to do things by halves.' For he was more confident, now, in his manner with her, he had grown used to having a woman about him again.

Mrs Kingshaw smiled, and opened the door and looked around eagerly, ready to be full of interest and admiration. The previous evening, at Warings, he had said to her, 'You need not fear that Charles will ever be at a disadvantage in this house. *I* shall not make any difference between the boys.'

Kingshaw walked a few steps forward, away from the others. He had not expected the place to be like this, he had expected it to be wild and open. He was afraid of it. It reminded him of his dream. He looked over at the lake. The water was quite still.

'What are you going to do?'

Kingshaw looked down at him coldly.

'Climb,' he said.

They were inside the ruin. The outer walls reached up very high, and there were odd bits of stone staircase, ending abruptly, so that you could step off into air, or on to parapets, and the remains of pillars, flat-topped like stepping stones. The surface was the colour of damp sand, rough and grainy to the touch, except where bits of moss and lichen grew out of the cracks.

'I bet you won't dare go up far.'

Kingshaw smiled to himself. He moved steadily from stone to stone, along the edge of one wall. He wanted to get as high as he could, up beside the tower.

Hooper watched him from below.

'You'll fall off.'

Kingshaw ignored him. He was sure-footed and unhurried, not afraid of any height. He looked down. Hooper was immediately below him. Kingshaw waved an arm.

'Why don't you come up as well?'

His voice echoed round the castle walls. Hooper had got his penknife out and was digging his initials into a slab of stone.

'*You'll* catch it if anyone sees you. You're not supposed to do that. They can put you in prison for doing it.'

Hooper went on scratching.

The walls were narrower here. Kingshaw went down on all fours, and made sure of the surface with his hands, as he went along, moving very slowly forwards. They had put new mortar between the spaces, though, so that there were no loose stones.

Now the wall went up about a foot, on to the next level. He manoeuvred the step, and then stood upright, carefully, and looked around. Outside of the castle, he could see the flat grass and the lake, and his mother and Mr Hooper, sitting on their bench at the far side. He felt high above them, very tall and strong, and safe, too, nobody could touch him. He thought, *this* is all right, I don't care about any of them here, they can't do anything at all to me, I don't care, I don't care. He felt lightheaded, exulting in the freedom of it. If he reached his arm up, he might touch the sky.

But even up here, it was warm and airless.

He shouted down to Hooper, 'I'm a bowman, I'm the head warrior of this castle. If I shoot an arrow, I can kill you.'

Hooper looked up.

'I'm the King of the Castle!' Kingshaw began to wave his arms about, and to prance a little, delicately, on top of the wall. If he walked forwards a few yards farther, he would come to a gap. If he could jump it, he would be out on the parapet, leading to the tower.

Far below, the tiny figures of his mother and Mr Hooper had begun to wave their arms, signalling to him. He thought, fuck to you, and then suddenly, shouted it as loud as he could, certain that only Hooper would be able to hear him.

Hooper said, 'You'd better come down, show-off, if you fall you'll split your head open.'

'Fuck to you. I'm not going to fall.'

At school, he had climbed on to the music block roof, at night, and along the ivy between one dormitory floor and another, he could get to the crow's nest at the top of the elm tree by South Gate. Nobody had ever done that before. It was the only distinction he had ever been able to secure for himself.

Balancing on the step, to judge the leap just ahead of him, Kingshaw thought, Hooper is down there because he's scared. He peered over the edge of the parapet. Hooper was wandering about among the pillars at the entrance. He looked up, catching Kingshaw's eye, and looked away again quickly.

'I *know* . . .' Kingshaw said to himself, whispering, 'I know . . .' He waited. Hooper shouted, 'I can come up if I want to.'

'Come on, then.'

'Those steps over there lead down into dungeons. *You* daren't go down to them.'

'Don't change the subject, Hooper. You daren't come up here and this is better than anything.'

Without warning, Kingshaw leaped over the gap between the stones of either wall and up on to the ledge. It was only just wide enough for his feet. He saw Hooper take in a sharp breath. His head was tilted back to watch, and the eyes and nostrils and mouth-hole were like black currants in his pale face. Kingshaw shouted, 'I bet you couldn't even walk along the first little bit of wall.'

Hooper turned away and walked across the open space below. He went under the broken bit of archway and towards a flight of steps. After that, Kingshaw lost sight of him.

He looked up covetously at the tower. He wanted to get there, to sit on top and look out. If he had a telescope, he could have seen anything at all, for miles and miles. He imagined enemy horsemen thundering over the grass towards the castle, hundreds of them, bunched tight together at the front and widening out behind in the shape of a fan. All around the castle walls, standing in the tall window slits and on the turrets, would be the archers, waiting.

But there was nothing. Nor could he see any way at all of getting up as far as the tower. He looked round him, at the dark fir trees on the hills surrounding the lake, and at his mother and Mr Hooper, only paying attention to each other, now. He thought, I am higher than any of you, I am higher than anyone in the world. No, that was not true.

He felt suddenly depressed, flat, cheated by the flash of excitement which had come to him as he climbed, and was now gone. He began to turn himself around cautiously, preparing to come down. Then he saw Hooper, some distance below him, balanced on a ledge.

'What are *you* doing?'

'You didn't think I could climb up.'

'You said you were going down into those dungeons.'

'You can't, they've put a gate up and locked it. So I started climbing.'

To get down on to the level below, Kingshaw had to slither over one of the jutting pieces of wall, and then walk along a ledge until he reached Hooper. He leaped across the gap, negotiated the wall on his hands and knees, and then lay down on his stomach. It was always better to drop down that way, feet first, arms holding on to the top of the ledge above, until you were quite steady, belly flattened against the wall. Then, one, two, three, down. He was quite used to it, sure of his own judgement. The only thing was not to rush.

Eventually, he reached Hooper.

He said, 'I'm going back now. They might have got the picnic out.'

Hooper didn't answer.

'Come on. You can do what you like, but I'm fed up with this place. There isn't anything else to see now, it's boring.'

Hooper did not move. Kingshaw looked at him closely. His face was green-white.

'Oh, hell – do you feel sick or something?'

No answer.

'Look, you'll have to go down first, because I can't get by you, it's too narrow.'

'I can't.'

'What's up? You haven't done anything to yourself, have you? Come on.'

'No.'

'Why not?'

'I want to get behind you.'

Kingshaw sighed. 'Thick-head, I've already told you. I'm stuck here till you move, and there isn't any other way down. You can't get behind me.'

He supposed that they must be quite high up. He hadn't thought much about it, before, because he didn't care. He never cared, however high he climbed was never high enough.

'Look, don't be a nit, Hooper, get moving.'

'I can't, I can't. I'll fall off.'

'Hell. If you didn't like it, you shouldn't have bloody well come up here, should you?'

Hooper stared at him in surprise. He was the one who swore, usually.

'*Why* did you come up?'

Hooper gave him a helpless look. His fingers were like claws, the knuckles showing white through the skin with the strain of clinging so hard on to his stone.

'You were just trying to be *clever*, weren't you?'

'It's your fault, you dared me.'

'I never did.'

'I'll fall off, I'll fall off, Kingshaw, my hands'll slip.' His voice was high and cracked with fear.

Kingshaw waited a second, thinking. Then he said, 'Now listen – you've got to do what I tell you, because I know how to get down from here and you don't, and I'm not scared and you are. You've got to do everything I tell you – right?'

'Yes.'

'O.K. First take your hands off that wall, then.'

'No, I can't.'

'You've got to.'

'If I do, I'll just fall, I will, Kingshaw.'

'Shut up and do as you're told.'

'I *can't*. Oh, Jesus, don't make me let go. Why can't you try and get past, and then I can hold on to you?'

'Because there isn't *room* . . . How many more times?'

'If I fall off here, I'll be dead.'

'TAKE YOUR HANDS OFF THE WALL, HOOPER.'

Silence. Neither of them moved.

'HOOPER . . .' Kingshaw's voice rang round the stone walls. Slowly, Hooper began to release his hold on the stone, finger by finger.

'Promise you won't make me fall, you've got to promise.'

'You won't fall if you listen and do as I say.'

'*Promise.*'

'Oh God, you are an idiot, Hooper. O.K., I promise. Now open your eyes.'

'No.'

'*Open your eyes.*'

'I don't like it, I don't like it. I don't want to see down.'

'You haven't got to look down, you've got to look at your feet and think about what you're doing.'

Hooper opened his eyes and at once, his gaze was drawn towards the ground below. He said, 'Oh God . . .' in a whisper, and shut his eyes again, screwing them up hard, until his cheekbones rose. He had not moved his body at all.

Kingshaw noticed the dark, damp stain of pee in the groin of Hooper's jeans. After a moment, drops of it came trickling down his leg and fell on to the stone on top of the wall.

He thought suddenly, I could kill him, I could make him fall off just by looking at him, or touching him, or telling him to take one step the wrong way. I am the King, I am the King, there is nothing I can't ask him for, nothing he won't promise me, nothing I can't do to him. Up here, *I'm the King.*

134

But he had learned enough, over the past few weeks, to know that any power he acquired would only be temporary. Like the thunderstorm in the wood, and the time when Hooper had fallen into the water and bashed his head, and then when he had had the nightmares. As soon as the situation had changed, everything went back to what Kingshaw had come to think of as normal.

He was half a head taller than Hooper, and standing one step above him on the castle wall. Their eyes met. Hooper knew. He said, 'Don't make me, don't make me,' whimpering.

Kingshaw was silent. He could see his mother and Mr Hooper, turned towards one another on the green bench, talking and talking. I can do anything I like to him, anything at all. I can kill him.

He thought of the dark shed, and the glutinous body of the unknown insect he had squashed between his fingers, of Hooper's voice mocking him through the tin walls, and the old pig smell and the monstrous puppet dream. He thought, I'm the King of the Castle, now. I can do *anything*.

He knew that he would not.

The thing was, he would have to take hold of Hooper and guide him, as best he could, letting him keep his eyes closed, if that was what he wanted, and just making him obey one order after another, moving him step by step to the bottom. He would have to be terribly careful not to say or do anything to frighten him.

Kingshaw reached out his hand. In terror, Hooper flinched and took a step backwards, swayed and fell.

Chapter Thirteen

Afterwards, what Kingshaw remembered most clearly was being ignored.

When it happened, it was like a film that went very slowly, and then stopped altogether. Hooper seemed to go on and on falling, in a peculiarly graceful sort of way, one arm flung out. They were only perhaps as high as they might be on the roof of Warings, but a long time seemed to pass before he hit the ground.

For a second, everything stopped. Kingshaw saw the grass, and the still lake, and his mother and Mr Hooper on their bench, and the body of Hooper lying sprawled beneath the castle wall. Nothing moved. He looked down and felt like a bird, or a god, poised above them all.

After that, everything began to go very quickly, like a speeded-up film, as the figures of the adults came running around the path and over the lawn, their movements odd and jerky, seen from so far away. From somewhere, a man in uniform appeared. He had a peaked cap with a gold badge on the front of it. They were all of them chattering at once, like birds, as they came near to Hooper.

Kingshaw stood, appallingly calm, just watching them. From behind the hills, through the low grey cloud, a rumble of thunder.

In the end, he thought that they would forget about him altogether. People ran about across the grass, blankets were brought, Mr Hooper raced off in a car and came back with another man, a white ambulance arrived. All the time, Kingshaw stood, motionless, on the ledge. Nobody had looked up or called out to him.

They were lifting Hooper on to the stretcher. His eyes were closed, Kingshaw couldn't see any blood. Then they set off towards the ambulance, a little procession, marching in time. The thunder rumbled again, faintly.

He was sure that Hooper must be dead. He had looked dead, heavy and loose, like the rabbit in Hang Wood. He was also sure that it was his fault, that he had killed him. He had reached out his hand, and Hooper had thought he was going to push him. Besides, he had thought about it, wished it, it was what he had *wanted* to do. Once you wished a thing, it took you over, and you couldn't stop it happening. Like the warts. The fact that he had decided against it, had put out his hand so that he could begin to help Hooper down, after all, would not count. Hooper had fallen. It would have looked like a push, from a distance. He wondered what they would do to him.

Then he saw his mother, waving and shouting something he could not possibly hear.

Slowly, Kingshaw began to climb down from the castle.

He went back to Warings with his mother, in Mr Hooper's car. They drove very slowly. Kingshaw looked out of the windows and counted each tree down the long green tunnel. Some of them had roots, clawing their way up out of the soil, thick and twisted and shiny.

He wondered what it had felt like for Hooper, falling through the air, whether it had seemed as slow as it had looked, and how much it had hurt him, hitting the grass. Perhaps not at all, perhaps he had just been alive one second, and dead the next, without any pain in between.

Suddenly he remembered the assembly hall, and Lesage, reading aloud to them, 'Whereupon the soul flew from the body.'

He could recall every detail of it. Outside, it was snowing and he had been sitting beside a radiator which was painted cream. There were faint, black marks of a rubber plimsoll, between the metal ribs. He had looked out at the falling flakes of snow, because he did not want to look at Lesage. Lesage worried him. He used to send Kingshaw on messages, stupid, unnecessary messages that involved his walking miles from one end of the school to the other. When he came back, Lesage fed him, with squares of nut milk chocolate, piece by piece, out of a blue tin. Lesage was Deputy Senior Prefect.

Once, he had told Kingshaw to lie down on the study floor. Nobody else had been there. Kingshaw had thought he was going to hit or kick him, and his mind had groped round desperately for the reason, trying to remember some terrible, unknown wrong he must have committed.

'Close your eyes,' Lesage had said. He had obeyed. He was eight, then, at the beginning of his second year, anxious to please and be thought well of.

Lesage had not done anything at all. The electric clock on the wall had whirred, for a very long time, and Kingshaw had just lain there. When he opened his eyes, fearfully, Lesage was standing over him, looking down, not moving a muscle.

He said, 'You'd better go, hadn't you?'

For a moment, Kingshaw had stayed there, on the ground, bewildered.

'Go on, get up, you've got to be at Prep in about three minutes.'

'Oh – oh, yes. Yes.'

He had scrambled up, then, and gone before Lesage could say anything else. The incident had disturbed him. He wanted to forget about it. But he couldn't, not altogether. Whenever he saw Lesage, he stared at him. And he went on remembering his voice. It was quite deep, even then, and oddly hypnotic, it went up and down in a rhythm. Lesage always read at the Carol Service, and Founder's Day, and once a term at least, in assembly.

'Whereupon the soul flew from the body.'

A clear picture of that happening had formed in Kingshaw's mind, as he sat cross-legged on the wooden floor, among the others, looking out at the drifting snow. You had to listen to Lesage's voice, and when you listened, you remembered.

Lesage had won a King's Scholarship to Eton, the only boy from the school ever to have done so, his name was painted in gold leaf on the Honours Board. Lesage. Kingshaw had never forgotten. 'Whereupon, the soul flew from the body.'

This afternoon, he had stood on the castle wall, and that had happened to Hooper, the soul had flown from his body. Yet there had been nothing, only the long, slow fall, and then the absolute stillness, the heavy, crumpled limbs.

They were still driving very slowly, but they were out of the tunnel of trees now, and on the road towards the village. A combine harvester rolled down a field like a dinosaur, corn disappearing into its great, scarlet maw.

His mother had not spoken to him at all. He kept glancing at her, furtively. She was biting the corner of her lip, and frowning, and she held the steering wheel slightly away from her, as though she were afraid of this car.

In the end, he could not wait any longer for the blaming to begin. He said, 'I *didn't* push him. I didn't touch him at all.' His own voice sounded queer.

'It was very, very silly to go up there at all, Charles. But we won't talk about any of it, now.'

He wondered why, desperate to make her understand.

'I didn't *push* him, I was trying to help him down and he was scared, he didn't dare go without me helping him.'

She leaned over towards him slightly as she heaved the car around a bend. Kingshaw shouted, 'It was his own *fault.*'

'All right, darling, it's quite all right. You've had a nasty shock.'

'He's just stupid, Hooper is, he's a show-off, he shouldn't have tried to get up as high as that.'

'Charles, dear, I don't think this is really the right time to say unkind things about Edmund, do you? I am very glad you understand how silly it was for either of you to start climbing. Mr Hooper and I shouted and shouted for you to come down and you didn't take any notice, you deliberately ignored us. It was very, very naughty. Well, now it is too late, and Edmund has had an accident. I am a little ashamed that you were not sensible enough to realize what might happen, in the first place.'

'Look, it wasn't me, I was all right, I keep on telling you, it was him. Listen, I can climb anything, I can go up as high as high, it doesn't matter *how* high. I've climbed higher than anybody else in the whole school.'

'That is nothing at all to boast of, you are very lucky indeed that you have not fallen, before now.'

'I mean, it's O.K. for me, because I'm not *scared*, but Hooper *is* scared, he can't climb anything, not even a chair I shouldn't think, because it makes him sick, he's such a baby.'

'Charles, don't you remember my telling you that it is not the very bravest people who are unafraid?'

Kingshaw almost wept. There seemed no point at all in trying to talk to her, no way that he could make her understand the truth of things, or what was going on in his mind. It was no use saying again and again that he hadn't pushed Hooper, that it had all been his own fault, that climbing was O.K. as long as you were not afraid, because being afraid was what made you fall. He would not be listened to, he would not be believed. He might as well give up, as he always gave up in the end.

They had reached the house. He wanted to ask what they would do to him, and what was happening to Hooper, if they would put him in a coffin straight away, and where he would go till after the funeral, he wanted to say, will they make me go and look at his dead body?

He said nothing.

'Now you are going to have a drink of milk and sit quietly, Charles. Mrs Boland is here.'

He stared at her dumbly, standing in the dark, wood-panelled hall.

'I am going back to the hospital, darling.'

He wondered why and did not ask.

'I want you to be very grown-up and help Mummy, I want you to do just as Mrs Boland tells you, without arguing or making a fuss. You can be such a good boy, and you are quite all right, now, aren't you?'

She was touching her hand to her hair and looking around for the keys of the car. Kingshaw stood and watched her agitation. She was thinking about the hospital, and Mr Hooper. Whatever they were going to say or do to him, would wait until they both came back.

She had reached the front door and opened it, but now, she turned suddenly and bent down, clasping hold of him, so that his face was pushed up against her breasts.

'Oh darling, now *promise* me you will never, never do anything so silly again. It might so easily have been you, I shall worry all the time, I shall never be able to trust you to do things by yourself, unless you promise me.'

He was alarmed by the embrace, because of its urgency, and the note of panic in her voice. There was no warmth or comfort. 'Charles?'

He said, 'It's O.K.'

'Mrs Boland will make you a nice, hot drink.'

'O.K.'

'Don't say "O.K.", darling.'

'All right.'

She hovered, saying vaguely, 'Yes . . .' and 'Well . . .', and then went, running down the path towards the car.

When the sound of the engine had died away from along the lane, Kingshaw began to tremble violently. He sat down on a cane chair in the dark hall and began to say, 'Hooper is dead now, Hooper is dead,' over and over to himself, in a whisper.

By the time it was dark, they still hadn't come back from the hospital. Kingshaw had gone into the sitting room with a book. But he hadn't read anything, only stared and stared out of the window on to the empty lawn.

He put his pyjamas on. The thunderstorm had faded away, and the air was still, hot and clammy.

In the back sitting room, Mrs Alice Boland looked at television. 'Can I have another drink?'

On the screen, people were dancing in a long line, with their arms round each other's shoulders, and singing as they bounced up and down. The girls wore dresses that sparkled, and kicked their legs high in the air. Kingshaw watched in fascination. He wasn't allowed to watch television very much. He sat on a chair at the very back of the room, not wanting to go upstairs to bed by himself, hoping that Mrs Boland might forget him. He wanted her company, and the noise and movement of the television programme.

A film was beginning. The fluorescent light flickered over Mrs Boland's thin, attentive face, and cast tall shadows up the walls. Kingshaw tried to drink his orange juice silently, eyes huge, mesmerized by the screen. A man was walking along a road. It was in the town, but at night, everything was empty and quiet. They just showed you his feet, and the slabs of pale pavement, under the street lights. He was going along beside a wall. There was no music yet, only the sound of the man's footsteps, going very steadily, and the tap-tap of his stick as well, poking forward along the pavement. It was a white stick. The man was blind. That was all you heard, step-step, tap-tap, step-step, tap-tap. After a while, the music did begin. Step-step, tap-tap. It was very quiet music. They didn't show you anything of the man's body, only his legs and feet and the white stick. The music began to get louder, you knew something was going to happen. There was a long, long time when the blind man walked right away and the camera didn't follow him, it stayed still, on the empty stretch of pavement, waiting. And then came the legs and feet of somebody who was following. This man made no sound at all. He wore soft shoes. The music went higher.

Kingshaw looked away from the screen, and down into his glass. The ice cubes had gone very small and smooth, bobbing up and down in the orange juice. He closed his eyes. But the music went on, getting louder and louder, and when he glanced up at the television again, for a second, he saw the feet of the man behind, closing in very fast on the blind one, and the stick going tap-tap, tap-tap, on and on.

He got up quickly, and went out into the kitchen. It was very bright and cool. He put his glass on to the draining board and stood, looking down into the white, white sink. But he could still hear the music through the open door. He had to do something. He went into the cupboard and opened a new packet of biscuits and began to transfer them, one by one, into the square, red tin. It had a picture on the lid, of woods in the autumn. There was a stream, and piles of yellow-orange leaves. That was how it would be in Hang Wood, soon. But he would be gone by then, at school. Only without Hooper, because Hooper was dead.

There was some terrible, human screaming from the television, the music was crashing and stabbing. Kingshaw heard Mrs Boland calling out to him. He put the biscuit tin slowly back into the cupboard.

'You'd best go up to bed now, dear, it's late.'

He wanted to ask if he could stay with her until they came in. But he only said, 'Yes. O.K. Good-night.'

Mrs Alice Boland thought, his face is peaky, it's the shock. But she had never really been able to make him out, not since he'd come here, he was very close. It made a difference for a boy, of course, not having a father. Perhaps being here with Mr Hooper was helping him. Yes.

Mrs Boland turned her attention back to the television set.

He knew that he must not pause anywhere, on the staircase or on the landings. He ducked his head and ran, not switching on any light, or taking more than a single deep breath, until he was in his room, and burrowing his whole body far down beneath the bedclothes. He didn't want to go to sleep, because of the dreams, nor to think about anything that had happened today, all he could do was force his mind into a deliberate, cold pattern of thought about the future.

The main thing was, he would not have Hooper. He could scarcely imagine that, now, it seemed that this summer had gone on for ever and ever, he could not remember the time of not knowing him. Now, he would be on his own, in this house. King of the Castle. All the strain of trying to make friends with Hooper and failing, of anticipating his cunning, all the fear of the unknown traps he might lay, would be gone. But most of all, he might not have to go to the new school. They wouldn't have any reason for sending him there, surely, he might go back to St Vincent's, his own place. A sudden longing for it flooded through him, surprising him. He wanted the familiar sounds of bells and desk lids and voices calling in the dining hall, the smell and the rows of faces.

It's going to be all right, he said anxiously, it is going to be all right. King, King, King of the Castle. He was acquiring a taste for the idea of it. He would have his mother and Mr Hooper, if he wanted them. King, King, King . . . As he fell asleep, the dreams began.

In the beige saloon car, driving home at midnight, Mr Joseph Hooper said, 'I cannot think how I would have managed without you. I cannot imagine what I would have done . . .'

Mrs Helena Kingshaw heard the warmth of his voice and flushed with gratification, relaxing into the thick, soft upholstery of the car. But she said, as she had said again and again, 'Oh, if only I had watched them, if only it had not been for Charles . . .'

'No,' said Mr Hooper, 'No.' and reached out a hand. 'I will not have that.'

'But . . .'

'No! There is to be no blame, no question of it at all.'

He did not move his hand away. The palm of it was very dry and hard. Mrs Kingshaw thought, I have missed a man, I have missed the reassurance, and feeling of strength through physical contact. I am not a woman who can cope easily alone.

Aloud, she said, 'How *kind* of Mrs Boland!'

In the end, he struggled free of the hands that clawed at him, trying to drag him back, and he ran, faster and faster, down a long tunnel. He could see the light ahead, but behind him were the voices, echoing around the tunnel walls, booming in his ears, and then the great wings began to beat and flap, everybody was gaining on him, the crows and the puppets with bleeding heads, and the ambulance men. It was so near, so near, he had only to reach the end of the tunnel, for they could not touch him once he came out into the open, he knew that, and he pushed on his aching legs, faster and faster, he thought that his head would burst, and then, suddenly, he was there, out in the daylight, but now he could not stop his legs, they went on running down the field, through thick, damp tussocks of grass, and out on to the cliff top, and still on and on, so that he was falling and falling, accelerating as the hard green sea came up to meet him, and he woke up, pushing his hands out into the air, to try and save himself.

He was sweating. His bedroom was quite dark.

He said, where am I, where am I, and couldn't make out why he heard his own voice, he couldn't force himself to come fully awake, and he began to struggle out of the sheets which were tangled up all about his legs. He was sobbing and trying not to, unable to get his breath. He groped his hands around the panels of the door, but when he did find the handle, it was no use, it was still dark everywhere, on the landing and along the corridor, and he dared not put the light on for fear of what he might see.

He had never gone to his mother before, not since he was only a baby, he had always held his breath and dug his nails hard into the palms of his hands, and in the end, it had always been all right, he managed.

Now, he didn't care, didn't even try, he whimpered like a baby as he fought his way through the darkness of the corridor. He thought about how Hooper had been, in the wood, sitting with his head pushed into his knees, all through the storm, and now Hooper was dead, he had really fallen, and he hadn't come awake, he couldn't come awake, his hadn't been a dream, he . . .

'Mummy . . . Mummy . . . Mummy . . . Mummy . . .' He half-fell through the door into her bedroom.

'Mummy . . . Mummy . . .'

The curtains were not drawn. He could make out the shapes of the furniture, and the pale sheen of the silk coverlet on the bed. It was empty. Nobody, nobody . . .

Kingshaw thought, it's late, it's the middle of the night, they haven't come home, and they won't come home, and Mrs Boland has gone. There is nobody at all. Turning, he caught sight of his own, pale mirror-reflection, as though in water.

'Mummy . . . Mummy . . . Mummy . . .' Though he knew that it was useless, that there was nobody, knew it inside his head, but he couldn't stop now, crying and crying.

At the end of the corridor, going towards the stairs, he remembered the white stick of the blind man, tap-tap-tapping along the street, and the follower with his soft-soled shoes, and then he dared not go on. He sat down on the top step and cried noisily, rocking himself to and fro.

When the door opened below, and he saw the light, he could not imagine who might be down there, or what would happen to him, he had reached the end point of fear.

Mr Hooper came up the stairs, two at a time, Kingshaw watched his long, thin legs, opening like scissors, and saw his long, thin arms reaching down for him.

'Now . . .' Mr Hooper said, 'Now, now . . .'

He lifted him and carried him downstairs. The lamps were on, making little soft pools of light on the pile of the carpet, and in the velvet folds of the curtains. But when Kingshaw took hold of the mug, his hands felt queer and trembly, and the warm, sticky Ovaltine spilled down his pyjama front and through on to his skin. He began to cry again, not caring.

'Now, now . . . it's all right . . . now, now . . .'

His mother brought a sponge and clean pyjamas, and Mr Hooper held the mug for him to drink from. Kingshaw thought, Oh God, I *have* to ask them, they have to tell me, Oh God . . . The sponge was cool on his face and neck. He began to say . . . 'It's Hooper . . . Oh listen, you've got to listen . . .' But it was a long time before he could make them understand him. The sitting room was very warm and quiet. He watched his mother's fingers fiddling one of the bracelets round and round on her wrist, and thought of all the private things she and Mr Hooper had between them. His mouth wouldn't say the words, now, he was sweating again, with the effort of trying to make them understand. They said, 'It's all right, it's all right', and in the end, he had to shout to get through the soft, woolly shrouds of their voices, soothing him, muffling his own words.

'It's because of Hooper – Edmund – listen, it's because he's dead, he fell and he was dead and . . .'

But they began to tell him, again and again, that Hooper was not dead. 'Silly boy,' his mother said. 'Silly boy! Of course he isn't dead, whatever made you think that he was dead, of course he isn't dead, *silly* boy.' So that in the end, he had to believe them.

Mr Hooper carried him back to bed, going up the stairs and along the corridors very slowly. Kingshaw was obscurely comforted by the long, thin, man's arms around his body, and the bumping rhythm of his walk. He thought, let it go on, let me not have to be put down yet. He began to cry again, weakly, out of shame and gratitude and relief.

After they had left his room, he lay awake, and was more ashamed than ever before, because of what he had felt, because it had been Mr Hooper, Mr Hooper . . .

But when he woke, and it was still dark, it was the other thing he remembered. He said aloud, 'Hooper isn't dead. Hooper is not dead.' For a long time, he did not go back to sleep.

Chapter Fourteen

'Now I am going back to the hospital, dear, in just a few minutes. But you will be quite all right with Mrs Boland.'

'Yes.'

Kingshaw discarded a piece of sky, and sorted about for another. All the pieces looked the same.

'Mr Hooper has gone to London.'

'Yes.'

'And he is not going to be back until tomorrow, so you will be very good by yourself, won't you?'

'Yes.'

He fidgeted about in the jigsaw box, rattling the pieces, willing her to go away.

'Of course I must go and see poor Edmund.'

'All right.'

'Perhaps tomorrow you might be able to come to the hospital with me – yes, now that *is* a good idea! I shall remember to ask Sister.'

'No,' he said hastily. 'I don't want to. Thank you.'

'Why ever not?'

'No.'

'It would cheer him up, I know, to have his friend visit him.'

'Look, I don't *want* to go, that's all.'

He tried to force a wrong piece into the jigsaw, and bent one of the cardboard prongs.

'Well . . . we'll see. . .'

'I'm not going.'

'Let's not argue about it now, Charles, please. And it is such a lovely day, I cannot think why you must sit in here doing a puzzle. That is a thing for a *wet* day, isn't it?'

He shrugged.

'I think you had far better go out and enjoy the fresh air and lovely sunshine, while you can. It will be cold again, before we know where we are.'

Kingshaw turned his attention from the sky of the puzzle, to the river part, on the bottom. But that looked nearly as hard. It was the only jigsaw in the house.

'Have you anything you want me to tell Edmund, dear?'

'No.'

'But I think it would be so nice, if you could just think up some little message, you know.'

He said stiffly, 'I hope he's feeling better.'

'Yes, I will say that, of course I will. Oh, and he *is*, you know, and looking so much better, I thought that yesterday – indeed, I said so, to Mr Hooper, I said, Edmund is a much better colour. He agreed with me, I really think that he did. Yes. Though of course he is still so anxious, poor man.'

He thought, please let her go, please make her go away now. He hated the voice she put on for talking about Mr Hooper.

Ever since the night after the accident, she had hovered about him, fussing, asking questions, and when she peered into his face, he flushed with shame, remembering. A picture kept slotting into his mind, of the dark corridor upstairs, and the way he had groped along it, crying and calling out for her, and of how he had let Mr Hooper carry him back to his bedroom. It made him think of Fenwick, and what he would have said.

Fenwick had gone to school at the same time as him. They had stared at one another defensively, not speaking. Kingshaw had thought, I wish he could be my friend. For a week he had kept trying to get near to Fenwick, to talk to him. Fenwick never replied. And then, he had had the fall.

The quad was on a slope, and a lot of them were running down it very fast, bunched up together, playing jets. Kingshaw had pushed his way through them, at the top of the hill, so as to be next to Fenwick. Half-way down, Fenwick had tripped, and gone down flat on his face, slithering forward several yards. When Kingshaw got him up, he had great, bleeding, gravelly scrapes all down his knees and elbows, and on his face. Everybody else had run on down the hill, making propeller noises, none of them had noticed.

'I'll go and get somebody, I'll go and get Matron, it's O.K., somebody'll come and take you to the San. You'll be O.K. . . .'

Fenwick had said, 'Shut up.' He was very pale, apart from the blood.

He had begun to walk slowly back up the slope. When Kingshaw had tried again to go off and fetch somebody, he had said, 'Shut up,' more violently, and then, 'Don't be stupid.' Kingshaw had followed him, un-asked, into the House block.

The blood had poured down Fenwick's leg, and left spatters on the gravel. Kingshaw hadn't known what to say or do. He was awed by Fenwick. If it had been himself, he knew that he would have cried, he couldn't have stopped it. Fenwick made no sound at all. His face was just very stiff, and white. Kingshaw was afraid of him.

In the San, Fenwick had sat on the hard chair, and Matron had not told Kingshaw to go, he thought that she supposed he was Fenwick's friend, and so he had stayed, because he wanted to, he wanted to be Fenwick's friend, and also because he was still uncertain how he must behave in this place, unless someone gave him a definite order.

All the gravel was picked out of the cuts and grazes, bit by tiny bit, with cotton wool and a bowl of water, warm and clouded like an opal with Dettol. It had taken a very long time. Kingshaw had stood by the door and felt himself near to tears, his own stomach had clenched every time he heard the swish of the water. Fenwick had not looked at him, he had sat, and not moved and not cried, only pressed his hands hard into the sides of the chair, and once or twice, sucked in his breath very softly, between his teeth.

'You can stay here and lie down, dear, until dinner-time.'

But Fenwick had said, 'I'm quite all right, thank you,' and got up and walked stiffly to the door. Kingshaw had followed him back to Form, and Fenwick had ignored him, walking as fast as he could, and looking straight ahead. His elbows and knees were covered in lint and flesh-pink plaster.

That night, he had come to the wash-basin next to Kingshaw.

'Fenwick?'

'What?'

'Does it – are you O.K. now? Do they hurt?'

Fenwick's eyes had narrowed. He said, 'Shut up, stupid.' Nothing else.

In bed, Kingshaw thought, that is the way you should be, that is the way. But after that he had avoided Fenwick because he knew that he never could be like it, he had tried and failed. All this summer he had failed, and there was no help for him. It was no real comfort that Hooper had failed too, because Hooper did not care, he lived by his own rules, Hooper was a coward and, afterwards, he lied and brazened it out, and there was nothing you could do to him, nothing you could prove, Hooper always won.

'Charles, dear, I do think it would be so nice if you were to buy Edmund a little present, out of your own pocket money.'

'What for?'

'Oh, now that *is* a silly question! I'm quite sure that if you had had such a horrid accident, and were in hospital all by yourself, *you* would like a present from your best friend.'

'Hooper isn't my best friend.'

'Oh, very well then, if you feel you haven't known him quite long enough . . . I do know you boys are very funny about things like that! But . . .'

Kingshaw stood up, tipping the jigsaw puzzle on to the floor in his agitation.

'Look, Hooper is not my friend at *all*, I hate Hooper, I keep on telling and telling you. He's a baby and a bully and I hate him, I wish I'd never seen him in my life, I wish he *had* been dead.'

He had known that she would go away after that. He squatted on the floor and began to pick up the jigsaw pieces, carefully, one by one. There was a wide band of sunlight coming through the window. After a bit, he left the puzzle, and lay down on his back inside it. He closed his eyes and felt the warmth on his lids. He thought, *this* is all right, this is all right.

They had left him alone most of the week. It had rained, and he had made a model of a helter-skelter, out of cardboard painted silver. It was shaped like the tower of a fort. You started a marble off at the top, and it rolled round and round, down the slipway on the outside, until it got to the bottom, and then dropped into a chute. It came out at a door, and then hit a drawbridge, and the drawbridge tipped up. There was a flag on the pole at the top. Kingshaw was proud of it, because it worked so faultlessly. He had been very content, making it by himself. Mrs Boland made him drinks, and meals, and brought him toffees, sometimes. It was all right.

It is only silliness, thought Mrs Helena Kingshaw, and a little bit of shock and hysteria after the accident, making him say those things about Edmund. I shall not get upset about it. He is only eleven years old, and there have been some upsets and disturbances in his life, I must not forget that. But I will not worry.

Mr Joseph Hooper had said, 'Children do not always understand what they are saying,' and she was grateful for his firmness, for the way he seemed to know. For his part, Mr Hooper heard himself and thought, perhaps, after all, I am not altogether a failure, perhaps I do know, perhaps I am a good deal more certain of many things than I realized. I have been losing confidence in myself, and *she* has made me see it, I have her to thank for many things.

He said, 'You have your own life to live, you must never forget that. You should make time for yourself and for your own interests and pleasures, apart from those of your son.'

Yes, she said, yes, and allowed herself to relax still further, to feel a little more hopeful.

'Our children will be all right, perfectly all right, children will always get along.'

Now, she thought, I shall be like a mother to Edmund, in so far as it is possible, I shall try to make no difference between the two of them, we shall be just like a family. In the market town, she parked the car and bought some crayons and drawing paper, and a box of home-made sweets.

For a long time, Kingshaw lay on the sitting-room floor, thinking of nothing, half asleep. The house was very quiet. At first, he had minded being left with Mrs Boland. Now he didn't, he was used to himself again. He liked it. Nobody could touch him.

The sun shifted, he felt the warmth and brightness sliding off his face. He got up, and began to break the completed jigsaw puzzle into bits, very deliberately, and put the bits back into their box. It was Hooper's puzzle. Kingshaw had been into his room and found it, and now he wished that he hadn't, he couldn't wait to get it back there. Because Hooper would know, even if he put it in precisely the same place, Hooper would be sure to know. It seemed the most stupid thing he had ever done, to go into that room and touch anything. He took it back.

When he came down again, he stood for a moment in the hall, listening. From the kitchen, he could hear Mrs Boland, scraping vegetables. Kingshaw went quietly outside, down the drive and then left, up the lane. He was very hot. He found an ash stick and began to beat the heads off the tall plants of cow parsley. He thought, this is all right, this is all right, make it stay just like this. He felt peaceful. He wouldn't think of anything terrible that was to come. Above his head, the black and white house-martins swooped and dived.

In the Memorial Hospital, Hooper lay with his broken leg hoisted up in the air, and played Snakes and Ladders with Mrs Helena Kingshaw. He thought, she comes here to see me every day, she feels she's got to, she would rather be with me than with him. He was pleased, even though he did not much like her.

Kingshaw stood on the gate for a long time, looking up the ploughed field ahead. But there was nothing happening, nothing to see. It was too hot, as well. He decided to go inside the church, partly because of that, and also because he had never seen it, it was something to do.

The edges of the grass were clipped very short and neat around the gravestones, and the hedge was straight. There were gargoyles on the tower, opening their cold stone mouths at him. Kingshaw stuck out his tongue, craning back his head. He would not be afraid of them in the daylight.

Inside the church, it smelled as though no living, breathing person had ever been there, the air was damp and musty and dead. Kingshaw walked slowly down between the pews. The hymn books were in two piles on a chair, with some of the spines and backs hanging off. His footsteps rang on the stone, and then were muffled as he came on to the red carpet by the altar rail.

He thought, this is church, this is God and Jesus and the Holy Ghost. After a moment, he dared himself to go and stand on the uneven tiles just inside the chancel. On either side of him, the wood smelled of oldness and polish. He remembered what he had thought and said about Hooper, how he had wished him to be dead. Now, he was afraid of what would happen, because of that. Things came back on you. You were never safe. There were the warts, still on his left hand.

He knelt down, abruptly, where he was, and began to say, O God, I didn't mean it – yes, I did, I did mean it, only now I don't mean it, I want to take it back and never to have thought and said it, and if I'm sorry, make nothing happen to me, make it all be forgotten about. I am trying to be sorry.

But he did not think it likely that he could ever be believed, nothing could change, because he had meant what he thought and said about Hooper, and still meant it. It was only being afraid of this empty church, and of the white marble warrior lying on his tombstone in the side chapel, that made him kneel down and tell lies. It was no good. He had wanted Hooper to be dead, because then things would have been better. His punishment was that Hooper was not dead, that everything was the same, and the thought of that was worse than anything. He acknowledged that he feared Hooper more than he feared anything in the world.

Please make nothing happen, please make it all right and I will never, never want anything else again, O God . . .

His knees were hurting from the hard tiles. He wanted to get out into the sunlight.

'What's the matter with you?'

Kingshaw spun round in alarm, and at once began to struggle to his feet.

'You're not supposed to go inside those railings.'

'I didn't touch anything.'

'All the same. It's where the parson goes, and *you're* not the parson.'

'No.'

'If you want to say your prayers, you should kneel down in a pew.'

Kingshaw began to move away. He dared not think of what might happen to him, for going in the forbidden part of a church. Something . . .

'I know who you are.'

He walked away very quickly down the aisle, and towards the big door, but the footsteps came behind him, and the voice. He felt spied upon, and ashamed of what he had been thinking, as though it had all been spoken out loud, in the dark church.

As he opened the heavy door and stepped out of the porch into the sunlight, two magpies rose up from the gate, and flapped through the air above his head. He felt his own heart thumping.

'Don't you ever talk?'

Kingshaw mumbled, kicking at a small stone on the path. The other boy's face was very small, and brown as a nut, he looked peculiarly old. His eyelashes were like spiders' legs.

'You live with the Hoopers.'

'So? What if I do?'

'Do you go to Edmund Hooper's school?'

'No. Not . . . no.'

'What school do you go to?'

'Boarding school.'

'Well, so does he.'

'Mine's different.'

'Why?'

'It's better than his. It's in Wales.'

'Do you like it?'

'It's all right. Yes.'

'I wouldn't. Day school's better.'

'Oh.'

'My father takes me and we have to leave at eight o'clock in the morning, it's about fourteen miles, I should think. But it's still better.'

They had begun to walk down the lane. Kingshaw found another stick.

'I know all about you.'

'No, you don't, you don't know anything. I've never even *seen* you before.'

'I've seen you, though, lots of times, I've seen you go by in a green car.'

'Oh. That's my mother's car.'

'I've seen her as well. She wears dangly earrings. You can see everything that goes by on the road.'

From where, Kingshaw thought, from *where*? He felt known and judged, surrounded by eyes. He said nothing.

'Our turkeys came this morning. Do you want to come with me and see them?'

Kingshaw looked sideways at him, startled. Where, he thought, what turkeys? He only shrugged.

'They're ten days old, that's all. They're good.'

A van came up behind them, hooting. The boy nodded and a man inside the van waved. Kingshaw thought, he knows everybody and they know him. He lives here, and I live here, now, but I don't know anyone or anything, except Mrs Boland and the woman at the post office. Hooper doesn't know anybody, either, we might as well be on the moon. He thought of Warings, surrounded by the high hedge, dark and inaccessible. All the time, this other boy had been watching, aware of him.

Now, he pulled up some plantains and knotted them quickly, and then began to shoot off the brown heads. Kingshaw tried it but the heads wouldn't go, the stalk broke.

'Don't you even know how to do that? Look, come here . . .'

They stood by the hedge. Kingshaw watched the other boy's thin fingers, twisting up the grass. His nails were very dirty.

'Now you do it.'

Kingshaw did it.

'See, it's easy. O.K., I'm the commander of this ship, and you're an enemy frigate and you've just started firing at me, and now I'm coming back . . .' The brown plantain heads shot into the air, hard as peas. One hit Kingshaw in the face.

'That was a direct hit, it was very bad, now you're holed and you're taking in water, you're sinking . . .'

'But I go down fighting and the lifeboats come out, we don't let you get away with it.'

They were crossing the bridge over the stream. Kingshaw stopped and undid the buttons of his shirt all the way down to the bottom.

'I've got fresh supplies of ammo, I'm coming at you from behind.'

Kingshaw said, 'What's your name?'

He looked astounded. Kingshaw thought, I should have known, I shouldn't have had to ask.

'Fielding, of course.'

Kingshaw said nothing. Fielding. He ought to have known. But the name meant nothing.

'Come on, you've got to run if you want to try and get out of my line of fire.'

Kingshaw ran. They gave up the plantain heads, now, it took too long, and they wouldn't fire far enough. Behind him, Fielding raised his arm.

'Ack-ack-ack, ack-ack-ack-ack-ack.'

Kingshaw didn't know where they were running to. The lane went through the village and out again, towards the Mildon road. He followed it, not thinking, enjoying himself. He pelted past a driveway.

'Where do you think you're going?'

Kingshaw stopped. Fielding was half-way down the drive. At the bottom, a farm.

'Come on, we're going to my house now.'

Kingshaw followed, no longer running, suddenly very aware of this new place, of the different shape and colour and arrangement of it. His feet made a scrunching sound on the loose gravel.

Fielding waited. 'There's a cow calving. Do you want to see?'

Kingshaw hesitated. Hooper would have watched his face, and known, and said scaredy-baby, scaredy, doesn't want to see, daren't go and look, scaredy-baby. For he did not know about seeing a calf born, everything here was strange, and potentially dangerous to him. He did not know.

'It won't have finished yet, I shouldn't think. We'll go and see and then look at the turkeys. Come on.'

Kingshaw decided to trust him, to let him make the decisions about what they were going to do. They went through a gate and across a concrete yard, and the air smelled thick, with cow dung and silage and straw. A thin cat raced madly away from them, across the yard.

Fielding said, 'It's in here.' Kingshaw thought, I don't want to go, I don't want to see, Oh Jesus, I . . . Fielding might have heard his thoughts. He said, 'It's O.K. But you needn't, if you don't like it.'

Kingshaw stiffened. 'I'm all right.'

The wooden door swung open. Inside, it was dark and steamy-warm.

Afterwards, he did not know what he had felt, he could not have said whether he had liked to look or not, whether he had been afraid or not afraid. He was mesmerized by it all, by the smells and the sounds, he could not have stopped looking even when he did not want to look. When he first saw the cow, he caught his breath, at the bony legs of a calf sticking awkwardly out from behind, and the rest of it still plunged deep inside its mother's belly. There was a man in Wellingtons, talking all the time in a strange, low voice, and a red-headed boy. They were bending down and pulling the calf by the legs, heaving at it like a cork stuck in a bottle. There was the sound of the cow panting and the breathing of the men, the sweet smell of sweat, and then a soft, quick suck, as the calf came out, slithering and unwieldy, and lay on the straw covered in blood and skin and long, colourless strands of slime.

Kingshaw found himself kneeling down beside Fielding, his chest hurting from the way he had held his breath, and strained and panted, with the cow and the men. They were very close to the stall. The cow moved, heavy as a camel, turned her head and began to lick the calf, covering its face with her tongue, and sucking up the mucus and blood. The calf snorted and snuffled, trying to open its eyes.

It is all right, Kingshaw told himself, it is awful, I am going to be sick, I shan't be sick, I am not afraid, it's *all* right. He looked at Fielding. The other boy was sitting back on his heels.

'Heifer calf,' he said casually. 'Nice and big.'

Kingshaw was filled with envy of his ease, in the face of the physical, the way Fielding knew and spoke and shrugged his shoulders. He had never imagined birth, would not have guessed at what it was like. He said, 'They have to pull quite hard.'

Fielding stood up. 'Oh, yes. Sometimes they need to use a rope. But Gerda's all right, she's calved twice before.'

'Oh,' Kingshaw said, 'Oh.'

The huge tongue was probing in and out of the stickiness inside the calf's ears.

'We'll go and look at the turkeys now. Come on.'

Kingshaw thought, he sees it every day, almost, it's nothing, he's forgotten all about it. I want to forget it now.

The turkeys were very small and fluffed and ugly, all packed together in wire trays, one layer above the other.

'What a lot.'

'We always have this many.'

'Oh.'

'You ought to be here when we do them at Christmas. There's a guillotine and I have to hold the dustbin to catch the heads when they fall off.'

Kingshaw's eyes pricked, he thought of each bird, as it saw the others going before it down the line towards the knife. He wanted to open the cages and take each one out, hold it between his hands, he wanted them all to fly away. Fielding saw his face. He stopped, by a pile of logs. 'Look, they don't know anything about it,' he said, 'it's very quick. It's not *cruel*.'

'No.'

'Do you want to see my hamster?'

Kingshaw nodded, numb before this battery of experience, bewildered by so many sights and smells and terrible truths, but still willing to be led by Fielding, to be shown everything at once. Later, he would be by himself, he would think about all of it.

They went through a wash-house, and into a kitchen.

'This is Kingshaw. He lives at Warings, you know. Can he stay to dinner?'

'If he likes.'

Fielding went to the window-ledge and lifted up a blue-painted cage.

'Oh, look, he's messed all that new bed stuff up again.'

The woman was quite tall and wore trousers. She said, 'He has his bed the way he wants, not the way you want.'

'I know. But it's annoying. Look, Kingshaw.'

Kingshaw was still watching Fielding's mother. Her hair was very straight. She smiled at him, and then looked away again, peeling potatoes. He thought, that is how you ought to be.

'Don't you want to see it?'

He was still standing just inside the doorway, unsure of things. Now, he went slowly into the room. Fielding had put the cage on the table and taken off the wire front. 'You can hold him.'

Kingshaw felt the small bones through the hamster's soft, pale body, and thin claws pressing into his hand. He didn't know whether he liked it or not.

'Are you *going* to stay to dinner?'

'I – I don't know. I'd have to ask Mrs Boland.'

'Oh, I know her. Where's your mother?'

'At the hospital with Hooper. He's hurt, he fell off a wall.'

Fielding did not seem interested. 'You can just go and ask her now, then, you can take my bike if you want, it'll be quickest.'

Kingshaw stroked his finger along the plushy back of the hamster. Its eyes were like jet beads. He thought, this is my place, mine, it will never have anything to do with Hooper. Fielding is *my* friend, mine. This is all right.

Beyond the window, there was a long garden, with fruit trees at the bottom. The colours and shapes of everything were very sharp and clear and bright, in the sun.

'My bike's in the shed, I'll show you.'

Fielding took the hamster and dumped it back inside the blue cage. 'Come on.'

Kingshaw went, running and leaping.

At Warings, he found his mother. She came out of the sitting room, clasping her hands together. She said, 'Oh, Charles, everything is going to be quite all right. Tomorrow, they are bringing Edmund home!'

Fielding said, 'Why don't you run away then?'

'I did.'

They were lying in long grass at the bottom of a field. A goldcrest was swinging on a branch of the hedge. Fielding turned over and looked at him suspiciously.

'I went up into the wood,' Kingshaw said.

'*Hang* Wood?'

'Yes. And farther than that, as well. Into the big one.'

'I wouldn't have.'

'It was all right.'

Kingshaw kept remembering it, thinking about the darkness and coldness.

'I wouldn't go into Hang Wood by myself, not for anything. Nor would my brother, even, and he's thirteen.'

'Nothing happened.'

'It might have. There's things in Hang Wood.'

'What sort of things?'

'I don't know. Just things. Ask anybody round here, they'll tell you.'

'There isn't anything. Only animals.'

'Oh, I don't mean *animals*.'

'We found a stream.'

'Who was we?'

Kingshaw sighed, pulling a flat blade of grass between his teeth.

'Hooper followed me,' he said. 'It's what he does. And then we got lost.'

The goldcrest flew away and the branch went on going up and down. Kingshaw half-closed his eyes, so that everything mingled together, greenness and heat haze and the moving branch.

'Are you afraid of Edmund Hooper?'

Kingshaw hesitated. Then said, 'Yes.' because he was not ashamed of admitting it to Fielding.

'But he can't *do* anything to you.'

'Yes, he can.'

'What?'

'He – he locked me in a shed. And into an awful room there is, with dead moths in cases.'

'They can't hurt you, though. Dead moths can't do anything to you.'

'He says things – I get scared from what he says.'

'Well, the more you let him see you are, the worse it'll be.'

'Yes.'

'But he couldn't actually *hurt* you.'

Kingshaw fidgeted, unable to explain. Everything that Hooper had ever done to him, all the things he reminded him of, the crow and the moths and the dead rabbit, the shed, and the way he had looked falling off the castle wall, were crowded inside his head, but it was impossible to convey how terrible they were, to say that it was not what Hooper really did, as what he might do, it was how he could make him feel.

'You needn't be frightened just of what somebody else *says*, need you?'

Kingshaw did not answer. Fielding was both right, and not right. He was sensible and matter-of-fact, and yet he himself knew what it was to be frightened of something, he had said that he would not have gone inside Hang Wood. But in spite of that, Kingshaw saw that he would never be able to make him understand fully, that there was an impossible distance between the two of them. The whole afternoon, he had gone on and on, trying to make Fielding see how things were, the terribleness of both present and future. It was pointless.

'He's coming home tomorrow.' Because the thought was like a black pit into which he kept falling, his stomach was screwed up tight into a ball.

'So what?' Fielding was shredding a dandelion. So what. Kingshaw could have wept for envy of his assurance. He thought, nothing will ever happen to Fielding, not ever, just because he doesn't care, because he is like this.

'You needn't stick around with Hooper if you don't want. You can come here.'

'No.'

'Why not?'

'They'll make me stay. They think we're best friends.'

'Tell them you're not, then.'

'They never listen.'

'Look, you oughtn't to let everybody boss you around so much,

Kingshaw, they can't make you do anything, if you don't want to, nobody can.'

'You don't know.'

'It's only your mother, isn't it?'

'I have to do what Mr Hooper says.'

'Why?'

Kingshaw shrugged. 'Because we live there. And my mother makes me. She likes him.'

'Oh.'

Fielding slit the dandelion stalk and green juice ran out over his thumb.

'I'm not going back to my own school any more,' Kingshaw said now, 'I've got to go to school with Hooper.'

He had not told Fielding this before, because he thought, somehow, that when you spoke a thing out loud, that was that, and if you didn't, there might be some mistake, some hope. Saying it, made it be true.

'Isn't it very nice there?'

'I don't know. But it won't matter what it's like if he's there, he'll make it awful.'

'Don't be stupid, there'll be plenty of other people, won't there? You don't have to stick with him if you don't want.'

'He'll make me.'

'You oughtn't to be so wet, then,' Fielding said furiously, and began to get up from the grass. 'Come on, we'll go and look for a slow-worm in the ditch.'

Kingshaw followed. He thought, perhaps Fielding's right, perhaps it will be O.K. I can say, shut up, Hooper, shut up and get knotted, stuff it, you don't scare me. I can tell the others about the thunderstorm, anyway, and how you peed your pants up on the wall at Leydell Castle, and everybody will listen, and then I can go off with them, you won't be able to scare me. Perhaps I can be like Fielding is, or Fenwick. Perhaps.

Fielding slithered down the grass bank ahead of him. 'I did find one,' he said. 'Once.'

Kingshaw did not know what a slow-worm looked like. He went after Fielding, poking about into the mud. The stream had dried up, here.

'Anyway, if Hooper's broken his leg and everything, he'll be in bed, won't he, and you won't have to stay with him the *whole* time.'

'No. I mightn't have to.'

'So you can come down here.'

'O.K.'

'He mightn't even be able to go back to school, might he, not straightaway? He might not be well enough.'

Kingshaw stood still, his heart leaping. He thought, Oh God, Oh God, yes, yes, and then it would be all right, I should be all right, I should have a chance, I should get there first and be able to find out about things, by the time he came to school, there would be other people.

The toe of his sandal touched against something hard. He bent down. Fielding was several yards ahead of him, poking in the reeds with a stick. Kingshaw said, 'I've found a tortoise.'

Fielding looked, and then came back. 'Hey – that's mine, that's Archie. He went away months ago. Hey, I thought he'd got lost.' He held it, and the snake-shaped, neolithic head poked forward, the mottled skin of the neck flaccid, like that of a very old man.

'Hey, thanks, Kingshaw! That was dead clever. Thanks.'

Kingshaw shrugged, and began to go along through the mud beside the hedge again, half-mad with pride and pleasure. He said, Fielding is mine, this is all mine, mine, it will be all right, over and over, inside himself.

Hooper did not come home the next day.

'It is so upsetting, such a disappointment,' said Mrs Helena Kingshaw, standing by the door of the kitchen. 'But perhaps if they are not quite sure, it is better not to have him travel here. He had a little bit of a temperature, the sister tells me. Oh, but *poor* Edmund, and now Mr Hooper will be back from London tonight, and feel so let-down, so anxious. Oh, dear!'

When he got outside, Kingshaw began to run, across the flat lawn and down the drive into the lane, exultant, afraid of nothing, racing through the sunlight.

Fielding said, 'I told you, he won't be able to go to school now. Come on, I've got some stuff to give the donkey.'

He was sucking a straw. After a bit, Kingshaw found one, and stuck it in the corner of his mouth, between his teeth. He must look and talk like Fielding, he must *be* like Fielding.

They went and found the donkey.

Chapter Fifteen

'You've been into my room,' Hooper said.

Kingshaw's glance flew to the jigsaw puzzle on the second shelf of the bookcase. It was still there, it looked the same. How did he know, then, *how did he know?* Hooper's eyes had followed the direction of his.

'*That's* what you had, isn't it? You took it and used it, and that's just the same as stealing. That game is my game, and it's my room. This isn't your house, Kingshaw.'

'It isn't yours either,' Kingshaw said, wearily. He stood, looking out of the high window, down onto the garden and the copse. Outside, it was still and very hot, the sky a brilliant blue. Kingshaw felt trapped.

'Now you must stay with Edmund, dear, you must keep him company. There are plenty of things for you to do, I know, plenty of games to play.'

'I want to go out.'

'That isn't very thoughtful, is it? Edmund cannot go out. I wonder if you really are so selfish as to forget that?'

'He doesn't want me to stay with him all the time. He doesn't want me at all.'

'Don't argue, Charles dear, I'm sure that you would want some company, if you had to be in bed all these lovely, sunny days, you would want to see a friend.'

'He isn't my friend.'

'Perhaps you would like to take up Edmund's drink, dear, when you go.' For she had decided simply to ignore it, this silly, persistent talk about their not being friends. That was the way boys behaved, it was a phase. She would take as little notice as she had taken when Charles had brought out his swear words, so triumphantly, as a very small boy. Mr Hooper had listened to her, and agreed. 'We shall take no notice,' he had said.

'Using somebody's things without permission is as bad as stealing. So you're a thief and a burglar. You're a burglar because you came into my room without me saying so.'

Kingshaw did not reply. He had been preoccupied again, ever since Hooper had come home, with thoughts of his fall, of how it had happened; there were endless questions going round and round in his mind, as though on a wheel. He wanted to ask what it had felt like, going through the air, how much it had hurt when he hit the ground, wanted to ask if Hooper had thought, I'm going to be killed, when I fall I shall be dead, if he remembered anything when he woke up, if he was frightened of going anywhere near high walls, now. Two of his ribs had been cracked, as well as the concussion and the broken leg.

'I was nearly killed,' he had said to Kingshaw, the first day they brought him home. 'That's what my father said, and the doctors. They said it was just luck I wasn't dead, that's all. Luck.'

Kingshaw thought, you should have been dead, you should have, it would be all right now, if you were dead, and then broke out into a cold sweat, at his own wickedness. He could not ask Hooper any of the questions that were in his mind. The old hostility was between them again, the first moment Kingshaw came into the bedroom, Hooper's eyes had stared at him and through him, knowing him, hating and scornful. And there was something else, too, something Kingshaw could not fathom. Hooper kept on watching him, as though he were trying to discover something, as though he wanted to make sure about what had been happening here, in this house, while he had been away.

Now, he was playing idly with a small, plastic puzzle. You slid rows of numbered squares about inside a tray, trying to get them into the right order. Earlier, he had said, 'This is what your mother gave me. She gave me a lot of things.'

Kingshaw had not replied. But he had been surprised at how much he minded, at his own angry jealousy. She is *my* mother, he had thought, mine. And was immediately puzzled, because he knew that in truth he did not care very much about her.

Mrs Boland had thrown some bread out on to the grass at the back of the house, and now the starlings had come down, jostling and fighting, and there was a crow, too, circling about overhead, waiting to dive. Kingshaw wondered how long he would be made to stay here. He was afraid all the time, now, even though Hooper could not move out of his bed. He was afraid of what was going on inside him, what he was planning, afraid of the way Hooper looked at him. What he had done in the past had only been a beginning, Kingshaw knew that much. But it had given him a satisfaction, he had seen how easily he could make Kingshaw afraid.

Now, he heard him shifting a little, in the bed, and turned round to look at him, though still he kept his distance, staying at the other side of the room.

He said, 'Does it hurt?'

Hooper glanced up from the puzzle. His eyes narrowed. 'It was your fault,' he said, for reply. Kingshaw flushed. They had had the argument before, over and over again, he knew that he was right and wanted to cry with frustration because Hooper still made him anxious and guilty.

'Don't be stupid, I've told you and told you you shouldn't have started to climb up there. You were scared and so you fell. People always fall if they're scared.'

'You pushed me off.'

'Liar, liar, liar, I never touched you. You were scared and you fell off, and you're a stupid liar. I was going to get you down, wasn't I? I was going to hold on to you because you were blubbing, you were so scared.'

For a moment, Hooper was silent. Then he said quietly, 'Something will happen to you. Because it was your fault and I told them, it's what they believe. You needn't think you'll get away. Something will happen.'

'You don't frighten me, Hooper, you're just trying to cover up for being scared, that's all.'

'You wait, Kingshaw. That's what.'

Hooper bent his head to the puzzle again. They were silly, stupid threats, the sort of things bullies said and didn't mean, and Kingshaw knew that they were true, that something would happen, either directly as a result of Hooper, or in spite of him. He waited for punishment, dreaded the start of every day, now, because of what might happen to him.

To stop himself thinking about it, and because Hooper didn't want him there, he was only ignoring him, while he fiddled with the puzzle, Kingshaw walked quickly across the bedroom, and out of the door. Hooper said nothing.

Walking along the landing, he tried to remember what Fielding had told him. It's only what he says, he can't *do* anything to you, you don't have to let him see you're scared of him. He can't do anything. But he can, he can – Kingshaw began to run, trying to get away from his own whirling thoughts.

'Something will happen to you. You wait.'

It would, that was certain. Hooper would wait until they both got to the school, and then it would all begin.

Once, only once in his whole life, Kingshaw had been beaten up. Crawford had done it, Crawford beat up everybody. It was down in the old pavilion on the lower sports field. It hadn't been much, not now he thought back to it, it could have been far worse. Crawford had been frightened when he heard footsteps and voices outside. But Kingshaw could remember vividly the feel of Crawford's fist punching into his belly, very deliberately, and then the way he had started to pull his little fingers backwards, farther and farther, could remember the sick, cold dread of what was coming next, how much worse it would be, and the bewilderment of not knowing why, why. He didn't even know Crawford, they were in different houses, Crawford was three years older. He'd just found him and made him go to the pavilion. It might have been anybody else.

Crawford had been caught. He was always hurting people, and being caught, and in the end, he had left the school and nothing like it had ever happened again. But he remembered. The worst feeling had been the aloneness, before they had heard the footsteps, the knowing that however loudly he cried out, there was nobody at all who could hear him. His terror of Crawford had been absolute. Afterwards, he had not dared to tell anyone.

Hooper wasn't like Crawford, the things he did were different, his threats were in many ways worse. His reign was one of terror, Crawford's had been one of simple brutality. But Kingshaw thought he knew that that would start to happen as well, sooner or later, with Hooper. Even though he would not beat up Kingshaw himself, he had friends, didn't he, other boys at the school. Hooper would only have to speak a word to them.

He crossed the hall, in the grip of his own thoughts. There was Fielding, that was all, he could run and run and there would be the farm, the sunshine, the animals, they could lie in the long grass at the bottom of the garden, they could feed the donkey, they could scrump the apple trees, anything. At Fielding's, he was safe, it was his own place. He turned the knob of the heavy front door.

165

'Charles!'

He spun round. His mother was standing in the doorway of the sitting room. Kingshaw began to edge his way around the front door, trying to get on the outside, not wanting to listen to whatever she would say, wanting only to get out, to get away from them all.

'Where are you going, dear?'

He stood still, not moving his hand from the knob.

'Charles? I asked you a question, didn't I?'

She spoke to him differently, now, he thought, there was a new sharpness and impatience, as though she had decided to change her way of dealing with him. It would be Mr Hooper, he knew, she would be doing it to please him.

'Where are you going?'

'To the shop. I want something.'

'What do you want?'

'Just – something.'

'Don't be secretive, dear, you know that Mummy doesn't like it.'

He squirmed, hating the way she spoke of herself like that, as though she were another person.

'I want an ice cream. I've got some money.'

'There is plenty of ice cream in the refrigerator, dear, go and ask Mrs Boland . . .'

'No. I don't want that sort. I want a different sort.'

'I'm quite sure that all ice cream is very much the same, you know.'

'I want to go to the *shop*.'

'Then you must go quickly.'

'What for? Why must I? I haven't got anything else to do.'

'And what about poor Edmund, lying all by himself upstairs? Have you thought of him?'

'He's . . . he's asleep.' But he felt himself flush, telling the lie. There was a little silence. Mrs Helena Kingshaw looked hurt. She said, in a quiet, disappointed voice, 'Go and get your special ice cream then, Charles.'

He moved forward.

'Charles?'

He was trembling, in his anxiety to rush away.

'You are not to go anywhere else, you know. I want you to come straight back here from the post office.'

He almost burst out at her in his fury at the unfairness of it, he wanted to shout, I'm not, I won't, I'm going to the farm to see Fielding and you won't stop me, it doesn't matter what you say because I'll do what *I* want, so.

He said nothing.

'Now, I shall just pop upstairs and make sure that Edmund is comfortable.'

Kingshaw closed the door carefully behind him, and then began to run. He thought, I hate them, I hate all of them, I hate them, I will do what I want.

He walked across the road, away from the post office, and stood by the small bridge, licking the drops of sticky, creamy liquid as they slid down the cone. The air above the dried-up stream was buzzing with insects, in the heat.

Last night, his mother had told him about London. He was to go with Mr Hooper to buy his uniform, for the new school. Nobody else would go. He thought about it. When that happened, the past would really and truly have finished, he would be wearing black and gold like Hooper, not sky and navy blue, there would be no way out at all.

Hooper had said, 'My father's going to pay for your school uniform. He's going to pay for everything, didn't you know? You should just think yourself lucky that he's got plenty of money, shouldn't you? You'll have to do what he says now, won't you?'

'Why?'

'That's obvious, stupid.'

'How do you know about it? You don't know. I don't believe he's going to pay anything at all.'

'Well, who is, then?'

Silence.

'Don't be *stupid*, Kingshaw.'

He had wanted to ask his mother, but he could not have brought off the words, and in any case, there was no need, because he knew it was true. His mother had always told him about how much it cost to keep him at his school, even in spite of the money from the Governors' charity, she told him how careful they had to be, and how he couldn't have so much pocket money a term as the others, she said, 'I have made a lot of sacrifices for you, Charles,' and then, 'As long as you make the very best of your chances, there, that is all I ask you, as long as you remember how lucky you have been.'

So he knew that there would have been no money for this other, better school, without Mr Hooper. His mother had told him how much better it was. Everything had been arranged by Mr Hooper. He did not understand why, there seemed to him no possible reason why Mr Hooper should want to spend his money on them, not however much he had. His mother was a housekeeper, wasn't she, and they had been here two months. Nothing like it had ever happened to them before. 'People are very mean and unthinking,' Mrs Helena Kingshaw had so often said. 'They do not understand how hard it is for people like us to live decently, they do not make allowances.'

But Mr Hooper did. She said, over and over again, 'Mr Hooper is very good to us, Charles, you must understand that. You should be very grateful to Mr Hooper.'

Why? Why?

He had looked at Mr Hooper surreptitiously across the dining table, and when he passed by him on the staircase, trying to understand. 'We are getting to know one another, Charles, don't you think? We are becoming very good friends.'

Kingshaw had shrunk back, not able to reply. But he could not forget the night Mr Hooper had carried him upstairs, after his nightmares, and how he had wanted to stay close to him. He was still ashamed of his own weakness.

He bit the bottom end of the ice cream cone in half, and stuffed the two bits into his mouth. Then he heard the sound of the Landrover. He saw Fielding.

'Where've *you* been?'

In the back of the van were three calves, tied up to a rail and stamping about, their eyes enormous, and rolling with fright.

Kingshaw said, 'Hooper's come back. They make me stay with him quite a lot.'

'Oh. You're not with him now, though.'

'I came out.' Kingshaw kicked the side of the huge tyre.

'We're going to market. You could come, if you want. Why don't you, that'd be O.K.'

'I – they'd make a fuss.'

'What for?'

'I'd have to ask them.'

'Go on, then, we can wait, can't we? We could come with you to ask.'

'No.'

'Don't you want to?'

Kingshaw did not reply.

'We're taking the heifer calf. The one you saw getting born, *you* know.'

'To the market?' Kingshaw looked at it again, bumping about in the Landrover, remembering how it had been.

'But it's not very old.'

'Ten days. They go at ten days.'

'But what'll happen to it? When somebody buys it, what then? Where will it go?'

He felt suddenly anxious to know about the calf, it was some kind of visible link between himself, and Fielding and the farm.

Fielding's father let off the handbrake of the Landrover. 'Veal,' he said, without much interest, 'they go for veal.'

Kingshaw waited in the road until they had gone right away, hearing the sound of the engine up the hill, and watching the dust rise, and then settle back again. After that, there was nothing he could do but go back to the house. He walked very slowly through the long grass beside the hedge, sending up sudden clouds of white butterflies every so often. He didn't even run going past the open space that led to the old allotment, though he turned his head away, not wanting to see the shed.

He had both wanted, and not wanted, to go to the market, sensing that the place would hold all kinds of new terrors for him, sounds and fears and smells. He didn't want to see the calves being led away. But he had wanted to be with Fielding, and Fielding's father, to ride in the front of the high Landrover, to be going away from here. None of them would have been able to touch him, then.

He turned up the long drive, between the rhododendron bushes. His mother said, 'I have made a cold chocolate drink, Charles, you can have yours with Edmund.' And she went ahead of him, with a firm tread, carrying the tray.

For a moment, he hesitated, standing in the hall. It was cool here. The door of the Red Room was slightly ajar, he looked in quickly and saw the first of the glass cases, with their outstretched, shadowy shapes.

'Charles . . .'

He went up very slowly, one step at a time, thinking.

Hooper was sticking a lot of new stamps into his green leather album. He had a bowl of water, and a pair of tweezers, laid out on the flat board they had put up for him, over the bed. When Kingshaw's mother had gone, he said, 'I know about a boy called Fielding.'

Kingshaw stared at him.

'*I* know everything, you needn't think I don't. Your mother tells me lots of things about you.'

The chocolate drink was thick and sweet, coming up into Kingshaw's mouth through the straw. He squeezed his hands tightly together to stop himself from crying, because Hooper knew, Hooper found out everything, he had nothing left that was his own, nothing at all.

He turned and looked out of the window again.

Hooper said, 'I can get up the day after tomorrow. I can come and sit downstairs.'

So he would be going back to school, then, there wouldn't even be that. Kingshaw put down his empty mug.

'Where do you think you're going?'

He didn't answer.

The full, mid-day sun was pouring into his own room through the glass. There was a smell of hot paint and plastic, from the galleon model on the window-ledge.

Kingshaw lay down on his bed and pushed his face into the cold silk quilt.

Downstairs, Mrs Helena Kingshaw sat in the drawing room on a chintz-covered chair, and shortened the hem of a cotton dress by one inch and a half. She thought, I am going to look younger, I am going to take very great care over my appearance, now, and then flushed a little, with the excitement of knowing how much it had come to matter.

Mr Joseph Hooper said, 'There was nothing *wrong* with your old school, Charles. I am very anxious for you to remember that. Nothing wrong at all.'

Kingshaw stared at him, not replying. The train was very hot – the sun shone straight onto his face, through the glass. He had never been in a first class compartment before.

'Your mother has had a bit of a hard time of it, life has not been easy for her, these past few years. You are quite old enough to understand that, I'm sure.'

He didn't like to hear Mr Hooper speaking like that about her, it made him seem a party to her secrets, made Kingshaw feel that he knew everything that had ever happened to them. The train shot into a tunnel, and he felt his eardrums block up suddenly, and then they were out again, into the sun.

'It is just that your new school, Edmund's school, will be very much better for you. Yes, indeed, better in every way. You will have *opportunities.*'

What for, Kingshaw thought desperately, what for? Why did everything have to change so often? He had always known that, when he was thirteen, he would have to win a good scholarship to a public school, and always known that he would not manage it, he was only good at plodding along by himself, not at competing.

'You must work very, very hard.' his mother had said. 'You can be a clever little boy, if you will only just concentrate. There will be no money to send you off to public school otherwise, Charles, you do see that, don't you? You do understand how we are placed?'

He wondered what would happen now, about the scholarships, whether it would be different, because of Mr Hooper. He didn't much care, it seemed to have nothing to do with him. They would decide, as they had decided everything.

'We are running through the suburbs,' Mr Hooper said now. 'There is always plenty to see from the windows of a train, plenty to interest anyone.'

Politely, Kingshaw turned his head to look out.

Mr Joseph Hooper thought, he is a good deal easier to deal with than my own son, that I must admit: he is quiet and withdrawn, yes, but there does not seem to be anything strange about him, as there has always been about Edmund, and there is no constraint between us. He is not a boy who says very much, and yet I think I know his mind, I think I can say that I understand him. His mother has told me what I need to know. Though, in truth, since the coming of Mrs Helena Kingshaw, he had felt himself a new man, his lack of confidence had faded away. He knew how to deal with Edmund, now; firmness, he had decided, firmness and directness, that is all that is needed, and then they are happy enough; boys are very simple animals.

He thought that he himself had gone through a bad patch, after the illness and death of his father, and the move to Warings, he had remembered the past, and his own childhood, and been embittered.

Perhaps, after all, he had exaggerated things, perhaps he had been happier. The memory played tricks, when one reached middle age, and then, the company of Mrs Helena Kingshaw had helped put everything into perspective again.

Mrs Kingshaw. He shifted a little on the seat, for he was not able to make up his mind, he was just a little anxious, just a little unsure. He thought that life had taught him not to make impetuous decisions.

On the opposite seat, Charles Kingshaw still looked out onto the back gardens of suburban houses.

Mr Hooper said, 'This is the Strand, this is Trafalgar Square, this is the Mall, there is Buckingham Palace . . .'

'I know.'

But the taxi skidded in and out of the traffic, and Mr Hooper did not listen, he recited the names of streets and buildings because of his belief in the usefulness and fascination of such facts.

Kingshaw said, 'We *lived* in London.'

'Ah, yes! Now that is St George's Hospital . . .'

He did not like being here with Mr Hooper. It was like being with a stranger, one of the masters from school, perhaps, it felt odd. He could think of nothing at all to say, except in answer to questions. They walked very quietly across the grey carpets of the department store, towards School Outfitting, and the rooms smelled of perfume and new cloth. He thought, I could run away. I could get into the lift and go down the other staircase, and out into the street, I would be lost.

But he would not do it. It would be worse, alone in the city streets, full of strange people, than it had been alone in Hang Wood. The noise confused him, the way everybody pushed about. He had forgotten London. Mr Hooper said, 'Well, now . . .' There was a man with striped trousers and a tape-measure. Kingshaw had never been shopping with anyone except his mother. He was measured and pushed in and out of the sleeves of blazers and the legs of shorts, and Mr Hooper and the man talked about him over the top of his head, he felt as though he was not really here, not really himself. He said nothing. But when he looked in the tall glass, and saw himself like Hooper, in the black and gold uniform, looked into his own eyes, he knew that there was no more hope for him, that it had all begun.

★

Hooper was playing with the silver cardboard model of the fort, rolling the marble down and letting it drop through the chute, over and over again. Kingshaw watched him for a moment, his fury rising, and then began to run, down the corridor and the staircase, across the hall and into the sitting room, clenching and unclenching his hands.

Mr Hooper was pouring out two glasses of sherry from a bottle. The windows of the sitting room were open onto the silent lawn.

Kingshaw shouted, 'It's *my* model, you gave him my model, the one I made, and you didn't even ask. I didn't want him to have that, you shouldn't give him *any* of my things.'

He saw the look that passed between his mother and Mr Hooper, knew what they were thinking of him, and it made him want to strike out at them, in rage, he felt misjudged by them. He thought, they don't want me, they don't want anything to do with me here, they want themselves and Hooper, there is no place for me.

'You've got to make him give it back. He's got plenty of things, he's got everything. He's got to give me back my model.'

'Charles . . .'

'It's mine, mine, *mine,* he isn't to have *anything* of mine.'

When Mr Hooper stepped forward quickly, and struck him across the cheek, he heard the sound of it sharply, through his own head, and out in the room, too, saw his mother's face, full of relief and shock, and Mr Hooper's, as he stood over him. And then the silence. None of them moved. Silence and silence.

The telephone rang. Mr Hooper went out of the door and into the hall.

'I think you had better go quietly upstairs, Charles. I'm sure you can understand why. And perhaps you will also try and understand how very much you have upset me.'

He did not look at her.

The door of Hooper's bedroom was closed. Kingshaw kicked it open with his foot, and stood there, breathing very fast. He could still feel the stinging on his face, from Mr Hooper's hand. The marble rolled, and dropped through the chute.

'Give me that back.'

Hooper looked up.

'It's mine, I made it. You'd just better give it to me.'

'Your mother brought it in, anyway.'

'I don't care! *Give* it to me.'

'And anyway, as well, you made it in *our* house, it's *our* cardboard and *our* paint, so it isn't yours at all, it's mine, you don't own anything that's in this house.'

Kingshaw began to walk towards the bed. He didn't care about Hooper, he didn't care what any of them said or did to him, he only wanted the model, because it was his, it had taken so long to plan and make, building it had been so difficult, and now it worked perfectly, nobody else should touch it.

'Give it back.'

Hooper held it high above his head.

'I'll punch you, I'll get it off you, Hooper, you'd better give it me before I do.'

'You daren't touch me, I'm ill and I'm in bed, they'd hear you. You can't do anything at all to me.'

Kingshaw lunged forwards. As he did so, Hooper hurled the model away from him, across the room. It hit the far wall and dropped, landing upside down on the linoleum beside the carpet. Hooper still held the marble in his left hand, laughing.

The top of the model was broken, the cardboard had buckled and the drawbridge was tilting sideways. The flag lay on the floor. Kingshaw knelt down and picked it up. As he got slowly to his feet again, his mother said from the doorway, 'I think that you should be very, very ashamed of yourself.'

Chapter Sixteen

'Oh, but it is *so* nice to hear from you, such a lovely surprise!' Mrs Helena Kingshaw's voice had an edge of excitement, she was a little out of breath, for she had not so very many friends, and did not really expect any of them to get in touch.

She had not allowed herself to feel at all lonely at Warings, because it had worked out so very well, the relief of coming here and finding it all so satisfactory, so *safe*, ought to be enough for her, and more. Though, in truth, she had thought that when Mr Hooper was in London, and the boys had gone off to school, it might not be . . . well, it was just a little isolated, and Mrs Boland was not exactly a woman with whom she could share any confidences.

But she would not think of that, for they had been so very fortunate, Mr Hooper was so very kind. And at the Sunday morning cocktail party, there had been just one or two women with whom she thought she might, perhaps, become friendly, after a time. They had seemed to accept her as something more than a housekeeper.

Now, Enid Tyson had found out their address, and was on the telephone, and she remembered that there was another world, outside this house and this village, a world in which she had lived and not *always* been unhappy, a world which had nothing to do with Mr Joseph Hooper. Mrs Enid Tyson was not widowed but divorced, in unhappy circumstances, and so they could talk to one another, there was an understanding. Mrs Kingshaw settled herself a little more comfortably in the hall chair.

From the study, with the door slightly ajar, Mr Joseph Hooper listened. No friend had ever telephoned before, and it came to him with a little shock of surprise that Mrs Kingshaw had been here for only two months, that she had a past about which he did not know quite everything, friends with whom he had nothing to do. He was a little resentful.

Charles Kingshaw came down the staircase and heard her voice, stopped.

'But of course not, no, my dear, of course you are right. We can never quite tell, one may be . . . yes, we may be *anywhere,* by then, we may not still be here. Oh, yes, we are very happy, and Charles has been a changed boy, you know, since he came here, it has done him so much good to have a companion. Though of course, there have been little upsets and frustrations, that is only to be expected . . . yes, little jealousies . . . No, I don't know, nothing is really settled, Enid. I have not quite made up my mind about the future.'

For she was anxious that Mr Hooper should hear her, anxious for him to know that she retained her pride. If there were any decisions to be made, then *he* should be the one . . . Even though she might allow herself to hope, to take a little notice of odd straws in the wind.

Very quietly, Kingshaw crept back up the stairs. He went up on to the second landing, and along the corridor, into the room with the dolls. After Hang Wood, he had not wanted to come in here, it had reminded him of his own failure, his ultimate loss of control over things, after all the careful planning. But eventually, he returned. It was the only place he had left, he had to make the best of things.

He was trying to mend the helter-skelter fort.

'I have not quite made up my mind about the future . . .' Kingshaw spoke the sentence over and over to himself, softly. 'I have not quite made up my mind about the future.'

He didn't *know* what it meant, he never knew, with his mother, it might mean anything at all, might have nothing to do with him. There had been something in her tone of voice, something in the over-emphasis of words, that made him suspect her. After all, he had been to London with Mr Hooper, the uniform had been bought. 'Men together!' she had said, coyly, when they had returned. There would be no changes in those plans, now.

But perhaps they would not always live here, perhaps there had been a quarrel, perhaps she had come to hate this dark house as much as he did, perhaps . . .

He began to wonder where else they might go. They had been to so many places. What had been worse than all the other people's houses – perhaps, in some ways, even worse than here – had been the private hotel. They had lived there for almost a year, and it might have been for ever. At school, Broughton-Smith had found out, he had said, 'Kingshaw lives in a *private hotel!*' and they had all stared at him, it had been an abnormality unknown to any of them.

It had been at the private hotel that he had known Miss Mellitt.

There had been a dining room which was always cold, and they had their own table, by the mirror in the corner, people said, 'That is the Kingshaws' table,' in odd, dispassionate voices. He had not liked eating every meal in front of so many other people.

There had been no other children in the hotel, visitors came and went, Mrs Kingshaw found strangers to take him to the zoo or into the park. Some were always there, like Mr Busby and Mr Taylor, who always sat together. Mr Busby had only one leg.

But it had been Miss Mellitt, Miss Mellitt . . . He looked up, suddenly, filled with dread at the memory of her. After his own bedroom, there had been a space, and then the last door right at the end of the passage, and that was Miss Mellitt's room. At night, Kingshaw had always heard her, coming up the stairs, and he had held his breath with terror until her footsteps had gone right past his own door, certain that there would be a time when she would stop, and turn the handle, and come into the darkness.

In the dining room, she spilled blobs of soup on to the front of her dress, and when Kingshaw had looked up, she had been staring at him. Her eyebrows had been very thick and dark, and her scalp showed through the thin hair, in patches. Every time he saw her, he had been forced to stare at the pink, shining skin, and then to look quickly away. He had been afraid of Miss Mellitt, she had come into his nightmares, and even now, when he was at school, doing something, miles and years away from her, he remembered. She had smelled oddly musty, like clothes left for years in a chest of drawers.

'Miss Mellitt is old,' his mother had said, 'old and rather lonely. You must be very kind and respectful to those who are old, Charles, I am sure they teach you that at school.'

'I don't like her.'

'That is not kind.'

'She keeps coming and talking to me. She touches me. I don't like her.'

'I have told you, darling, she is just a little lonely. I daresay that she likes to hear what a nice, polite young boy has to say about things.'

He had not replied, after that. Only run away from Miss Mellitt and lain in his bed at night, sick with fright as she had come slowly past, down the long passage, and started again and again in horror, at the bits of bald scalp.

Now, he realized why he had remembered again. It was not only wondering where else they might be going to live. It was because of the smell. The dolls in the glass cabinet smelled of Miss Mellitt.

Kingshaw bent his head forward, closer to the model, breathing in the thick, acrid fumes of glue and metallic paint quickly, trying to forget.

'Of course, we may not still be here . . . I have not quite made up my mind about the future.'

Mr Joseph Hooper stood before the wardrobe mirror, hands up to his neck, undoing his tie, anxious. He thought, there is something wrong, something she has not felt able to tell me, she is not altogether happy here, after all.

He leaned forward, and peered closely at his own face, at the seaweed-coloured eyes, and jutting nose, at the fine, thin lines drawn across his forehead, and around his mouth. He thought, there is nothing much to be proud of, nothing so very special about me.

Yet there was something between them, a tension, an understanding, he had seen it in her, and felt it in himself, he thought that he was quite sure . . .

'I have not made up my mind about the future.'

Well, it is my own fault then, for I have been indecisive, worried about taking any steps I might regret, or that it might all be too soon. Even though, when I advertised for a housekeeper, I had it in mind that . . .

He walked away from the mirror, unbuttoning his shirt, guilty at what he had had in his mind, as he was always guilty. He looked at the shaded, sombrely-papered bedroom, with the neatly made double bed in which he slept alone. The pictures began forming in his mind. He thought, I am an intensely sexual man, and so there is a strain, an unease, that is the reason for everything.

He had been afraid of coming to terms with himself, of admitting the whole truth. Now, there was Mrs Helena Kingshaw, in this house, sleeping upstairs by night and moving about the rooms by day, looking at him, choosing her clothes carefully, shortening her skirts, and he had watched her and been disturbed.

He thought, I have never had what I have wanted, it has never been right. There had been the politeness of his marriage, the elaborate courtesy of the double bed, he had suffered from the cold gap between his permitted behaviour, and his desires.

178

But after that, afterwards . . . he sat down abruptly on the chair beside the bed. Afterwards, nothing. Only that he sat on the underground trains and looked at the legs of the girls sitting opposite to him, imagined silk-stockinged buttocks and thighs, curled in different positions, and in the evenings, he walked down sidestreets off the Charing Cross Road, looking for the pictures of breasts and mouths in the windows of bookshops, and outside the erotic cinemas.

There were opportunities, he knew that. But he had never taken one, never would, he was alarmed by himself, and uncertain where to begin. He only slept, and sweated through his dreams and woke to the guilt of the morning. Nothing else. Nothing.

Now, Mr Hooper sat and thought about Mrs Helena Kingshaw, in this house, in the room upstairs, thought of the pleasure of her company, the pride and satisfaction it gave him to see how relieved she was to be here. And there was the way that she looked at him, he recognized something of his own need, there was something . . . He undressed. He thought with excitement that a physical marriage to Mrs Kingshaw would not be like what he had had with Ellen, for Mrs Kingshaw would answer to him, without the niceties and the restraints, she would bridge the gap between fantasy and life.

The idea that she might not, after all, be intending to stay at Warings, the idea of living once again in this house with only the unappetizing cold meals left by Mrs Boland, and the memories of his own childhood, to occupy him, shocked Mr Hooper out of his indecision.

Tomorrow, he said, climbing into the cold bed, tomorrow . . .

He was anxious. They were driving somewhere, all of them together in Mr Hooper's car, and he did not know where they were going.

'It is a *surprise*. This is a very special day, and you are going to have a lovely treat,' Mrs Kingshaw had said.

'Where are we going to?'

'Oh, now, you will have to wait and see!'

'I want to know. I don't like it when I don't know.'

'You are a funny boy, Charles. Whoever heard of someone being told about a surprise before it happened? Edmund is *very* excited, he doesn't want to know. It is like trying to peep into parcels, before Christmas morning.'

And so she would not tell him anything more about it, only smiled secretly, and nodded her head, and now, they were driving away from the village. They had been made to put on their best long, grey trousers. Hooper had only been out once before, since the accident. He had to sit with his leg up along the back seat, so that Kingshaw only had a small amount of room. The underneath of Hooper's plaster was grey and smudged.

It was like the day they had gone to the castle, all over again, the smell of the car reminded him of the long, green tunnel of trees. But today it was raining and cold, and they were driving in a different direction. The trees had a tinge of yellow, with the start of autumn.

Kingshaw had said, 'Why do we have to go somewhere?'

'Ah, well that is a secret too. But you will find out about it, all in good time.'

He already knew. He had always known. But now it was happening, it was the truth. The reality of it was no worse than the anticipation had been. When Hooper had come and told him, he had been neither surprised nor angry.

He was starting on a new model, in the room with the dolls, drawing it out very carefully on graph paper, first, to see whether it could work. It was a good deal more complicated than the helter-skelter fort. They had told him that he must play chess with Hooper, but he had come in here, he no longer cared what they said or did to him. Hooper didn't want him. He was making lists of battle regiments.

When the footsteps came along the corridor, Kingshaw had remembered Miss Mellitt, fumbling her way towards his room, and for a moment, he was terrified, uncertain of where he was. The fusty smell seeped from out of the chinks in the dolls' glass cabinet, into the room. Then, a hump. Hooper, kicking against the door.

'Hiding . . .'

'I can do what I like in here, and this is all mine, my mother gave me the money to buy all the things for it, so, it's got nothing to do with you, Hooper.'

Hooper came forwards into the room, limping heavily. Kingshaw was standing beside the table, his arm outstretched over the drawing of the model, defensive.

'I don't want your stupid model. That's a baby thing.'

'You broke the other one. You played with it and then broke it, and you're not touching anything else of mine.'

'Shut up, I've just heard something. I know something you don't know.' His expression was cunning, secretive. Kingshaw waited, not moving from the table. He had learned enough about Hooper, now.

'You won't like it when I tell you. *If* I tell you.'

'What did you come here for, then?'

'I told you something would happen.'

Silence. Kingshaw thought, *everything* has happened, whatever it is can't make any difference, can't be any worse. But his stomach turned over with dread, watching Hooper's face.

'Aren't you going to ask me? Don't you want to know?' His voice sang with mockery. Kingshaw pressed his lips together until he felt his teeth cutting into the skin. He wasn't going to say anything, wasn't going to ask.

'Maybe I'll just let you find out, then.'

Slowly, Kingshaw turned and sat on the chair in front of his table. He stared down at the lines of the drawing. Now, Hooper would tell him.

'He'll be your *step-father.*'

Silence.

'He's going to get married to your mother, and it's going to be soon, it'll be before we go back to school. They were talking about it. I heard them. It's what I told you was going to happen, I told you ages ago.'

Kingshaw felt nothing. Only that he had known, and now it had come. He had been waiting for it. He said, 'You can go away. I'm busy.'

'You needn't try and be clever, Kingshaw.'

'Shut up.'

'You needn't think you won't have to do what my father says, now, because you just will. *And* what I say.'

'Shut *up.*'

'Anyway, I don't have to have your stupid mother here for ever, I don't want to have anything to do with her. Or you. You're just stupid.'

His tauntings washed over Kingshaw, they sounded babyish, he didn't care at all what Hooper said.

'You *wait.*'

Kingshaw did not answer, did not move. He realized that it was Hooper who was angry, Hooper who minded about it. He had never wanted them to come here, to his house. On the first day, he had sent down that note. 'I didn't want you to come here.' And now they were to stay, and he was powerless to stop it, his house would be their house. Kingshaw thought, I ought to be glad because he minds. But there was nothing at all. He felt alone inside himself.

But later, in the middle of the night, he had woken up suddenly and remembered it, and then he had realized that it was really true, it was going to happen. He thought, there will always be Hooper, now, for ever and always, Hooper and Mr Hooper. He began to weep, pulling his knees up to his chin and rocking himself. The worst of all was this house, with the dark rooms and the old furniture and the cases of moths, he would always have to come back to it. And in his mother's own room, there would be Mr Hooper.

But still they had not told him. At breakfast the next morning, before Mr Hooper went to London, there had only been looks, passing between him and Mrs Kingshaw, and the talk of an outing, a surprise.

'Well, now,' Mr Hooper said, 'Here we are!' And stopped the car behind rows of others, in a muddy field.

'At least you boys are going to be quite safe this time. There are not going to be any chances for you to go climbing and falling today!'

Kingshaw looked out of the windows of the saloon car, through the streams of rain. When he saw it, he thought Oh God, Oh God, let us not be going there. He knew that they were. His throat tightened. Hooper was watching him carefully. Kingshaw saw the way his eyes had gleamed, suddenly, with triumph. He had known at once, he always knew.

Mrs Helena Kingshaw stepped out of the car and unfolded a lime-green umbrella.

'Now, Charles, you will have to run ahead as best you can, dear, make a quick dash through the puddles. There is no sense in us all getting wet. But I shall have to come behind with Mr Hooper and help poor Edmund.'

Kingshaw walked away from them quite slowly, ignoring the rain. He thought, this is the worst thing in the world, nothing could have been worse than this. Why didn't they know, why didn't they *know*? He tried desperately to think of a way of escape, he would have done anything at all not to have to go inside.

Behind him, coming through the muddy field, Mrs Helena Kingshaw said, 'Now, when Charles was a very small boy he used to be a little bit frightened. But of course all that is quite forgotten, and this is going to be a simply splendid treat. And it doesn't matter *what* the weather does to us!'

*

When he closed his eyes, it made no difference, it made it worse, because then he could imagine everything, it was all whirling round inside his head, and he could hear the noises more loudly, smell the smells.

Mr Hooper had bought the best, the most expensive seats, very close to the ring. Kingshaw looked up towards the darkness at the top of the tent, where the ropes and ladders for the acrobats hung, limp and still, and then down and down at all the rows of people, at the bobbing white faces and staring eyes. He gripped his hands tight on the arms of the seat. I can't get out, I can't get out, I can't get out . . . it will come down on us, everybody will fall and there is nothing I can do. His mind filled with confused pictures of the canvas billowing and blanketing down, and of the bodies of all the people, piled up together, crushing him.

The smell was one he had remembered, of wet clothes, steaming, and sawdust and hot arc lights, of canvas and animal dung, and the noises were the same, too, banging through his head, and behind his eyes, when he closed them, the cracking of whips and the rolling of drums and the terrible braying and roaring and trumpeting of the dancing animals. It went on and on, everybody was laughing and laughing.

'Charles, whatever is the matter, dear. Take it, don't be in such a dream, take it, *take* it . . .'

His mother was leaning towards him, whispering urgently, and then he looked up and into the white, shining face of the clown who stood on the edge of the ring, in front of him. The white paint was like a skin stretched over it, glistening with sweat, and there was a huge scarlet mouth, opening and shutting like the mouth of the carrion crow, there were the eyes, staring into his own. The clown was trying to give him a yellow balloon, with soft, rubbery ears. On the other side of the row, he could see Hooper, smiling slightly at him, knowing. And then the clown had gone, and they were putting up the steel tunnels for the lions, and he wanted to scream to get away, he waited and waited for the animals to go mad and attack the man inside the cage with them, waited for the roaring to burst open his own head.

In the interval, Mr Hooper bought them multi-coloured ice creams on sticks, and chocolates for Mrs Helena Kingshaw.

'Oh, I feel just like one of the children! What a treat!'

Sitting beside her, Kingshaw waited for the turn of the lumbering, gentle elephants, and when they came, almost wept, because of the tasselled caps they were made to wear, and the docile expression in their eyes . . . He held the uneaten ice cream in his left hand, and it dripped away down the side of the seat, and on to the floor, in a sweet, sticky trail.

It is just for the sake of the boys, Mr Joseph Hooper thought, for he shifted in his uncomfortable seat and was bored with the circus. But when he craned his head up obediently to watch the leaps and somersaults of the Four Flyers, he saw that the bodies of the girls rippled and shone, in watery satin, and that their bodies arched, their legs moved and swung. He put out his hand and felt for the silken knees of Mrs Helena Kingshaw.

In the covered tunnel leading out of the circus tent, among the pushing crowd of people, Kingshaw was violently sick.

'You should have *said* something, Charles, you should have said something, or else just tried to wait for a moment.'

Outside, in the cold rain, he thought Oh God, Oh God, it's all right, it's gone, it's finished, and stood, shivering at the memory.

'I have been to see Mrs Fielding.'

Kingshaw stared at her in horror, not wanting to believe what he had heard.

'We have met once or twice, of course, about the village, but now I have been down to the farm and introduced myself.'

He stood in the kitchen doorway, white-faced. His mother was unpacking her basket of shopping.

'What did you have to go there for? You *shouldn't* have gone there.'

'Don't speak to me like that, dear, I have told you about it often enough. As a matter of fact, it was all on your behalf. I wanted to ask Anthony to tea, one day next week. Before you and Edmund go off to school.' She paused, glancing sideways across the kitchen to Mrs Boland, 'before the wedding.'

'I don't want Fielding to come to tea here. I don't want him to come at all.'

'Oh dear, Charles, I really cannot keep up with the way you boys fall in and out in this silly manner. I thought you were supposed to be such great friends.'

'He's *my* friend.'

'Well, then . . .'

'I don't want him to come *here*.'

'Well, you have been there a good many times. I know, his mother was very kind to you, while Edmund was in hospital and you were all alone. Having Anthony to tea is the very least that we can do. And besides, now that we are going to live here always, it will be so nice for you all to play together, in holiday times.'

'He won't want to come.'

'Oh, he told me that he would love to!'

Kingshaw went out of the house by the back door, and down the path through the yew trees, towards the entrance to the copse. Hooper had gone to the hospital, to have his plaster seen to.

To the right of the narrow, grassed-over track that led into the copse, there was a small clearing, within a circle of beech trees, and hidden by them from view of the house. He came here sometimes, when he could get away from Hooper, because there were grey squirrels, darting and leaping about in the trees, and he liked to watch them, he liked their soft, agile bodies and swaying tails. Since the accident, Hooper hadn't been able to follow him without making a din, because of having to drag his plastered leg, and it wasn't much good for him down here anyway, it was muddy after almost a week of rain.

The leaves and soil were mulched together underfoot, and the grass was wet. Looking up between the trees, he could see puffy bits of cloud, and patches of blue sky, and the pattern of them kept changing in the wind. But today, there didn't seem to be any squirrels.

The idea of Fielding coming to the house, eating tea at their table, having to play games with them in the sitting room or on the lawn, the idea of his being watched over by Hooper, was unbearable. Fielding and the farm and everything there had been his, he had found them. Now, his mother had been there, walking down the drive and up the path to the front door, seeing everything, asking questions of Fielding's mother, intruding and spoiling. He knew that Fielding would come to Warings, because Fielding was easy, he liked to go anywhere and do anything, things pleased him, he would be friendly with anybody. Kingshaw had seen that from the beginning, and only thought that he must keep Hooper away. When he had talked about Hooper, Fielding had listened, and believed him, and yet it would make no difference, he was too careless about things to put up any barriers. And Hooper would not be able to do anything to him, either, nothing at all, he would not even try. He could neither frighten nor humiliate Fielding, because his temperament would reject all of it without trouble, he would not bring out the worst in Hooper, as Kingshaw himself did. Fielding was invulnerable.

All this, Kingshaw felt, rather than reasoned out, he was certain of it inside himself. He could not hold Fielding, nobody could, he would try and try, and Fielding would slip away, and make friends anywhere, share anything. So that was the last thing.

They had been talking about the wedding. On Thursday, September 10, they would go to the Registrar's office, in Milford, all of them together, and then there was to be a celebration lunch at the George Hotel, 'a *family* lunch,' Mrs Helena Kingshaw kept on saying, 'the four of us together.'

After that, they would all go to the school in Mr Hooper's car. Mrs Kingshaw had said, 'I shouldn't like him to go on the train, not just this first time, even though he will have Edmund. Oh, yes, I know he is eleven years old, but that is not so very big, is it?'

'No, no,' Mr Hooper had said. 'No, no,' and patted her knee. She felt comforted.

So she had said, 'We shall all go to the school together, and see you nicely settled in, Charles, and after that, Mr Hooper and I will be going away for a few days.'

Kingshaw felt queer inside, dull, imagining it all, knowing how the day would be. There would be the strange building and the crowds of unfamiliar faces, he would be alone with Hooper, after the car had gone. It would all begin.

Inside an alder bush, just ahead of him, a family of wrens was darting and hopping about, their tails sticking upwards like Indian head-dress feathers. After a while, he got up and started to creep towards them. He wanted to catch a bird and hold it between his hands. A twig snapped under his foot. The bush went still, the brown feathers of the wrens merging with the branches. When he moved clear, they were already flying away. He heard the sound of Mr Hooper's car, driving up to the house.

'Do you want to see something else now?'
   'Yes.'
   'Something I bet you've never seen before.'
   'O.K.'
   'You might not like it, though.'

'Why?'

'You might be scared.'

Fielding looked surprised. He said, 'I'm not frightened of much.' Hooper paused, looking into his face, trying to make up his mind if this was the truth. He had not yet got the measure of Fielding, had not met anyone so honest about himself, and able to say and do anything at all.

'Kingshaw's scared of them.'

At once, Fielding turned back. 'We won't go then, if you don't want to. It's O.K.'

Kingshaw stood apart from them, hands in his pockets, proud and at the same time scornful of Fielding's kindness.

'I don't care what you do.'

'Is it something alive?'

'No,' Hooper said, 'they're dead things.'

'Oh, well, I don't mind *that*. I don't mind anything much. Only . . .'

'Look, I've said I don't care, haven't I? It doesn't bother me what you do with him,' Kingshaw spoke furiously, resenting everything about the way Fielding was, with Hooper.

Inside the Red Room, Fielding said, 'Hey – it's butterflies! Great!'

'Moths,' Hooper said, 'Moths are different. They're better than butterflies.'

Fielding was peering down eagerly into the first case. 'I can see them properly, now. I can see all the hairs on their bodies.'

Kingshaw stiffened.

'My grandfather collected these. He was world-famous, he wrote books and things about them. They're worth thousands of pounds.'

'Liar.'

Hooper turned on Kingshaw. 'You just stuff it, scaredy. You don't know anything.'

At once, Fielding glanced round, anxiously. Kingshaw refused to meet his eye. Hooper was moving over to the display cases, looking closely at Fielding's face again. 'Dare you *touch* one?'

Fielding looked puzzled. 'Yes. They're only dead things. They can't hurt you.'

'Go on then.'

'It's locked, though.'

'No, it isn't, you can lift the lid up.'

'Wouldn't they get damaged? We might get into trouble.'

'*I* dare touch one. I lifted one out, once.'

'Oh.'

Fielding had walked to the next case. From the doorway, watching them, Kingshaw thought, Hooper believes him, he isn't going to make him open the case and put his hand on one, he isn't going to make him prove it, he just believes him. That's the way Fielding is, that's the way you should be.

It had been different with him. Hooper had known, from the very first moment he had looked into Fielding's face, that it would all be easy, that he would always be able to make him afraid. Why, thought Kingshaw, *why*? His eyes suddenly pricked with tears, at the unfairness of it. WHY?

Now, Fielding was standing up on a chair, touching the back of one of the stuffed weasels. His hand came away, grey with dust.

'If somebody doesn't clean them, they'll drop to bits, I should think. They sort of rot.'

'Do you like them?'

Fielding climbed down. 'They're all right,' he said, without much interest, 'they smell a bit funny.'

He went to the next case of moths and began to read the names out, as though they were something ordinary, Kingshaw thought, as though they couldn't hurt you or frighten you, like a list of the names of ships or dogs or wild flowers. Nothing. It was just that Fielding was happy to discover anything new, happy to do whatever anyone else suggested.

He had only said, 'They smell a bit funny.' It was the smell that Kingshaw hated most of all. When he went past the door of the Red Room, he remembered the night Hooper had locked him in there and the rain had beaten against the window, and the moth had flown out at him from the inside of the lampshade.

Not long ago, Mr Hooper had been talking about the moths. 'I have thought seriously of getting in an expert, having them valued. I have thought of selling them, they are of no use to any of us, none at all.'

'Oh, but they are *heirlooms*, family things, when the boys are a little older, might they not begin to take a real interest in them? Surely you ought not to get rid of anything so unusual.'

Kingshaw had listened to his mother saying it, and despaired, for everything she thought and believed and said and did seemed, now, to have less to do with him than with anyone in the whole world. And in spite of himself, he minded, he wanted bitterly for her to be different, to be *his*, at the same time herself, and yet a different sort of person. He thought now, it was better than this before we came *here*.

But that was not true, either. For, before this, she had clung to him, she had said, 'You are all I have now, Charles, I do so want you to do well, you do understand that, don't you?' He had struggled to get out from under the weight of meaning behind her words.

Hooper said, 'We could go and do something else now.'

'All right. What?'

'I don't know. We could look at my battle plans. It's all the regiments set out on a chart. They're in my bedroom.'

'What are they for?'

'Battles.'

Fielding looked uncertain.

'It's what I like doing.'

'Do you want to?' Fielding asked, turning to Kingshaw. His nut-coloured face was full of concern.

'I don't care.'

But Hooper had changed his mind, he was saying 'No, *I* know, what we'll do is, we'll go to the attics.' He started up the stairs.

The crow, Kingshaw thought, the stuffed crow. And there might be other things, they might lock me in there. God.

'Kingshaw daren't.'

'Shut your face, Hooper, I'll punch you.'

Fielding looked from one to the other, shocked by the violence in Kingshaw's voice. Hooper turned his back again, on Kingshaw, speaking to Fielding only. 'Come on, it's good in the attics, there's all sorts of things.'

Kingshaw watched them, not moving.

'*Aren't* you coming?' Fielding asked gently.

Kingshaw was silent.

'O.K. We won't then.'

'He's just scared, you needn't bother about him. Look, come on, Fielding, I want to show you something. Something private.'

Fielding hesitated. For a moment, it might have gone either way. Hooper might have won or lost. Kingshaw felt the tension between them, and felt Fielding's concern for him, too. He wanted to say, I'm all right, you can just go with him and leave me alone, you can do anything and I don't care, I've finished with you, I'd rather be just me, me, me.

Abruptly, Fielding jumped back down three stairs at once, his face full of sudden pleasure, at an idea he had had. 'We'll go to my place,' he said, 'that's what we'll do. There's a new tractor, it came yesterday. We'll go and see that.'

He went off through the front door and into the drive. It was sunny again, now, after the last shower of rain. The gravel shone, slippery with wetness. Fielding looked back and shouted impatiently, 'Come on.'

Hooper went, he could move much faster, now, on the plastered leg, but Fielding waited for him all the same. Kingshaw stood just outside the door, moving his toes about in the loose gravel, listening to the soft, rough sound it made. He wasn't going to the farm. He wouldn't go there again, now. Hooper could go. He didn't care about Fielding, none of it belonged to him any more.

He thought about the first day he had gone there, the strangeness of it, the way he had trodden about warily, like a cat, smelling out new things. There had been the calf, ugly and slithering and wet.

At the bottom of the drive, by the gate, Fielding was waving for him to follow them. Hooper was already out of sight behind the hedge. For a moment, Kingshaw watched, not moving. The wind blew into his face across the lawn. He wanted to go, more than anything he wanted to go, because he wanted it to be as it was before. But it wouldn't be. That was gone. He made himself say it out loud.

He went back into the wood-panelled hall, and closed the front door behind him quietly.

Fielding waited, puzzled, he thought that he should go back for Kingshaw. He had been funny, all the afternoon, distant and cold and angry. It worried Fielding, he was only used to people who behaved as he himself behaved, people to whom things were easy. He didn't know what to do. Perhaps Kingshaw felt ill.

Hooper had walked back. 'What's the matter? Look, don't wait for him, he's batty, he's just stupid.'

'But . . . there might be something wrong.'

'No, there isn't, don't be a nit, he's only *sulking*.'

'What for?'

'It's what he always does. That's what Kingshaw's like.'

Fielding was still unhappy.

'Look, when we've got to your farm, he'll come after us, he's bound to. He always does come.'

In the end, Fielding believed him. They began to walk through the long grass of the ditch. It was very wet. Fielding was still looking for a slow-worm.

Kingshaw went up to Hooper's bedroom. The battle chart, with its coloured pins and flags and symbols, was propped up on its easel. On the table were Hooper's long lists of regiments, written in different-coloured biros. The letters were big and round.

Kingshaw rolled them up carefully. Then he took down the chart, and peeled off the Sellotape from around the edges, so that the sheet of paper came away from its cardboard backing. He rolled that up, too.

When he got downstairs again, he could hear his mother and Mrs Boland talking in the kitchen. He went out of the front door, and then around to the back of the house, through the yew trees. In the clearing by the entrance to the copse, he squatted down and began to tear up all the paper into small pieces. It took a long time.

He scraped a patch of ground clear of wet leaves and twigs and put the little pile of papers on to the soil. He had brought the matches left over from Hang Wood. After using up three, the paper caught, in a sudden breeze, and then began to burn steadily.

Kingshaw watched the blue-edge of flame creeping and flickering and expected to feel exultant, but there was nothing much, it scarcely interested him any more. When the paper had all burned, he ground the charred bits up with his foot and covered them with a pile of wet leaves. His hands were wet and covered in mud. Though it made no difference whether he hid it or not, Hooper would still know.

He stood for a moment in the clearing, listening to the water dripping down off the beech leaves, and then realized what he had done, and what would happen to him. He had thought that he couldn't be afraid of anything again, but now he was afraid.

There were five days until September 10, five days until they went to the new school. It was not worth thinking about it, not now.

It began to rain again.

Chapter Seventeen

All through the day, Hooper kept looking at him. But he said nothing.

The house was full of suitcases. Mrs Helena Kingshaw ran up and down the wooden staircase and along the corridors, flushed in the face, thinking at once of the labels on grey socks and black and gold blazers, and of the soft pile of dresses and petticoats and cashmere cardigans, lying upon her own bed. It is all so quick, she thought, all so sudden, now that we are come to it. But there was the security, the sense of arrival.

In his study, among the letters and newspapers, Mr Hooper thought, I have made a good choice, and then twitched with desire for that day, and the next, to be over, for the register to be signed and the boys settled.

Outside, rain and a high wind, tearing through the yew trees. Mrs Kingshaw packed a long-sleeved woollen dress, thinking of outings along the promenade at Torquay.

Hooper had said nothing about the disappearance of the battle plan and his lists of regiments. He had come back from the farm in the Landrover, with Fielding's mother, and talked and talked, gloating. Kingshaw had waited. Nothing. He was alarmed, it was not like Hooper, he had expected a roar of fury, and then the tale-telling, and the punishments. Nothing.

For a while, he clung to the thought that Hooper might simply not have noticed, might have lost interest in the plans. But there was the empty sheet of white cardboard, propped up on the easel, the table-top clear of papers. He was bound to have noticed. But, nothing. Hooper had just watched, keeping his distance, and Kingshaw knew, then, that he was waiting. He turned over and over between his sheets at night, attacked by the horrifying dreams, and then, when he woke, by the recollection of the truth, that waking was no better than sleeping. It would happen. Something.

He almost went to Hooper and talked about it, to get the thing over with, almost said, I took them, I did it, *look* what I did, so. It would have been a relief, no matter what had followed. But he was numbed, unable to say or do anything. Only to look down into the open suitcases, at the neatly folded black and gold uniforms, and see the labels on the handles, C. J. N. Kingshaw, Drummond's School, written in Mr Hooper's handwriting.

He took a book about fossils and went to the window-seat in the drawing room, and through his mind ran pictures of what the school might look like, how the faces of the boys would be. But he could not imagine anything other than St Vincent's, because that was the only place he knew, and the faces in his mind were those of Devereux and Crawford, and Broughton-Smith.

'Now, you are both to have an early night. There will be enough excitement and to spare, tomorrow, you need to be fresh and rested.'

His room looked bare, everything packed away, it was as it had been the first day he had come into it, the day he had fought with Hooper and punched him in the face.

His mother stayed with him for quite a long time, that night, she kept on touching him, asking him things, and when she had gone, the air all around his bed smelled of her smell. Rain was beating against the windows.

Kingshaw woke suddenly, almost as soon as he had fallen asleep. There was a noise. He moved in his bed, expecting to see the stuffed crow, or something else, to find something in the room. But there was nothing. Silence. Then, a bump, and a soft scraping sound, of paper. He lay absolutely still. After a moment, a creak of floorboards and the footsteps going away. He waited again. There was no sound from downstairs. No sound except the rain outside.

In the end, he switched on the lamp and slid out of bed. The sheet of paper was folded over once, and lying on the floor just beyond the edge of the door.

'Something will happen to you, Kingshaw.'

The letters were printed in thick, black felt pen, and underlined again and again. In spite of the fear that had gone on and on for so long, it was suddenly worse again now, as he read Hooper's message, it darted through like a fresh toothache, and he screwed up the paper and sent it as far away from him as he could across the room, and then flung himself into his bed, pushing his face under the covers and trembling.

The nightmares began.

The moment he came awake, it was just dawn, and he remembered, and then he knew, quite suddenly, what to do. It was because the morning reminded him of the time before. The house was quiet. When he looked out of his window, it was clear and grey.

The open suitcases seemed to have nothing to do with him, now.

Outside, it was cool and the air felt moist, though it had stopped raining and the wind had dropped. But once he had climbed over the fence and begun to trudge up the first field, the grass was thick and wet. The only difference today was that there was no mist, he could see a long way ahead, the sky was smooth and pale.

They had cut the corn, and burned the stubble, and the field seemed much bigger, the trees on the edge of the wood looked a long distance away. The outer edges were fringed with yellow and brown, but inside, it was dark green and thick, the leaves hadn't started to fall.

At first, when he stepped inside the wood, he stood still. He was not certain of the way, now, beyond the first bit. They had turned and changed direction so much, after following the deer. He tried to remember the way the men had brought them, when they came out again.

The smell was familiar, the one he had smelled when he crawled out from under the bush, after the thunderstorm, fresh and cool, but sweet-rotten, too, from the soil and the leaf-mould.

He felt suddenly excited. This was his place, it was where he wanted to be. It was all right. He said to himself, again and again, *this* is all right, *this* is all right. He began to push his way slowly through the damp undergrowth.

At Warings, Hooper slept, flat on his belly, his mind blank, but on the floor below, his father moved and tossed, excited by dreams. Waking, Mrs Helena Kingshaw thought, it is today, and this is the best thing that could have happened, the best thing for both of us. I shall not be a struggling, lonely woman now, that is all past, all done with and forgotten, and we are going to be happy, all of us together. Everything is about to begin.

She got out of bed and looked at the oval travelling alarm clock. On the wardrobe door, the cream-coloured linen suit hung, showing palely through its polythene. Mrs Kingshaw thought, there is plenty of time for everything, plenty of time. And sat down on the edge of her bed again, to smoke a cigarette. It was a little after seven o'clock.

Kingshaw had found the clearing now. The stones were still there, piled up, from when they had built the fire. It seemed a long time ago. He didn't stop to look.

On the bank of the stream, he took all his clothes off, and folded them in a pile. He shivered and the water was very cold, silky, against his body. For a second, he hesitated, part of his mind starting to come awake. And then he thought of everything, of what else would happen, he thought of the things Hooper had done and what he was going to do, of the new school and the wedding of his mother. He began to splash and stumble forwards, into the middle of the stream, where the water was deepest. When it had reached up to his thighs, he lay down slowly and put his face full into it and breathed in a long, careful breath.

It was Hooper who found him, because he had known at once where he would have gone, they all followed Hooper, trampling and calling. The rain had begun again, dripping down on their heads and shoulders through the dark leaves.

When he saw Kingshaw's body, upside down in the water, Hooper thought suddenly, it was because of me, I did that, *it was because of me*, and a spurt of triumph went through him.

'Now, it's all right, Edmund dear, everything is all right,' Mrs Helena Kingshaw put an arm out towards him, held him to her. 'I don't want you to look, dear, you mustn't look and be upset, everything is all right.'

Hooper felt the damp cloth of her coat, pressed against his face, and smelled her perfumey smell. Then, there was the sound of the men, splashing through the water.

PENGUIN DECADES

Penguin Decades bring you the novels that helped shape modern Britain. When they were published, some were bestsellers, some were considered scandalous, and others were simply misunderstood. All represent their time and helped define their generation, while today each is considered a landmark work of storytelling. Each is introduced by a modern admirer.

50s
Scenes from Provincial Life/William Cooper (1950) Nick Hornby
Lucky Jim/Kingsley Amis (1954) David Nicholls
The Chrysalids/ John Wyndham (1955) M. John Harrison
From Russia with Love/Ian Fleming (1957) Christopher Andrew
Billy Liar/Keith Waterhouse (1959) Blake Morrison

60s
A Clockwork Orange/Anthony Burgess (1962) Will Self
The Millstone/Margaret Drabble (1965) Elaine Showalter
The British Museum is Falling Down/David Lodge (1965) Mark Lawson
A Kestrel for a Knave/Barry Hines (1968) Ian McMillan
Another Part of the Wood/Beryl Bainbridge (1969) Lynn Barber

70s
I'm the King of the Castle/Susan Hill (1970) Esther Freud
Don't Look Now/Daphne du Maurier (1971) Julie Myerson
The Infernal Desire Machines of Doctor Hoffman/Angela Carter (1972) Ali Smith
The Children of Dynmouth/William Trevor (1976) Roy Foster
Treasures of Time/Penelope Lively (1979) Selina Hastings

80s
A Month in the Country/J. L. Carr (1980) Byron Rogers
An Ice-Cream War/William Boyd (1982) Giles Foden
Hawksmoor/Peter Ackroyd (1985) Will Self
Paradise Postponed/John Mortimer (1985) Jeremy Paxman
Latecomers/Anita Brookner (1988) Helen Dunmore

DECADES 1970s

The 1970s was a decade of anger and discontent. Britain endured power cuts and strikes. America pulled out of Vietnam and saw its President resign from office. Feminism and face lifts vied for women's hearts (and minds). And for many, prog rock, punk and disco weren't just music but ways of life.

I'm the King of the Castle/Susan Hill (1970)
'In the dark and taunting world which Susan Hill creates … the instruments of torture, with which one child persecutes another, are simple but nonetheless effective ... [She] is a master of suspense, leading us on with flashes of hope, and a sharp insight into the tormented child's state of mind' – Esther Freud

Don't Look Now/Daphne du Maurier (1971)
'A tale of perception and premonition, of second sight...No one explores the relationship between the physical and the psychological, the visceral and the emotional, like Daphne du Maurier' – Julie Myerson

The Infernal Desire Machines of Doctor Hoffman/Angela Carter (1972)
'Surely her real, still underrated, classic … It is swooningly romantic, indifferently and knowingly beautiful, vigorously philosophical and cunning beyond belief' – Ali Smith

The Children of Dynmouth/William Trevor (1976)
'A generation before Patrick McCabe and Irvine Welch, *The Children of Dynmouth* reveals Trevor at his most ruthless, macabre and *grand guignol* … Trevor's gift of conjuring up evil and obsession, and making them utterly convincing, is central to this consummate novel' – Roy Foster

Treasures of Time/Penelope Lively (1979)
'With characteristic subtlety and wit Penelope Lively explores intricate themes of appearance and reality, of the power of memory and of the warping and shaping that occurs with the passing years' – Selina Hastings

He just wanted a decent book to read ...

Not too much to ask, is it? It was in 1935 when Allen Lane, Managing Director of Bodley Head Publishers, stood on a platform at Exeter railway station looking for something good to read on his journey back to London. His choice was limited to popular magazines and poor-quality paperbacks – the same choice faced every day by the vast majority of readers, few of whom could afford hardbacks. Lane's disappointment and subsequent anger at the range of books generally available led him to found a company – and change the world.

'We believed in the existence in this country of a vast reading public for intelligent books at a low price, and staked everything on it'
Sir Allen Lane, 1902–1970, founder of Penguin Books

The quality paperback had arrived – and not just in bookshops. Lane was adamant that his Penguins should appear in chain stores and tobacconists, and should cost no more than a packet of cigarettes.

Reading habits (and cigarette prices) have changed since 1935, but Penguin still believes in publishing the best books for everybody to enjoy. We still believe that good design costs no more than bad design, and we still believe that quality books published passionately and responsibly make the world a better place.

So wherever you see the little bird – whether it's on a piece of prize-winning literary fiction or a celebrity autobiography, political tour de force or historical masterpiece, a serial-killer thriller, reference book, world classic or a piece of pure escapism – you can bet that it represents the very best that the genre has to offer.

Whatever you like to read – trust Penguin.